S0-AGF-152

THE ABDUCTION OF SMITH AND SMITH

THE ABDUCTION OF SMITH AND SMITH

A NOVEL

RASHAD HARRISON

Huntington City
Township Public Library
255 West Park Drive
Huntington, IN 46750

ATRIA BOOKS

New York   London   Toronto   Sydney   New Delhi

ATRIA BOOKS

A Division of Simon & Schuster, Inc.
1230 Avenue of the Americas
New York, NY 10020

This book is a work of fiction. Any references to historical events, real people, or real places are used fictitiously. Other names, characters, places, and events are products of the author's imagination, and any resemblance to actual events or places or persons, living or dead, is entirely coincidental.

Copyright © 2015 by Rashad Harrison

All rights reserved, including the right to reproduce this book or portions thereof in any form whatsoever. For information, address
Atria Books Subsidiary Rights Department,
1230 Avenue of the Americas, New York, NY 10020.

First Atria Books hardcover edition January 2015

ATRIA B O O K S and colophon are trademarks of Simon & Schuster, Inc.

For information about special discounts for bulk purchases, please contact Simon & Schuster Special Sales at 1-866-506-1949 or business@simonandschuster.com.

The Simon & Schuster Speakers Bureau can bring authors to your live event. For more information or to book an event, contact the Simon & Schuster Speakers Bureau at 1-866-248-3049 or visit our website at www.simonspeakers.com.

Cover and interior art by Michael Yakutis

Manufactured in the United States of America

10   9   8   7   6   5   4   3   2   1

Library of Congress Cataloging-in-Publication Data is available.

ISBN 978-1-4516-2578-3
ISBN 978-1-4516-2580-6 (ebook)

For Isaac

". . . a civil war is, we may say, the prototype of all war, for in the persons of fellow citizens who happen to be the enemy we meet again, with the old ambivalence of love and hate and with all the old guilts, the blood brothers of our childhood."

Robert Penn Warren, *The Legacy of the Civil War*

THE ABDUCTION OF SMITH AND SMITH

1

Embarcadero Port, San Francisco. 1868.

Moonlight rippled on the black water. The sounds of the Barbary Coast saloons filled the air and met them on shore. Jupiter watched the rocks. He aimed his lantern at the shadows. Something moved underneath the sand. "They're here," he said to Clement. The earth parted, light shined through the crack, and a hand emerged beckoning Jupiter and Clement. The trapdoor under Maggie's saloon opened and an unconscious man slumped to the shore. He was young, about twenty or so, and strong. His palms were pebbled with calluses, no stranger to work on a ship. He'd fetch about twenty-five dollars, a tidy sum, but Jupiter searched the man's pockets anyway. No money, just a crooked deck of cards and loaded dice. Poor boy had tried to trick the wrong people and ended up on the bad end of a vanishing act. Jupiter nodded to the man underneath the earth. The hole closed and all was dark again.

Jupiter put the shady paraphernalia in his pockets, then he and Clement dragged the boy to their boat and dropped him on top of a pile of three other unconscious men. The lad was all muscle; maybe they'd get an even thirty for him.

They pushed off. Clement manned the oars and Jupiter held the lantern, waving its beam in the darkness until the masts of the *Halcyon* became visible. She was bound for the Philippines; a ton of pepper in her hull, she needed a crew badly.

• • •

"What have we here?" asked the first mate as he looked at the three unconscious men at Jupiter's feet. Clement spoke up. "We've got a carpenter, a cooper, and one able-bodied seaman—skills to be determined on deck."

The ship's crew buzzed about.

The first mate scratched his beard. "Are you sure these men have sailed before? Last lot you two provided were so fond of land that they damn near had tree trunks instead of legs."

"It's our promise," Clement said, "to provide you with the most skilled seamen available at the time."

"Aye, and I'm sure you'd swear it on your mother's soul," the first mate grumbled.

"Well, I'm glad we are in agreement," said Clement.

"How much?" asked the first mate.

"Fifty dollars for the lot," said Jupiter.

Clement looked at him. "You heard the man."

The first mate spat. "Highway robbery, this is," but paid Clement accordingly: fifty dollars—ten to Jupiter, fifteen to Clement, and twenty-five to Maggie.

"Be careful of this one," Jupiter said, pointing to the man as he climbed back in the boat. "He likes to beat women." Judging them made it easier for Jupiter. If they had done bad things, if they were bad people, then they must deserve what was happening to them. In places like Maggie's there was an ample supply of men who did terrible things.

"Oh, does he?" asked the first mate. "Too bad for him—and the lot of us—that there ain't any woman aboard. Although, these long trips do tend to play tricks on your mind. Some of these younger lads may get mistaken for mermaids."

• • •

The ship vanished into the fog as if by some natural sleight of hand. Jupiter was no magician, but he was quite good at making men disappear.

They brought the boat back to shore, secured it, then walked onto the portside road, merging with a crowd teeming with sailors, drunks, and thrill seekers.

Jupiter could feel Clement staring at him as they walked. "Something on your mind?"

"I feel as though I should ask *you* that question," answered Clement.

Jupiter hated when Clement acted as though they were friends. It was closer to indentured servitude than a relationship, and he wasn't foolish enough to think otherwise.

"Where were you the other night?" Clement asked. "Had to hire off the docks for muscle."

"Had a prior obligation."

"Tea with the Queen? I don't see a note pinned to your shirt."

Jupiter stared him down. Clement had seen Jupiter kill a man once. Jupiter gave him a look to remind him of that fact. Clement stared back as if he remembered but didn't care.

"Did you say anything to Maggie about it?" Jupiter asked.

"No, I didn't. There's me saving your ass again," said Clement.

"Fine. Thanks to me, we got double what we expected for those last ones. Just take what you spent out of my share."

Clement spat in the road and barely missed the shoe of a passerby. "Damn right I will. Listen to you acting like you don't need the money."

He always needed the money. He had strong-armed his way across the country, tarnishing whatever honor remained in his uniform. During the day, Negroes, old and young alike, had waved at him as he passed in his tattered blue coat. At night he stole food and rifled through the pockets of unconscious drunks. By the time he arrived in San Francisco, smelled the briny air, and saw the harbor—a forest of masts—he had turned desperation into an art. He had killed countless men during the war, only two since its end. Maybe he was becoming a better man.

"And we're still one man short," said Clement.

"Or we can take what we have and call it a night."

"Call it a night, he says. This isn't that kind of job, now is it?"

Jupiter was walking. "Did you hear that?"

"Hear what?"

Something faint and shrill floated over the ironworks. "*That*. It was a scream."

"So what if it was," said Clement. "Screams are popular this time of night."

Jupiter heard the sound again and walked toward it.

"Jupiter, don't bother—"

At the end of a dark alley, he found the source of the sound: a Chinese girl, about thirteen or so, pinned to the wall by a man three times her size and three times her age. "Ease up, honey," the man growled. "The more you fight the longer it'll take." There was a tipped-over basket of laundry, clothes strewn on the ground.

The girl screamed again. She looked up and saw Jupiter. She began shouting at him in her language. Jupiter had not picked up much Chinese, but it was obvious that she was screaming for help.

The man slapped her into silence. He looked over his shoulder and saw Jupiter. "Get out of here, nigger. This doesn't concern you." He put his hand between her legs, forcing them open.

"I think it does. Why don't you leave the girl alone? Go to one of the saloons up the street, plenty of willing women there. I'll even buy their time for you if you let that little girl take the laundry back to her family."

"Ain't this somethin'. Why would you care what I do with this little whore?"

Jupiter looked at her, then the clothes; small clothes, the clothes of children. "How much do you want for her?"

"What?"

"You said she's a whore. How much do you want for her?"

Clement had caught up with him. "Jupiter, let's leave this man to his business. We have our own to attend to." He grabbed Jupiter by the arm.

"Best listen to your master, dog."

Jupiter snatched his arm back. "If she's a whore how much are you going to pay her then?"

He seemed confused. "Not a goddamned thing. I've never paid for Chink slit in my life. Why start now?" The girl took advantage of the distraction, gathered her things, and ran away.

The man walked over to Jupiter, an inch from his face. The man had no teeth, which put Jupiter at ease: men with teeth like to use them when a fight does not go their way. "You just cost me my entertainment for the evening," he said, poking Jupiter's chest upon each syllable. "What are you—"

Jupiter grabbed the finger, bent it back until the man was on his knees. Clement flung his coat open, drew his blackjack, and swung it against the man's head. His face hit the ground before Clement brought his arm back.

"Christ, why did you start that?" said Clement, searching the dark windows and doorways for witnesses.

"You said we need another man. His finger's broken, but I think he'll do just fine." Jupiter knelt and struggled to lift him. "Aren't you going to help me?"

"Oh, The Mighty Jupiter needs help?"

"What are the two of you up to?"

Jupiter knew it was a policeman. He turned around while trying to hold the man upright.

"Our friend has had too much to drink. We're just taking him back to his room."

"Too much to drink, you say?" The policeman walked over to the man and lifted his chin, which dropped promptly once he let it go. "Unless the man has swallowed a bathtub full of liquor, I'd say he's been done in by something stronger than drink. What house did you say you're taking him to?"

"Clark's on Geary."

The policeman stroked his mustache. "So if I were to stop by in a couple of hours, I'd find him there, sleeping like a baby?"

Jupiter looked at Clement. "Yes, you would, officer. You see the state he's in."

"Oh, I see the state he's in, but something tells me he's headed outside of California." The officer gripped his baton and moved closer to them. "Listen," he said, "I know the routine. The world's a cruel place—makes good men do bad things. I don't know what this man did, but he has done something, and I'm sure it would make my job easier to have him off the streets. However, the problem is that this man is wanted."

"Wanted?" said Clement. They struggled with the man's body.

"Aye, for chopping down cherry trees . . . and a large fellow's beanstalk. There's a reward for him. I'd hate to miss out on that reward."

"Just how large is that reward, officer?" asked Jupiter.

He tapped his palm five times with his baton. "Oh, I'd say about ten dollars."

"Christ," said Clement

"Shouldn't take the Lord's name in vain, son. It shows a lack of character."

• • •

San Francisco was a rough city, a city that broke you if you were weak. A night of carousing in a saloon, and you might awake the next morning on a ship headed for Australia. Close your eyes while enjoying a woman's charms—the sweetness of her kiss, the safety of her embrace—and you would open them in the cramped quarters of a vessel charting a course for the East Indies.

There were ships out there that needed crews; supply failed to keep pace with demand. About twenty or so gangs specialized in shanghaiing—snatching unsuspecting sailors off the street—even other ships—and selling them to ships bound for distant ports. Some were coy about it; in other places it was blatant. Yet everyone looked the other way. Things had become so dire that it wasn't just sailors in danger of the crimp: any able-bodied man who dared to enter a brothel or saloon made himself a potential victim. Shipmasters were duped into believing they were purchasing the skills of true sailors, not just the insolence of drunkards and louts.

"Tracking down deserters," is how Clement explained it at first, but Jupiter soon learned the truth.

It was Jupiter's idea for Maggie to be more discreet in her endeavors. To him, the brazenness of the crimps and tricks played on the shipmasters seemed misguided. If skilled seamen were needed, it made sense to seek them. Why shouldn't Maggie keep her intentions secret? Since sailors were fearful of being shanghaied from every dive on the waterfront, why not create a place that offered the illusion of safety, one where they could have a drink without the fear of receiving a club to head or dope slipped into their drinks?

Jupiter learned that the hard way. Soon after his arrival, some white men began following him. During a night of drinking, one of the men attacked him. The war had unlocked a desperate lust for survival in Jupiter: when threatened, he was unmatched.

He grabbed the man's windpipe and squeezed until the rigid tissues collapsed in his grip. His victim thrashed violently; he tried to scream, but no sound came.

Clement watched all of that unfold and shot the remaining attacker. He approached Jupiter, offering to help him remove the bodies. Yes, Jupiter had acted in self-defense, but there was no way—even after emancipation—a black man who killed a white man could avoid the noose.

After helping Jupiter, Clement said he needed a favor. He explained that the man Jupiter killed had worked for Maggie. He was her best man; the fact that Jupiter killed him so easily would both anger and amaze her. She would want to be repaid for helping him and for the man's death.

•   •   •

Ace of spades. Ten of diamonds. Queen of hearts . . .

He looked at his watch. He had memorized the entire deck in two minutes. A good memory was prized back on the plantation. By the time he was thirteen he could recall the order of a deck in less than ten minutes. The Colonel had a prodigious memory—as did the Colonel's father, he was quick to let you know. Colonel Smith considered memory to be the cornerstone of a superior intellect. He taught his son, Archer, memorization techniques handed down from the ancient

Egyptians and Greeks, as well as the Freemasons. Jupiter would listen to the two of them, father and son, undetected—the door cracked just enough to let through a sliver of candlelight, and their voices were a soft chant of words and numbers.

● ● ●

He had bought some land out in San Joaquin. No home on it yet, just the lean-to, there before he'd come along, dusty and empty. It seemed right. It overlooked a creek. It felt like the kind of place that she deserved: unmarred by history, brimming with promise. Thinking about it usually comforted him, but sometimes that comfort gave way to dread. What if he found her today? Or the next day? The next month? The next year? There was just land, no home for her.

He'd bought the land and gave up, as if he never truly expected to find her. How could he? That would require a drastic change of luck. Wherever he looked for her, the old plantation, San Francisco, it seemed that he always ended up hurting someone. He had crimped another man. He tried to let go of the memory but there was no getting free of it. It had already dropped its anchor.

He once tried putting up posters that bore her likeness, but the drawings never did her justice and, despite his romantic notions, it made her seem like an outlaw. Lately, the idea had revisited him, begging for attention.

He leafed through the incomplete sketches. Noses, eyes, and lips drifting unmoored from the face that should have held them.

There were two other items seemingly out of place: a notice—preemancipation—for a runaway slave, and a document detailing the profitability of a plantation nailery. He turned them over carefully and read the script, scrawled in charcoal and already beginning to fade.

September 16, 1864

Jupiter,

I have been practicing my writing like you taught me. I have not heard from you in so long I do not know if you are alive or dead. I imagine you using that mind of yours to do whatever it takes to make it out of the War. I imagine you coming back here to find me, and hopefully finding this letter. We have gone west to San Francisco. We hear the War did not reach that far, and there are places of hope for colored. I so wish I could be there to greet you, but with the War ending, we could not stay on the plantation much longer, and in the south there is no place for us—

He went to the next page.

I pray you can forgive me. I pray you will read this and still join me—

The pages were numbered 1 and 3; the second page was missing. Whenever he read what he had of the letter, he would speculate what might have been on that missing page. A name? Some other detail that would help to find her? Clara told him this was all that Sonya left. He was so grateful to have some part of her that he did not question the old woman's honesty.

•   •   •

San Francisco was a hard place to get used to. He often wondered why he'd chosen it. The desperate immigrants working the docks, the tardy prospectors still looking to stake a claim, the din of confusion from the strange screeching sounds of foreign languages, the grifters and con-men, the outlaws and robbers, the shanghaiing crimpers. The brothels. The earthquakes. Why would she have chosen this place?

He wondered if she was passing for something other than Negro—a Mexican or Spaniard. She was a shade or two darker than he was. He couldn't pass for white, but it was obvious he was something else besides Negro. In San Francisco, it was common for him to be addressed in Spanish or French, Arabic occasionally, but also a half dozen other languages he had never heard before.

2

Jupiter sipped his whiskey and watched the girls work the room. One of them walked over to him. "You want some company, stranger?"

It had been quite a while since he was with a woman. He had spent the last few years under a hazy spell; then, one day, he woke up, and no matter how warm their words were, he became all too aware of the coldness of their touch. Even body to body, there was still a vacancy and distance in their eyes.

"No. I'm fine by myself."

"You don't like me?"

He took another sip of his whiskey and put the glass down, but behind the woman propositioning him he saw a vision that made him swallow hard. "No, I don't want you. I want her."

• • •

Fletcher was an artist who sketched lewd scenes for a well-heeled clientele—scenarios custom ordered by men too private, too concerned with their reputations, to patronize a brothel.

Made to order with exact specifications, Fletcher's drawings needed compliant models. Maggie gave him access to a private room that he used as his studio. His clients paid well, but he had a weakness for fine liquor and gambling: his money always went back to the house.

Jupiter walked in without knocking. A woman wearing a maid's uniform caressed the shoulders of a nude woman wearing only a tiara fashioned out of wire, and holding a rolling pin as if it were a scepter.

A half-finished reflection of the two of them appeared on Fletcher's canvas.

Fletcher looked up at Jupiter. "I'm doing work for a client," he said. "I'm so sorry, ladies. He'll be leaving right away."

"Don't bother me none," said the queen. "Neck's starting to get stiff anyway. Why don't we just come back tomorrow?"

"That won't be necessary. He's leaving right now. And he's sorry for making you uncomfortable. Isn't that right, Jupiter?"

"I'm hungry," said the maid.

"Don't worry, Fletcher," the queen said. "We'll be back to get our money. No need to worry about us skipping out on you. You don't enjoy our company that much. We'll be back tomorrow."

The girl with Jupiter watched the nude queen follow the maid.

"What do you want, Jupiter?" Fletcher asked after the women had left.

"Excuse me, Fletcher, but you don't seem too happy to see me."

"Forgive the hostility, but you interrupt my business and you come in here with a girl who doesn't seemed all too pleased to be in your company. But it's good to see you've given up on your obsession. It's about time you've moved on."

"Actually, I haven't," Jupiter said. "That's what I'm here about—the sketch. You couldn't get the eyes right before. These are the eyes."

Fletcher sighed, "These are the eyes?"

The girl looked scared, but she didn't say anything. "Don't worry," Jupiter said to her. "I said all he'll do is draw you, and that's all he'll do."

"May I have a word with you, Jupiter?"

"Don't go anywhere," he said to the girl. "I'll pay you for your time; just wait right here."

He followed Fletcher behind a row of covered easels. "Sonya has eyes just like hers. Get those eyes on that sketch so I can make a poster, and maybe find her. But you have got to get those eyes right."

Jupiter hated the pitiful look Fletcher gave him.

"It's been *years* since the war's over," said Fletcher. "If you've found a woman with her eyes why not just count your blessings. Maybe that's as close you'll get. Why can't you see it as a gift and accept it?

12

She is for hire, I presume?" Jupiter wanted to break Fletcher's hand for saying that, but Jupiter needed his skill.

"You of all people should know it's not that simple. Where's your woman since Louise died?"

Fletcher's eyes danced. "All right," he said finally. "Young lady, could you come over here please?" Fletcher leafed through a stack of sketches, all of them incomplete in different ways. Some were missing a mouth, or a nose, or a frame of the face, but then he found one that only missed the eyes. "Sit still," Fletcher said to the girl. She looked over at Jupiter. "No, no, don't look at him. Look at me."

She looked down at her hands.

"Look at me, darling. Lift your head and look at me. Look at me like you've just been in the company of a very wealthy man, and he's promised to take care of you and you'll never have to see this godforsaken place again."

She tilted her head and opened her eyes. Jupiter watched as Fletcher drew them and captured—recreated—every bit of their radiant gleam.

3

Jupiter's cup rattled against the saucer. He sipped his tea and placed it down carefully, briefly remembering his training and the many times he had served this kind of china at Colonel Smith's plantation.

"Do you like your tea?" Maggie asked.

"It's fine."

"It's strange how you can be a man of so few words, but then at other times . . . not few enough."

Jupiter's hand moved slowly from the teacup as he looked up at Maggie. "I'm just a man. I'm sure you'd find those traits in others."

Maggie dabbed the corners of her mouth with the white linen, then laid it neatly on her lap. "Isn't it amazing how men can say, 'I'm just a man' as a way of dismissing or even excusing their shortcomings, yet they expect all the power, expect so much to be granted to them because of their gender—because they are men. How many problems could I get out of by saying 'I'm just a woman'?"

"You would never say that," Jupiter answered.

"No, I would never say that."

"Well, I'm not making excuses."

"No, I would never say 'I'm just a woman' as an excuse to forget my integrity or as an excuse to lose my hold on reason."

"It's just a thing people say," said Jupiter.

"It's just a thing that *men* say. The same men," said Maggie, "that use their manhood to excuse the weaknesses of their character, those same men are looking to take everything I have left. Everything my husband left me when he died. They're looking to take it all. You wouldn't let that happen to me, would you, Jupiter?"

He took a long pause, maybe too long. "No, Maggie. I wouldn't."

"No, you wouldn't, but that wouldn't stop plenty of men from trying. Who knows what sort of scoundrel I would have married—if my association with you hadn't made me a pariah."

Jupiter squinted. "Pariah?"

"Pariah . . . it means outcast . . . misfit."

"I know the word, just don't like the sound of it."

"Of course you know the word. You know many things. You know many words."

"I see you've been talking to Clement," he said.

"Jupiter, there are men out there who want to take everything I have. Everything I'm building. All that we are doing, all of our successes, have to be gained without attracting attention. My way of doing things has been designed not to attract attention. That's why I have you, Jupiter, because they don't see you coming. You and I are invisible. No one sees us coming. That's the problem with us, I guess. People like you and I, we want to be seen—it's part of our nature. But sometimes, quite often in fact, our natures do not operate in our best interests. You have to remain invisible. They don't see you out there. You are a shadow, and before they see you, who you really are, before they see what has cast a silhouette, by then it is far too late. You must remain the shadow. Funny thing about shadows, the thing common to all of them is that they do not speak. They do not give an explanation as to why they cast their darkness on other things. They are silent. They require no explanation. You have a keen mind, Jupiter, but you . . ."

"But you need me because I'm good with my hands," he finished for her.

"Yes, you are indeed good with your hands." Her face reddened. "You find me hideous, don't you?"

"I don't think you're hideous, Maggie. *You* think you're hideous. You're the one who called yourself a pariah."

She cleared her throat. "I think I'm finished with the matter. Let's change the subject, shall we. Any news about your family?" she asked.

Jupiter glared at her. She wanted to hurt him, invoke the personal hell he carried within him. He thought about his visit to Fletcher and the word *family* and everything it meant.

"No," he said. "No word."

Maggie reached slowly for Jupiter's face. He did not move. She came close to his cheek but closed her fingers and withdrew her hand.

"My, you are so exquisite, Jupiter. I see so much in you. So much of the kind of strength and character my late husband possessed. I see it in you, even though I'm not supposed to. Do you think there ever would have been a war if more white people could have looked across the cotton fields, plantations, and servants' quarters, just looked over and seen themselves in you, in your people, do you think the war still would have been fought?"

"Plenty of white folks saw themselves in us. Can't say that would have stopped it—it most likely caused it."

"No, I don't like this subject either." She checked the state of her hair in the mirror behind Jupiter. "I need you to stop talking so much during the course of business from now on. If these men, once they get back to shore, spread the word to keep an eye out for a colored crimper it would not only hurt my business, it would damage the thin barrier that keeps the races from killing each other."

•   •   •

Maggie lit the lamp, then snuffed out the match. "What do you think, Clement?"

"I think he's developing a conscience."

"Bad time, wrong cause."

"If he's putting you at risk . . . You know I would do whatever it takes to protect you. He's my problem. I brought him to you. If you want me to take care of him, I will."

"And just like that our problem would be solved," said Maggie.

"I understand your connection to him. I pass no judgment."

Maggie turned away. "No, it's not that. He helped me once, through a very difficult period." Her mind drifted to that night when she was shivering and clammy, fighting off the withdrawals from opium . . .

•　•　•

"Here," said Jupiter as he handed her a cup of some foul-smelling liquid. She brought it to her nose and vomited.

"How dare you come into my room," she said, puke still on her lips. "This time of night . . . if anyone saw you . . ."

"You need help. It's obvious. No one'll think twice about a Negro coming to the aid of a white person in need of his services."

"It's the kind of services offered that might be troublesome." She managed a putrid smile.

"Drink what's left in that cup. Hold your nose if you have to. It'll get you through the night. The early ones are hardest, but this will make it easier. During the war, it worked for plenty of men in my regiment."

She sipped it, then spit it out.

"You don't sip it. You swallow it all at once."

She braced herself, tilted back her head, and emptied the cup. She felt better almost immediately. "Don't judge me."

"Oh, I promise you I won't. You ladies of privilege and means get bored and develop a taste for the exotic, for adventure. You try things. Occasionally you go too far."

She laughed. "I can assure you I did not go too far." She undid the first three buttons of her top.

Jupiter looked away. There was the jagged scar where her breasts used to be. "The cancer went too far. Morphine was the least the doctor could do after they took my flesh away. They failed to tell me how I'd depend upon it long after the wound had healed."

"I'm sorry. I didn't know. I'll be back tomorrow night with another batch."

She nodded.

"Evening, Clement," she heard him say outside her room.

•   •   •

"What do you want me to do?" asked Clement as she returned from the memory.

"Watch him closely, for now. Don't do anything rash. I'll be giving you my word soon."

4

Archer sat up and shielded his eyes. It felt as though the sun blared from behind his lids.

"Lazarus has risen." She was angry but still poised, still beautiful.

Archer reached for her. "Forgive me, my love, but I had—"

"—another one of your episodes?"

"That's right. This one was especially painful—like electric eels fighting inside my skull."

She came over to him, ran her fingers through his hair, still damp from night sweats. He closed his eyes and pressed his cheek against her stomach.

"Were you in Chinatown?"

He looked up at her; those eyes were inquisitive yet trusting. "Yes, but you know I only use it for the pain."

The little boy walked in. "Mother, may I go and play with the other children?"

"Did you finish your lesson?"

"No, but I promise I'll finish it later."

"You may not play until you have finished your lesson."

Archer rubbed his temples. "Oh, go on and let the boy play. I wish I had played more as a child, but I was surrounded by serious adults—serious men who wanted me to be a serious boy. Now look at me. Am I one to be taken seriously?"

The boy smiled. "*See*, Mother, Mr. Smith says I should play more."

"You've heard my answer, now run along."

"You should be easier on the boy," Archer said, once the child left the room.

"Mr. Smith, I would appreciate it greatly if you did not tell me how to raise my son."

Archer squinted. "So, it's 'Mr. Smith' now, is it? If I remember correctly, not two nights ago, it was *Archer*—both whispered and screamed."

Her face reddened but she did not turn away. "Don't be crass."

He thought of his mother, her humorlessness and impatience with men and the games they played with a woman's dignity and loyalty. "My apologies," he whispered, remembering how he met the woman and the boy.

•   •   •

Archer's train reached San Francisco. He ached for opium. He had been sick most of the journey west. Shivering, cold sweats brought on by the opium drought. His first thought was to find lodgings but somehow he found himself, with clothes bag in hand, wandering into the more debauched section of town where the green dragon could be found in its dark dwellings.

Amongst the dim light and strangers, he nestled into his muse. Everyone was half-lidded and languid. The only sound was the occasional moan. Archer's mind went swirling. A nocturne that sent him coasting over the battlefields on a flying horse. And jousting with the Colonel, now a surprisingly agile bearded skeleton. The Colonel's lance brushed Archer's temple and his Pegasus screeched and flew away.

When he awoke, he had no idea how long he had slept: his watch was gone. So was his clothes bag. He would have been distraught had he not remembered to tuck his money into a hidden compartment of his vest. It made sense to do this while traveling, and he had merely forgotten to take it out.

He wandered out of the opium den onto the busy streets, stumbling past the comers and goers who paid him no mind or looked at him in disgust when they saw from whence he came.

Just across the way, he saw a church and a young woman handing out pamphlets and preaching a sermon not quite gospel but close to it.

"Greed and sin and fornication and prostitution and the China-man's drug will keep you farther away from Jesus."

He didn't realize he was walking to her. The little boy by her side handed Archer one of the pamphlets. "Will you come to Jesus?" he asked Archer.

Archer looked at the boy, thinking back on a time when he too was full of innocence. He looked at the woman, whose beauty could not be hidden, despite her struggle to appear plain. For some reason he thought of his mother, even though he had long since forgotten what his mother looked like. But the new memory, the replacement memory of his mother's face, very much resembled this woman. "Yes," Archer said, looking at the woman. "I would like to come to Jesus."

The woman took in boarders, but only on an evangelical basis. They had to agree to give their souls to Christ. There were other men around doing household chores and whatnot. Archer regarded them as virtual eunuchs. It was easy for Archer to tolerate them. He liked looking at the woman. She fed him, and he pretended to read the Bible and go to Christ, all while lusting after her. Until one day, he realized the ache for opium had gone. It had gone and been filled by a genuine love for Christ . . . and for this woman. She must have seen it too, for on that night, she allowed Archer into her bed.

The next morning Archer looked at the latest edition of the newspaper, lamenting the decay of the city in bold ink. He looked at the date under the masthead: he had been in San Francisco for three weeks.

• • •

She left his embrace and went to the window. There was a parade of some sort on the street below. "Have you heard anything about the man you are looking for?"

His temples throbbed. "I have. Does that disappoint you?"

She did not answer right away. Two men carried a large slab of meat, practically an entire carcass. One of the men struggled with his end and it fell into the mud. Another man came to their aid and they managed to load it onto a wagon nearby. "I thought you would have given up on all of that."

"The man killed my father, Elizabeth. That isn't something one easily forgives."

Why should a man have to explain such things? He thought back to that insolent Pinkerton who irritated him so, failing to see the importance of his mission . . .

Atlanta. August 1865.

Archer needed laudanum badly. He was already plagued with frequent tremors. But he was meeting the Pinkerton at noon, so he managed some restraint. Not that he had much choice; laudanum, let alone whiskey or a good brandy, was hard to come by in these parts now. But he would need something soon, before the sickness would overwhelm him.

The Pinkerton met him in an empty office, formerly occupied by a lawyer. Seated at a large wooden desk, the Pinkerton adjusted his waistcoat, attended to aiming a small torch at the bowl of his pipe, then said, "Mr. Smith," without looking up.

"What do you have for me, Mr. . . ." Archer thought a moment. "Forgive me. I almost called you 'Mr. Pinkerton.' But, of course, that is not your name."

"Pinkerton will do just fine. My own name is for family and friends. And even if I bother to tell them, I am always *Pinkerton* to my clients." Archer had already accepted that, not feeling up to dueling wits or verbal jousting. He grew weary at the thought of it. "Indeed," said Archer. "So what do you have for me?" Archer had already met with the Pinkerton a few days prior and told him what Cora had said about Jupiter's heading west.

The Pinkerton got his pipe good and prepped and sent a fragrant cloud through the anonymous lawyer's office. "The darkie's headed out West."

Archer shifted in his seat. Anger and fatigue weighed on him. "Forgive me, sir, but I do believe I have already provided you with that information."

"Indeed you have, Mr. Smith."

"Forgive me, once again, if I fail to see the sense in providing you with payment as well as information. I assumed our relationship would be quid pro quo."

The Pinkerton smiled a grin of smoke. It came out of his nostrils and wisped at the corners of his mouth. "Indeed, sir, we are in agreement. You told me he was headed out West, but through my contacts, I know what route." There was a long silence between them as the smoke began to cast a hypnotic haze over Archer, with all its spinning, twirling, and dancing. The haze reminded him too much of an opium dream. He was beginning to long for it.

"Please, Pinkerton. Forgive me if I wish to end the suspense."

"He's headed up the Cherokee Trail with a group of other freed slaves and soldiers."

Archer sat up straight, feeling sober only briefly. "I assume, Mr. Pinkerton, that you have your men dispatched to this trail with the intent to seize him . . . with the utmost haste."

"You could assume that, Mr. Smith, but you would be wrong." Archer could see that the Pinkerton was playing games with him—why, he did not know—but his patience was wearing thin. "And why haven't you?"

The Pinkerton leaned back and puffed his pipe. "The war is over, Mr. Smith. And you are still fighting battles."

"That animal killed my father."

"Yes, indeed. And like so many other animals, he has probably already littered the trail with his carcass."

"What are you saying?" asked Archer.

"I do not intend to send my men out into the woods to kill a nigger that may already be dead."

"That is not for you to decide. I am paying you to bring this man to justice. He killed my father, a *Colonel*. The Smiths have been in this country since its founding. I'm giving you good money to find him and bring him to me." Archer was getting dizzy. He did not know if he looked it, but he felt green.

The Pinkerton breathed through his pipe so that it flared a bright diamond of fire with only a hint of smoke and looked at Archer with pity. "I should remind you, Mr. Smith, that you have given me no money. Pinkertons take payment upon completion of their duties. With that being said, you should see to yourself, sir. . . . It seems that you have your own demons to wrangle with."

"My demons are none of your concern. And since you have proven to be of no help, I shall see to them as I see fit. Good day, sir."

"Good day, Mr. Smith. And good luck to you."

5

"Hello, Mrs. O'Connell," he said.

"Mr. Dalmore," said Maggie, "to what do I owe the pleasure?"

"May I sit?"

Maggie nodded. "Mr. Dalmore, I feel compelled to remind you that our last meeting began with the same formalities. I lost a great sum from our last dealings," Maggie said. "I shan't like to repeat it."

Dalmore crossed his legs. "Your money is not lost, it is *invested*. The concept is more than sound—it is the future. When the right time presents itself, we shall be up and running. It is still a viable concern."

Maggie leaned back in her chair. "You and your ships and guns. Haven't you been paying attention to anything? Railroads are the future."

He smiled. "Yes, railroads are good for the country, and many men will get wealthy by them. However, my dear, with ships and guns, one can rule the world. Railroads are not the future, they are the present—another gold rush with iron as a substitute. Now the skies, they are another matter entirely. The skies are the future—but until then the seas will have to do. When they can lay track across the Pacific from here to China, then I will be impressed."

"Mr. Dalmore, you are quite the visionary, but your contempt for railroads doesn't permit you to lie to your investors and allow them to think they are part of a railroad company when, in fact, you have made them unwitting arms traders, while you lay track that will ultimately lead nowhere."

"I lose no sleep over the matter, and as long as my investors make money, neither shall they . . . including you, Mrs. O'Connell."

"I have no cause for concern?"

"My dear, the *Cressida* shall be finished, and she'll be a *fine* ship. I have always been frank with you. It pleases me to have someone in my life with whom I can be completely honest. Despite your displeasure, I have noticed that you have kept the secret about the railroad between us. . . . I haven't even told that idiot Grayson."

"Your partner would object to being called an idiot." Maggie smiled.

"There's a good girl. We are in this together. Which brings me to the reason for my visit. A problem has come to my attention," Dalmore said.

"What sort of problem?"

"You've heard that Hutchins is still missing?"

Maggie shifted in her seat. "Missing . . . not dead?"

"I thought *you* would tell *me*. I've been direct with you so far; continue to be so with me."

"Of course."

"Our friend in Chinatown, Mr. Lin, may be involved with Hutchins's disappearance." He waited. "Hutchins was behind most of the anti-Chinese legislation, as well as the organized harassment of Chinese workers. The motive is obvious."

"Indeed it is. You employ a vast number of Chinese at your shipyard as well as your faux railroad."

Dalmore arched an eyebrow. "Yes, Hutchins has been a thorn in my side. He's got the Irish riffraff thinking that they should earn as much money as regular white men. Please, my dear, take no offense."

Maggie blinked slowly.

Dalmore continued. "Our arrangement for *enticing* crew has kept costs manageable. No, I'm afraid this affects you as well."

"I do not follow."

"One of Lin's men was beaten and he said a great deal." Dalmore looked around the room. "Is that Negro that works for you—what's his name? Neptune? Is he here?"

"Jupiter. No, he is not."

"Ah, yes, Jupiter. Probably for the best— He was spotted in China-town coming from Lin's place sometime before Hutchins's disappear-ance. Lin's man said Jupiter was paid a nice amount for the job."

Maggie swallowed hard and clasped her hands to prevent them from trembling. "Mr. Dalmore, you speak so disapprovingly of the evils of *my* business. I assumed that we are in the same business. Are we not?"

Wood floor planks creaked. Dalmore leaned back in his chair and rolled an unlit cigar between his fingers. "No, Mrs. O'Connell, we are not in the same business. You are in the business of calling attention to yourself, so that a man like me must come to speak to you about your childish mishandlings and give you a proper spanking like the petu-lant brat that you are. I am in the business of setting the terms and telling you that you have no choice but to follow them. Indeed, Mrs. O'Connell, we are not in the same business."

"Well, Mr. Dalmore, you've certainly said a mouthful. Would you be kind enough to tell me what these terms are that you speak of?"

"Someone from your operation needs to answer for this—it shouldn't be you. I have been known to be magnanimous on occasion . . . the choice is yours."

Dalmore left. Maggie stayed in her seat for a while. She noticed that Dalmore had left his hat on the divan. It made her feel spied upon. She caught her reflection in the two-way mirror and spat at it.

"Clement."

The door opened. "Yes?"

"Mr. Dalmore has left his hat. See that he gets it."

"Right away."

"Before you go, send up a bottle of whiskey. My mouth feels dirty."

"Of course."

"And Clement, make sure it's Irish."

6

Dalmore had just entered his carriage when Clement caught up to him.

"Mr. Dalmore . . ."

"Yes?"

"Your hat, sir."

"Oh, of course." Dalmore eyed the hat suspiciously before accepting it. "Many thanks. Good night to you, Clement."

Clement positioned himself between the door and the carriage as if to enter. Dalmore extended his cane and pressed it against Clement's chest. "Let's not make a scene," said Dalmore. "You are fine where you are."

Clement stepped away. "Can you see to it that no harm will come to her?"

"Yes," said Dalmore, "if she comes to her senses."

"This is not what we planned."

"No, it isn't what *I* planned exactly. I admit things have gotten a bit messy, and I have had to improvise, but I thought your man, Jupiter, would have done the deed. I understand that Lin can be very *persuasive*—few people deny his requests. I'm surprised Lin let him live."

"What will you do about Hutchins's men?"

"That Negro will have to be sacrificed. That should appease them."

"And if it doesn't?"

"There are many ways to quiet a barking dog."

Clement watched the streets flow in streams of people. "She's the strongest woman I've known . . ."

"And she'll be even stronger when we combine our resources. Richer and stronger."

"I see that. It's what she deserves, and it's what Mr. O'Connell would have wanted for her. The things that woman has done for me . . . She's too young, of course, but she's like the mother I never—"

Dalmore raised his hand. "I hate to interrupt you, Clement, but I sense a sad story approaching, and I abhor sad stories. Didn't we all come to this country to escape them?"

"Of course. I got a bit carried away."

"Oh come now, Clement. Sentimentality is ill-suited for a man of your height and width."

Clement stayed silent.

"Clement, forgive my indiscretion for a moment, but I am aware of Mrs. O'Connell's . . . affection for this Jupiter fellow. I trust that nothing unseemly has happened between the two of them?"

Clement's fingers curled at his side. "Maggie is a respectable woman."

Dalmore smiled. "Indeed. I trust that once she and I have married you'll continue to keep your feelings for her under control."

Clement looked down, then nodded.

"Good. I think we are done here." Dalmore closed the carriage door. "One more thing. Tell me, did Hutchins make a lot of noise or scream at all?"

Clement stared. "No, he was as quiet as a church mouse."

"Imagine that. I guess there is a first time for everything."

Dalmore signaled for his driver to move on. Clement watched as it descended a hill and was no longer visible.

7

They stopped when the braided man offered Maggie a handful of dried chicken feet. Jupiter watched as she went over to his cart and pointed at the glistening ropes of pig intestines slick with blood.

"Fresh?" she asked the man.

He nodded. "Always fresh. I just get today."

"Let me think on it. I'll be back." Their walk recommenced. "I like to go easy on them," she said once they were out of earshot. "Turn them down, but leave them with reason to hope. I feel compelled to be polite to them. They make their offers so sweetly."

Jupiter squinted at a man juggling what seemed to be at least eight oranges. "Some might call that toying with them."

Maggie smiled. "I could be more direct if you would prefer."

The eyes were like a fawn's, and the smile like a viper's. "No, we wouldn't want that," he said.

"It seems as though you don't appreciate my attempts at kindness. You've been so unfair to me as of late. Continuing on your crusade for absolution and compromising me in the process. That isn't fair to me."

"I think I've been more than fair with you, Maggie. Do your dirty work. Line your purse. If you're unsatisfied with me, just tell me to go."

Those eyes again. "If it were only so simple."

They passed a small shop. "In here," she said. A young Chinese boy waited inside and rang a bell when they entered. A lean and polished man in a black smock emerged from the back.

"Mrs. O'Connell," he said as he bowed. "I have your order ready."

He handed her a black pouch tied with a red string. A smell, strong and medicinal, came from it. "This will keep the sickness from returning."

"Thank you," she said, returning the bow.

"Always a pleasure," he said, smiling.

Jupiter nodded at the man, but he was met with an icy stare.

"He saved me," she said, once they were outside, "when doctors couldn't. They said I wouldn't live. They were wrong, he was right."

"Was he right when he gave you all the opium in Chinatown?"

"I told him about your concoction. He said I should have come to him first."

"I'm sure he did."

"I'm loyal to the people that help me, Jupiter. Maybe to a fault. The people I care about are a part of me. You are a part of me. I shall never forget all that you have done for me. Which is why I am giving you this advice—you are a part of me, but if any part of me was to become infested with tumors again, I would not hesitate to cut it out."

Jupiter believed her. He thought about the last time he was in Chinatown, about a month ago.

• • •

Red lanterns painted with Chinese characters, shelves filled with anonymous containers. The guide led him to a room in back—so dark that Jupiter hesitated to enter.

"Come," he said with a smile. "No problems."

Jupiter followed him through a long dimly lit corridor. They stopped at a bolted door. Chinese words were spoken, a slot opened, and eyes appeared. The slot closed and the door opened. A large man nodded, and then stepped aside.

"Please, follow me," said the guide.

The room was exquisite. A long mahogany table with roaring lions carved into the legs. Pure jade sculptures, a man riding a horse, almost life-size. Paintings on silk of such detail and color: scenes of tranquil lakes, a battlefield and its bloody aftermath.

Jupiter heard something in Chinese come from the shadows. It was as if one of the statues had spoken.

The guide pulled a chair from the table. "Sit." He and the large man that opened the door went into the shadows.

They emerged with an old man, small and ancient. So old that he seemed ghostly. Jupiter was reluctant to look at him.

The old man looked at Jupiter and spoke in Chinese.

Jupiter looked at the guide, then the old man, and waited for him to finish.

"Gao Lin thanks you for coming. He apologizes for the theatrics. Not much could be shared with you outside of this room." He flashed an innocent smile.

Jupiter squirmed. "What does he want?"

The guide turned to Gao Lin.

Again, Gao Lin spoke in Chinese.

Even though Jupiter did not understand a word, he felt a growing awareness of the intent. He did not like what he heard.

Gao Lin spoke for a long time uninterrupted. The guide waited patiently.

When the old man finished, he nodded at the guide. "These are hard times for our people. We come to this country and offer no malice, just our hard work. We are beaten, killed, and are granted no legal recourse. We are treated like dogs—"

Gao Lin grunted.

"*Worse* than dogs," the guide corrected.

"I've noticed these things. You speak the truth, but why am I here?"

"Gao Lin needs you to—"

Again, Gao Lin grunted, then spoke to the guide smoothly.

"Gao Lin is asking humbly, respectfully, for your assistance."

"How can I help?"

"There is a man that comes here, and he beat like a savage one of the girls."

"Sounds horrible," said Jupiter. "A man foolish enough to do something like that down here, one would guess he'd never make it out alive. Where do I fit?"

Huntington City
Township Public Library
255 West Park Drive
Huntington, IN 46750

"We want you to remove him."

"Remove him?"

Gao Lin spoke to the guide and displayed his irritation.

"Excuse me, my apologies," said the guide. "We want you to make him disappear. Gao Lin is willing to compensate you for your services."

Jupiter smiled at Gao Lin. "I appreciate the offer, but I don't kill for money."

The old man laughed. The guide began to speak, but Gao Lin raised his hand. "So you kill for free?" he asked Jupiter in English. "You were a soldier, were you not?"

How does he know that? Jupiter thought. "I was."

The old man nodded. "I only said *disappear*. He is a problem that needs a solution."

"Why are you asking me to do this? Am I wrong in thinking that you are more than capable of handling this yourself?"

Gao Lin nodded at the guide.

"This," said the guide, "is not something we can do ourselves. The law in this city is already looking upon us with so much scrutiny. They blame us for so much already—perils that are not even real. One white man dies here and we invite risk to our entire community. Usually when one white man dies, other white men come looking for him. They would have to die too. It would be a vicious cycle and we would be on the losing end of it."

"It's true that I was a soldier," said Jupiter. "But I think our cultures must have a different understanding of what a soldier is. I am not an assassin."

Gao Lin slammed his fist on the table. Jupiter felt the transferred reverberations.

"I know exactly what you do," Gao Lin said in English. "You work for that Irish woman. You drug the sailors that come in there and subdue them somewhere off the premises, so that she will not appear culpable. And then you sell these men to the shipmasters looking to fill their crews. I believe you call it 'shanghaiing.'" Gao Lin looked at the guide, and the two of them laughed. *"Shanghai!"* He put an end to the laughter and looked at Jupiter. "I know very well what it is that you do.

You have proven to be skilled at it. I am asking you to do it for me. The man we wish removed is powerful in his own right."

"His name?" asked Jupiter.

Gao Lin stayed quiet.

"Hutchins," said the guide.

He could hear the blood rush to his head—the same sound children foolishly believe is the sea when a shell is brought to their ear. He had spent enough time in the presence of this kind of power. The kind of power that watches patiently and does not feel the need to speak. The kind of power that audaciously asks you to make a man disappear and does not feel the need to conceal it. Jupiter knew that he and Hutchins would not be around for much longer.

8

Fletcher had done a good job on the eyes. Jupiter remembered them being like amber: a luminous brown that stopped all things in their path. The poster was the closest he had been to Sonya in seven years.

HAVE YOU SEEN THIS WOMAN? SHE GOES BY THE
NAME 'SONYA.' CONTACT J. SMITH AT THE O'CONNELL
HOTEL. ANY INFORMATION WILL BE REWARDED.

Yes, the eyes were exactly as he remembered them. Seven years is a long time. Did she still look this way? He put the poster up in the colored part of town. They all watched him as he carefully applied each poster. He made sure to count out the amount of space between each bill, placing them in the usual well-passed areas—saloons, general stores, and whatnot. Even though it pained him to do so, he also put them up in front of the brothels. Jupiter cringed at the possibility. Maybe he had already found her and lost her without knowing it. Maybe their paths had crossed, but they each had changed so much that one didn't recognize the other. Maybe in the search for her through other women he had been with her, but the reality and its absence of intimacy prevented any kind of connection or recognition.

The eyes were just the same. It was seven years ago when Jupiter had left Colonel Smith's plantation for the war . . .

"Why are you going off to fight in a white man's war?" Sonya had asked him. "You don't believe all that talk about the war being over for us, do you? Come away with me."

"I'm going to fight for my freedom," said Jupiter. So earnest, he was. Did he believe it? What did he know about *fighting*? Honor. Valor. Those were the things he overheard the sons of plantation owners talk about as they played soldier with their wooden swords. What did he know of it? He was simply a mockingbird with his wings clipped, singing a song in which he mimicked the sounds but couldn't grasp their context.

"I'm going to fight. About time I started," he said.

She clutched his hand then. "Don't go. If you go anywhere go with me. If you want to leave, leave with me. North or South, what kind of freedom you think white folks'll give us? It ain't somethin' that we need to be given, it's somethin' we have to make. It's not something we have to prove we deserve by doing their shooting and killing for them, it's something that we have to make for ourselves. It's not out there on some big battlefield, it's right here, in this little space between us— that's where we'll make it."

"What country have you been living in, Sonya? Whatever we make, they take," he said. "I've learned well. I'm going out there to get what's mine."

She slapped him. He immediately saw the regret in her face.

"You're already free," she told him through her tears. But the anger came back and she tried to slap him again, but Jupiter caught her wrist. "You're making a *choice*. You're already free."

9

He had not heard any information about Sonya. He began to accept what he must have already known. Seven years is a long time. Seven years ago, the country, even though war-torn, was a big one. Seven years later, it was even bigger. A lot of ground can be covered in seven years, plenty of places to lose yourself or someone. Jupiter knew that better than anyone. At least he had money. Wasn't that the point, to start a life once he found her? Get a plot of land, raise some cattle, maybe a general store or something like it, start a family? Yes, that was his plan; maybe it was her plan too. Lots of people have the same plans. Maybe her plans were realized already, and the woman he was looking for was long gone, transformed in the cocoon of time. Maybe she was somebody else's woman now, with a different name and a different look, different dreams—dreams so different from his that they camouflaged her so much he couldn't recognize her, and she would forever remain hidden. But that is the thinking of a man resigned to reason, the kind of sense that should make you turn around, go in the other direction, see the sense in staying down. It had the opposite effect on Jupiter. It made him stand up and go down to the colored section.

•   •   •

All the posters of Sonya that Jupiter put up were gone. Someone had removed them. They were taken down, but there was no evidence of them on the litter-strewn streets. The posters had just disappeared.

He put up more posters in the places with the most passersby. An AME church opened its doors and the congregation filed in. Since the war, maybe even before, he had felt a repulsion to churches. Why was it left up to man to administer God's justice, only to be burdened by the aftermath? How many men can you bury under a cross until you are sickened by the sight of them? This time something was different. He felt compelled to follow the congregation in and sit amongst the parishioners in the pews. He put the remaining posters inside his coat. The pastor began his sermon by directing everyone to Mark, chapter 13. Jupiter did not bother to ask for a Bible nor did he need to, fortunately. It was one of the many passages he had committed to memory.

No brother shall betray the brother to death, and the father the son; and children shall rise up against their parents, and shall cause them to be put to death.

He recalled the passage, but as the pastor spoke, Jupiter drifted into the empty space of Colonel Smith's plantation—a memory of a place that housed other memories. There, in the dining room, he saw two women—his mother and the wife of Colonel Smith—share a look, brief but charged with contempt. In a dark corner of the kitchen where he first felt Sonya's touch—a soothing caress on the back of his hand after getting too close to the fire. The drawing room, his own hands closing the dead eyes of the Colonel.

Jupiter looked around the church. Within the congregation were some of the most impressive Negroes he had ever seen. Looking at the sophisticated bunch, he would not have been surprised to see Sonya beside one of the men, child in tow. He had always pictured her in that sort of company. But as he scanned the crowd, he encountered not her, but another ghost from his past.

A part of the church needed repairs. A three-man team worked at the cracks brought on by a mild earthquake. One of the men hummed a tune that took Jupiter back to hot nights on the plantation when he could listen to the singing that came from the slave quarters. The field hands were farther down the hill, but their songs could still be heard up at the main house. Jupiter turned his back to the church and hummed along. One of the slaves had made up some bawdy lyrics for it. Jupiter smiled as he recalled them. Lewd and lurid details are the easiest to remember. He mouthed the words softly, but stopped when he heard the words coming from one of the men behind him. He turned to look at the man and felt a chill.

"Titus?" The man stood when Jupiter said his name.

"Not here. It's best we go someplace private to talk."

• • •

Jupiter was confused. He had come all this way to find his long lost love, only to find his enemy. Somehow, it made sense that Titus was here—wherever Sonya was Titus would be close by. Back on the Colonel's plantation, Titus had never made a secret of his affection for her. Sonya was always fond of him too; Jupiter knew that. So when he'd gone off to war, Titus was more than willing to fill the void Jupiter had left behind. He took Titus to Maggie's. He wanted to be on familiar territory for their conversation.

"Where is she?" Jupiter asked.

"Boy, that's how you greet me? After seven long years? I thought sure enough you was dead," said Titus.

"Well, obviously I'm not."

"No you not. Not yet."

"Where's Sonya, Titus?"

"Man, when you left for that war, I thought for sure you'd never make it. I thought 'what is he doin'? That house nigger ain't cut out to be no soldier.'"

Titus smirked. Jupiter could tell he was trying to get under his skin. He was hiding something.

"Well," said Jupiter, "some of us had to stand up and be men while the rest of you scared niggers ran off to God knows where."

Titus shot short bursts of air through his nose. "Well, while you was playin' dress up, switchin' one uniform for another, playin' tin soldier, some of us had to look after the women and children when them plantations was knocked down to rubble and the fields set on fire."

Titus was right. While Jupiter, and men like him, were off fighting one war, another battle was being waged in his absence. So, in a sense, Titus was another kind of veteran in his own right. Jupiter had to give that to him.

"Titus, I know we were never what you would call friends, but I've been looking for her since the war ended—here for the last three years. You are the closest I've come to her in seven years. Now, a lot of questions are racing through my mind, a lot of feelings. There's so much I want to say to you, none of it polite or gentlemanly. But this is a favor for me, my own piece of mind. Just tell me where she is. Is she all right? Can't we just start with that?"

Titus looked away. "She ain't here no more. She left."

The barkeep put down two whiskeys. Jupiter finished his in a gulp.

Titus pushed his glass away. "Some of us came here from the old plantation. Thought there'd be work—"

"Titus, I know all that. Sonya left a letter for me with Clara."

"She left you a letter?"

"That's how I knew to come here. What about Sonya? Did she come with you?"

"Yes, she did." Titus kept looking over his shoulder. "You come in here a lot? Not too many colored."

Jupiter squinted at the crowd, mostly sailors and longshoremen. "I guess it depends on your perspective. Those two over there are Mexican. That one smothered in tits is a Laplander, I think. The one by the piano is definitely a Turk. In the back, three Irish. And those two are either Italians or half-breed Navajo. Who knows how many languages are spoken here."

Titus shrugged his shoulders. "Not sure, but I know they can say nigger in each one."

Jupiter stared at Titus. "Yeah, none of them look like us, and they damn sure don't look like Sonya. Where is she?"

"Well, most of us spread out after we got here. Some went to San Joaquin, Sacramento, Oakland, but Sonya . . . word is she been gone about six months now."

Six months. Jupiter claimed the orphaned whiskey. In his mind, he had already set out after her. He wasn't that fond of San Francisco anyway. There was a time when their presence in the city had overlapped. He could have bumped into her at any moment. He must have known it on some level—that explained the recent intensity of the search. He could sense her.

"Where?"

Titus ran his hand over his mouth. "Africa."

Jupiter lunged at him, grabbed his throat. "Don't play with me, Titus. It'll be your last game. I've been to hell and back. I learned a thing or two while I was down in them flames. I know how to break a man. And let me tell you something, Titus . . . white or black we scream just alike."

"It ain't a game. She went to Africa. Liberia. Now take your damn hand off me." Jupiter let him go. "She said ain't no way America would be a safe place for colored. Not in our lifetime."

Africa. She might as well be on another planet. "Why'd you let her go?"

"C'mon, you know how Sonya is. She got that wanderin' spirit. Suppose that's why she never stuck to me like she stuck to you. Guess ya'll alike in that way. Nah, our people been here too long, gave up too much of our blood and sweat to be runnin' off to some place we don't know about. This here is where I need to be."

Africa. At least there were plenty of ships in San Francisco. Maybe there was one bound for the Ivory Coast or Sierra Leone. But that would mean going down the coast and around The Horn. Who knew how long that would take? Six months? Maybe he should just hightail it across the country, find passage on a ship in North Carolina or Maryland. He felt his mouth getting dry as he thought about the journey that awaited him. How would he do it? Foolishly, he looked at Titus as if he had the answer.

A man came up to Titus and kicked out the chair from underneath him. Jupiter stood as Titus fell.

"I didn't fight a war for niggers, just to fight Chinamen for work," the man yelled. An empty sleeve where his arm should have been was folded and pinned to his shirt.

Jupiter spotted the barkeep making a slow reach under the bar. He raised his hand and signaled to him to keep the shotgun hidden.

"What was your regiment?" asked Jupiter.

"What?" He was drunk. He turned to Jupiter with his arm cocked to fight.

"I was in the 55th. You?"

"The 48th."

"Hell-raisers, that's what the 48th were. Hell-raisers. You saved our hides in Petersburg at Fort Elliot."

The one-armed man stared at Jupiter for a moment as if recalling a memory, then another man put an arm over his shoulders. "C'mon back to the table, Sam. We've got whiskey and women. The world's a better place over there."

Titus made a move, but Jupiter held him back.

"My apologies," Sam slurred as they went back to their table.

Titus pushed Jupiter away and snatched his coat from the floor. "We've talked enough. Hate to be the one bringing bad news. I wish you well," Titus said, "but I got to go. Been nice catching up with you. Real nice."

As Titus put on his coat, Jupiter felt the urge to ask him to stay—but he resisted. His mind was assaulted by fragmented images of the past. He was brought back to the present by a seemingly innocuous sight: a folded piece of paper where Titus had fallen. As he went to retrieve it, he felt a strange calm when the paper unfolded. It all made sense when he saw the spark of the eye, captured so beautifully by Fletcher, stare back at him. Titus was lying.

• • •

Jupiter went after Titus. He couldn't see him on the street. He pushed his way through the crowd, hoping that he was headed in the right direction. Someone yelled, "Move," up ahead. Titus moved briskly through the crowd. "Titus," Jupiter called to him. He looked at Jupiter over his shoulder and ran. Jupiter chased him through the muddy streets, down the alleys, hopping over drunks and prostitutes, through Chinatown, around the pig-pens, and hanging animal carcasses and meat shops, and, finally, to the docks. The man was strong, pushing people out of the way as he ran, but he was winded. Jupiter was too, though not as much. He still had some fight in him. The war had made Jupiter fit for such things. It had made a hunter out of him. Just not a good one. He lost Titus in the crowd.

• • •

Jupiter went back to the church. The men were completing repairs on the rear wall. He walked over to one of them—a young man, tall and smiling—and hit him in the jaw. The other men, wielding their tools as weapons, jumped between the fallen man and Jupiter.

"You got trouble with him, you got trouble with all of us." He was a large man. Jupiter felt he recognized him from the bare-knuckle circuit. He helped the man up. "You all right, Henry?"

Henry nodded.

"I don't have a problem with you. Just him." Jupiter pointed at the man nursing his jaw. "He's bedding my wife."

"That true, Henry?"

Henry spat a blood-tinted stream of saliva. "I never laid eyes on your goddamn wife."

"Titus told me. He said the tall one called Henry was the man I'm looking for."

"We've known Titus for some time now, and that don't sound like him. What'd you say your wife's name was?"

"Sonya." Jupiter held his breath.

The men looked at each other. "Sonya?"

Jupiter nodded. "When the war ended, I went back to the old plantation looking for her. Folks said Titus forced her to come with him. I tracked her here from Georgia."

"I know Georgia. What parts?"

"Atlanta."

"Atlanta . . . I heard there ain't much left of it. You say you tracked her all the way here?"

Jupiter reached into his pocket and retrieved one of the posters. "Here, see for yourself."

He took it and squinted at it. "Can't read, but that sure looks like her."

"Look, what's your name?"

"Morris."

"Morris, my name's Jupiter. I am just trying to find my wife. It's clear that Titus lied to me and sent me over here to cause trouble. You tell me where he stays and I'll handle it myself."

Morris looked at the other men. Henry looked away, but said, "Go on and tell him."

"He stay over in Millbrae," said Henry. "Just past Miller's Dry Goods."

"Millbrae," said Jupiter. "Thank you. Thank you kindly, and sorry about that jaw, Henry."

Morris handed over the poster. "Good luck to you—"

Henry snatched the poster away. "I can read, and this here says something about a reward."

"Does it, now?" said Morris as the three of them encircled Jupiter.

• • •

On the road to Millbrae his knuckles bled, but he did not feel the pain. He saw Miller's Dry Goods first, and then he spotted the boarding house that welcomed Negroes. A black man walked out and Jupiter approached him. "Do you know a man called Titus? Big fella. Dark."

The man almost answered Jupiter, but when he saw those bloody knuckles, he shook his head and walked away.

"Just tell me if you know him!" Jupiter yelled.

The man picked up his pace and never looked back.

Jupiter looked in empty doorways and darkened windows, and watched the faces in the street. "Titus. Does anyone know Titus?" People gave him strange looks.

"Hey, you lookin' for Titus?" asked a voice from above. Jupiter looked up to the second floor of the boarding house. An old black man, thin with wisps of gray on his mostly bald head, peered out of the window.

"Yes," said Jupiter. "Is he in there?" He made a fist at his side.

"No, I ain't seen him around much lately. Think he got a girl in San Francisco or something. Damn fool left food in his room for weeks. Had rats all through the place. I never saw one rat as a slave. As a free man, I've seen more rats than free men."

"When did you last see him?" asked Jupiter.

"I don't know. Been a while— Now that I think about it, I used to see him with this little boy. A colored woman—well-to-do—weren't ever no slave—she teach colored children out her house. Towns. No, *Tinsley*. Her place is right up the road."

•   •   •

Jupiter found the Tinsley School for Colored Children. The streets were crowded; some fraternity for professional men of color had just let out. They hobnobbed and strolled leisurely. Jupiter plowed through them, but where was he headed? There were so many people. Something entered his field of vision, and Jupiter stopped. A boy, lifted by large hands, rose above the crowd, and was placed in a horse-drawn wagon. Once the boy was secure, Titus followed him inside. They were only a few yards ahead. The horse picked up its pace, and so did Jupiter, getting close enough to see the boy's features. He looked all too familiar, even though Jupiter had never seen him before. Just looking at him Jupiter knew that his own blood flowed through the boy's veins.

He ran faster, pushing aside anyone who got in his way. He picked up speed, feeling weightless as he gained ground, but then the boy turned around and looked at him. Jupiter became aware of his pounding heart, his lungs struggled for air, his legs felt like hot lead weights. The boy continued to stare. As the distance between them grew, Jupiter felt raw and naked, weak and powerless. He stopped in the road, panting and watching until he could no longer see them.

". . . and did Grayson say anything about when his leg of the railroad would be finished?" Miss Ellen rocked slowly in her chair.

"He said sometime within the next six months." Sonya leaned forward a bit. "He thinks that's two months ahead of his rivals." Miss Ellen did not seem pleased with that information. Sonya thought hard. "He also said something about the stock."

Miss Ellen stopped rocking. She brought her head into the light, revealing her wrinkles and the hints of red-brown in her mostly white hair. "What did he say, child? Think carefully."

Sonya tried to remember the details; she wanted to be specific. She wished she had Jupiter's memory, or even Jacob's, but all she could remember was how confused she was by Grayson's jargon. She parroted the words linked to that feeling, unsure if they were right, unsure if they mattered. "He said that once everyone hears about the completion date, he'll be able to sell his shares."

Miss Ellen's eyes narrowed. "Child, are you sure?"

Now Sonya was certain, even recalling what color shirt Grayson wore on the day.

Miss Ellen looked down for a moment, then sucked her teeth and smiled. "That rascal's spreading lies to get his stock price up so he can get out unscathed . . . and then buy the rival's stock when it falls. That track of his probably won't be finished until Jesus himself returns. Oh he's a slippery one. He and Dalmore fooled me once—but never again. Good child. Good . . ."

Proud that she had done the old woman some good, Sonya smiled.

• • •

Of the letters she sent him, all but one remained unopened. There were six of them, one for each month she was gone. She read the letter, recalling the frame of mind she was in when she put pen to paper, sending them off to her little boy, pleading with him as if he were the governor and she the convict begging for a pardon.

Please do not be angry with your mother. I know being separated is hard. It is ever so hard for me as well. But know that I am doing this for the both of us, so that we can have a chance at a better life . . .

She folded the letter and placed it back amongst his things. She wanted to, but it was hard to feel guilty. Mr. Grayson had offered a generous sum to be the traveling maid for Mrs. Grayson. He was a businessman who traveled often to Chicago and New York.

The things she had seen. She could not help but to smile. Each city—large, mysterious, sometimes indifferent or unwelcoming, but, more often than not, enticing. They hinted at just how big the world is, how little she had seen of it, and how much she wanted to share it with her son.

She got the job through Miss Ellen, the richest colored woman she had ever met—in fact the only rich colored woman she had ever heard of. No one was certain how she made her fortune, but that was less important than how she kept it. Miss Ellen did favors for the powerful: politicians, bankers, and businessmen, they all asked her for loans to avoid ruin when a bubble burst, a campaign failed, or a venture went belly-up. There was even a rumor that she had funded John Brown's raid. She kept her power by pretending not to have any, never allowing a white man to be embarrassed for asking her for help—that and strategically placing the right woman in his orbit. Any service job for a wealthy family or establishment went through her. She helped countless newly emancipated women like Sonya, immigrants, and destitute women find employment. Her only requirement was that the women kept their ears open. She decided where you were to be placed, and you repaid her with information—that was a secret one would take to their grave. The San Francisco elite never suspected that they were being spied upon by their women from the margins.

She remembered the first time she met the woman. Sonya arrived at the big house on Octavia Street. She went to the back and knocked on the door of the servants' entrance. An old, brown-skinned black woman wearing an apron answered the door. Obviously the head housekeeper, Sonya thought. The woman offered no greeting.

"Hello, ma'am. My name is Sonya. I understand that there is an opening for a maid position."

The woman looked Sonya over and nodded in what seemed to be approval. "Follow me," she said. They went through the large kitchen and into an even larger study. The woman took a seat while Sonya stood.

"Tell me about yourself, child."

"Well, ma'am, I've worked as a laundress and domestic at various places around the city. I can provide references, if necessary."

"*References.*" The old woman laughed. "I'm sure you can . . . and they will all be glowing."

"Yes, ma'am."

"Well, that's not too impressive, is it? To have so many references from people who were supposedly so satisfied with your performance but are very eager to see you move on."

Sonya swallowed hard. "Ma'am, I left all of my employers on good terms."

"Oh, I am sure you did, but how aggressive were they in keeping you on?"

"Well . . . a Mrs. Dunleavy fell on some hard times—not to spread her business—but she was no longer able to afford a large staff. Mrs. Carmichael wanted to bring on a cook . . . specializing in cuisine I was not familiar with."

The woman nodded and held up her hand. "*Mr.* Dunleavy is a foolish man who thinks things get cheaper when you have less money. His staff are *my* people. You don't pay my people what they're worth, then I tell my people to move on. As for Mr. Carmichael . . . well, he's got a weakness for pretty young Negresses. Mrs. Carmichael can look the other way only for so long. Tell me, child, if I've said anything untrue."

Sonya stared hard and stayed silent.

"Good. You know how to hold your tongue," Ellen said. "You were a slave before the war?"

Sonya nodded. "On the Smith plantation in Georgia."

"I bet you had a hard time with the Colonel chasing you around the place."

Who was this woman? "You know everything about me, don't you?"

Ellen smiled. "Just everything you've chosen to tell."

A tall white man—obviously of means, likely the owner of the house, Sonya thought—entered the room. "Excuse me, Miss Ellen . . ." He looked over at Sonya. She bowed her head ever so slightly.

Miss Ellen's demeanor did not change. "What is it, Thomas?"

Sonya's lips parted. No sound came. Call a white man by his first name and no repercussions—who was this woman?

"There is a matter," said Thomas. His eyes skirted to Sonya, then back to Miss Ellen.

"What kind of matter?"

Thomas raised his chin a bit and added some rigidity to his posture. "Some gentlemen from the *bank* . . ."

"I am having a conversation with this woman. I'll be with you shortly."

Thomas lingered a bit too long.

"Tell them to wait, Thomas. That will be all."

He left. Miss Ellen looked at Sonya. The slyest smile formed on Ellen's face. Sonya couldn't help herself. She smiled too.

• • •

The Graysons needed a maid and they needed a cook. She got that job as well. The money was good, an amount that she could never refuse. They had refined taste. Back on the plantation, the Colonel had nurtured refined tastes as well. He'd developed a liking for French cuisine and had the cook of one of his guests train Sonya in how to prepare the rich Parisian dishes.

Mr. Grayson's palate appreciated the training given to Sonya by her former master, although he abhorred slavery.

She had resented making those meals for the Colonel, just as she had resented the Colonel. In fact, she was full of resentment and, even though it pained her to admit, it was the boy that conjured up a good portion of that resentment. He made her think of Jupiter.

•   •   •

Supposedly this was a new country after the war. She was not hopeful about its chances. As far as the way they treated the Negro, it seemed nothing had changed. San Francisco was to be a new beginning, but the hatred toward the Chinese did not beacon anything new; it was something old, something angry, something familiar. And now Miss Ellen, the most powerful woman—of any color—she had known, was worried. Maybe it was time to leave. More than a few respectable colored people were going to places like Canada, Africa, and even Mexico. Africa—at least Liberia—always had a certain mystical allure. Her cousin had gone there per the conditions of her manumission. She still had the letters Mary sent to her from the new country—close to ten years ago. She read them when times were hard. To her, they were totems of faith and optimism, a fairy tale of a captive princess freed by the death of her oppressor and whisked away to a magical land where she lived happily ever after. Titus would tell her it was childish to harbor such fantasies, but he always had an issue with her as of late. Her arrangement with Miss Ellen, her desire to better herself by improving her reading and writing skills—it all seemed to irritate him. But she didn't care.

His anger had started to scare her, and she made him leave. He got a room at a boarding house in Millbrae near Jacob's school. He apologized, said he'd change, and was just starting to work his way back into her life.

Maybe it was the way she didn't take his new name, Freeman, and held on to her slave name, Smith. Titus said it was because of Jupiter, and he was right, partly. All the people she knew and loved were called Smith. Most of them she would never see again. Yes, she was no longer in bondage, but she did not want *that* chain to be broken. And she liked that when she thought of Smith work came to mind—work on a higher plane than the toils of slavery. Work that was respected: there was skill and craft, heat and hammer in it. She considered playing with the spelling: maybe a silent "e" at the end, something to distinguish her from all the other unrelated Smiths. For all of Titus's symbolic name changing, she thought it tragically ironic that he would call himself Freeman in a country where he still was not truly free.

Titus had been a valuable asset to a woman alone in that savage country, this wild city. His size thwarted most of the direct threats, but they were still susceptible to the same perils and dangers as other Negroes. This was the first time in her life that she felt protected. It was a new feeling for her. So much so that she didn't even know how to put a word to the feeling that she had never felt before.

Her mind raced. She alternated between slicing potatoes—almost cut herself, twice—and tending to the laundry, soiling the clean clothes with her dirty hands. She looked at Titus's pants; big and wide like a carnival tent. He wasn't wiry and muscular like Jupiter—she did remember that about him—more like big and brawny. Yet it had been so long since she had last seen Jupiter. She could not even remember what she loved or missed most about him—she did not have the kind of memory that Jacob had. Jupiter had been on her mind so much lately—especially with Jacob's fascination with memory games. It made her think about those years just before the war when the savage institution of slavery was losing its thin veneer of civility, yet Jupiter and Archer continued to challenge each other with quotes from Shakespeare or some Greek play she had never heard of while the Colonel watched approvingly.

• • •

Titus came in with Jacob.

"Well, you two are here a lot sooner than I expected." She reached for the boy and he walked past her.

Titus seemed out of breath. "There was a wagon for let. Seemed like a good idea. Been working all day. . . . The boy seemed to like it."

This is when a woman should kiss a man, greet him with love and affection. The urge should have been there, but it wasn't—it rarely was.

She went back to the laundry. There was something in the pocket. It was like a flower that had yet to open. She let its square petals bloom. She unfolded the piece of paper. She almost fainted when she saw her own face staring back at her.

"Titus, what's this?" she asked him. "Titus?" She held up the poster.

He was silent.

"Say something." She pointed to the black letters.

"You read better than me," Titus said.

Jacob came over to eye the poster. "It says J. Smith, mamma. J. Smith. 'Have you seen this woman?'" the boy read. "'Looking for Sonya Smith. Please contact J. Smith at the O'Connell boarding house. Mamma, why is J. Smith looking for you?"

She jerked her head at Titus.

He looked away.

"Titus, is this Jupiter looking for us?"

He nodded.

"How do you know? Titus? Have you seen him?"

"Saw him not too long ago. Been putting up posters all over town. I took down every one I could find."

"You mean to tell me Jupiter's not dead?"

"Wish it were so, but he ain't."

"And what'd you tell him? Titus, what'd you tell him? Did you tell him about Jacob?"

"No. He don't know about the boy."

Sonya balled up the poster. Hit his chest. Slapped him as hard as she could. The hits were more like the flutter of butterfly wings to Titus. He grabbed her hands. "How could you do this to me? You knew I thought he was dead. Knew how I felt about him."

Titus threw her hands back at her. "Yeah, I know how you feel. Yet I still took care of you and your boy like he was my own. And I been looking after you. Making sure you were safe. All while you held on to some dream, some ghost."

She turned away.

"Yeah, he still a ghost, even though he come up. Half of him is in this world, the other half's in another. Yet you long for him like he's some sort of perfect man."

"You don't understand, Titus," she said. "It ain't as easy as that."

"So now I ain't smart enough to understand? Look here, you want to run off and chase that nigger, then go ahead."

"What'd he say? Where'd he go?"

"Well, I told him you run off to Africa. Liberia."

She fell to her knees. Jacob comforted her.

"Sonya," said Titus. "I love you. I didn't mean what I said before. I did all that sacrificing 'cause I love you. I know what kind of man I am, what kind of man I can be. I'm sorry I lied to you. I just want to take the best out of this world, however much it will let me, and give it to you. But Jupiter ain't gonna promise you that. Go ahead and see him. You'll see the man he's trying to become, and the man I already am. If you got any sense, you'll stay right here with me."

"I know you are a good man, Titus. I know, but you're not good for him." She looked at Jacob. "And what's not good for him can't be good for me."

He grabbed her arm. "Maybe I ain't good for him, but maybe you not good for him neither. Maybe you not good at all. Gone for six months. What kind of mother leave her son like that?"

"Stop it, Titus."

"Stop what? Telling you the truth you can't stand to hear? All my life I had to hold my tongue. Get mad—don't say nothing. Treated bad—don't say nothing. Watch you and the other pretty yellow gals up the hill do what you do to get in Ol' Colonel's good graces, and I don't say a word. And you think you the one so damn good." Titus pushed her against the wall.

Jacob took a step toward him. "Let go of my mother," he said.

"Don't move, honey," Sonya advised. "Mamma's all right."

Jacob began to cry.

Titus grabbed her throat and squeezed. "How much more money

will it take to keep you here? What price Miss Ellen set for you? Don't think I don't know what you do for that old whore."

Titus held his grip. Her throat struggled to make a sound. "I am not a whore, and neither is she."

"You are what I say—" Titus stopped.

Sonya felt his grip loosen as he looked down. A red peony bloomed on his shirt. She pushed the knife in a bit deeper. "My son is watching this. You know what kind of memory he has. He'll probably never forget this moment. But how he remembers it is up to you. This can end with you letting go of me and letting Jacob and I walk out that door, or it can end with your guts hanging out your belly and you bleeding to death."

Titus let go. He winced as Sonya withdrew the knife. He clutched his stomach. The wound wasn't deep enough to kill him, just deep enough to scare him. He backed away and Jacob ran to his mother. He lingered at the door, the fantasies of life with her now overwritten by the sight of her holding a knife stained with his blood in one hand and her son in the other. "You just remember that when we were crossing this country, when the mules gave out, or when we couldn't hitch a train and you got too tired and your legs gave out, it was *me* that carried you. Both of you."

Sonya stared at him and held her boy tighter.

Titus put his hand on the wound, then looked at the blood on his palm. "I'm sorry," he whispered as he left.

11

It was dark in that place, yet his eyes still burned when he opened them. Whatever alchemy went into that strain he indulged in, it was strong—almost strong enough to make him forget his name. Almost. Lately he had been craving his opium on the more powerful side. He stood, slowly, feeling as if someone was still pulling him down. He flung the doors open, met with the bright light, only intensifying the pain behind his eyes. A strong light, accompanied by sounds of foreign tongues. Every word seemed screamed. Light and sound, so oppressive that it seemed supernatural. He had crossed paths with one of those "slant-eyed men with braided hair." Haunted is what they called him— or at least that's what he heard—but that was to be expected of a man who had to dig his father's grave after finding him murdered.

Memories emerged, all too clear: The things he wanted to forget as well as those things that he didn't. The reason he came to this city, the man he was looking for, the things he wanted to do to him once he found him, all vivid.

He walked through the city, which wasn't easy—too many hills. He stood outside a church contemplating if he should go in or if they would be willing to receive someone like him. He liked to do this, stand outside churches and consider the possibility of redemption waiting for him in one of the pews, but he never went in.

A woman walked out, young and beautiful. His eyes followed. Before he knew it he had followed her across the street, but then she disappeared. He lost her somewhere in the loud, bright crowd. There were too many people in this damn city. He had seen her before, haranguing people outside the saloons to find the Lord. He noticed her beauty then but avoided her fiery sermon—he already had another pretty proselytizer to deal with—now here she was again. There were no coincidences: his father taught him that. Everything was connected.

He leaned against a wall. His leg bothered him. When he thought of his leg, he thought of the war; and when he thought of the war, he thought of his father; and when he thought of his father, he thought of the man who killed him.

He looked at a wall and noticed a poster; on it he saw the familiar face of another woman. He read it:

Have you seen this woman? Contact J. Smith at the O'Connell Hotel.

He trembled as he reached for it, then swiped it down and into his pocket, as if stealing some precious jewel.

12

Jupiter went back to his room. Maybe the boy would tell Sonya that he saw him. . . . But how could he? He didn't know Jupiter from Adam. Maybe Sonya would see one of the posters and come looking for him. There was that possibility—wasn't there?

● ● ●

There was a tall Irishman at Langley's who liked to accept challengers from the crowd. "Who here can take the Scourge of Dublin?" Shirtless and his arms held open, he stalked the crowd in circles. He looked sculpted out of pink marble. "I see many people but no men. . . . At least none worthy of my skill." He threw a flurry of punches that sliced the air. An old man, short and broad, emerged. "I'll take ya," he spat. "And I'll knock that smile off your fat Irish mug—and have a helluva time doing it!" The crowd cheered.

Jupiter tapped the man on the shoulder and raised his own hand to the crowd. "No. You gentlemen came to see a fight that matters, one with real stakes, not just a pointless brawl, but a fight where the outcome affects all of our lives. I challenge the Scum of Dublin."

Silence.

A man with a white beard tinted with dust came close to Jupiter and squinted. "Yep. He's a nigger."

The crowd erupted in a din of cheers and betting.

"Aye," said the Scourge, "I see we have a mongrel that likes to bite. Well come on over here, you half-breed mutt, and let me put you out of your misery." Jupiter didn't wait for the crowd to react. He sent a punch to the Scourge's face that made him shut up and get to work.

During the war, Jupiter had engaged in many fistfights of this sort—most of them against men in his own regiment. He wasn't worried about losing; he knew too many weak spots on a man's body. Enough pressure on the kidneys and they fall like a shack on a windy day. He didn't think about the money. As he inflicted more damage to the Scourge's kidneys than rotgut whiskey, he thought about coming home to find Sonya, only to kill a man he had known all of his life.

13

Archer walked through the crowd. He did not know why, but he felt like searching the faces. He had settled into this life easy enough—but he was already thinking of ways to free himself. He thought of how badly the boy and his mother would be hurt if Archer were to suddenly disappear from their lives.

Many Negroes passed by on their way to work the docks, clean stables, or foolishly pan for gold. Until one of those black shadows was more *distinctive* than the others. Something about the sight seized the movement of Archer's muscles.

He followed him past the general store, past the tannery, staying just two or three people behind him. All the world seemed to drift away—an optic iris locked on the back of the man's head, the rest of the world pushed to the edges. Archer kept following. His heart began to race as he got closer. He followed the man into an alley that led to the dock, then past the docks and into a tavern. Down in the tavern was a large fight pit. Archer blended into the crowd and watched the Negro, waiting to see his face. The Negro traded words with what looked like a large Irishman. The crowd urged them on. A fight commenced. Over the flurry of punches Archer only watched for the Negro's face. It was as if he were the one in that ring. One of the fighters must have landed a good punch because everyone screamed. The Irishman moaned on the floor. The Negro stood over him. He turned to face the crowd. Jupiter raised his hand in victory.

• • •

After the fight, Archer followed him for a long while, and eventually to a boarding house. All Archer had to do was be patient. He had tracked him out West and now he finally had him. He waited in an alley across from Jupiter's boarding house, trying to fight off sleep in the darkness.

Come dawn, Jupiter finally walked out. To pull out a gun in that crowd would send women and children screaming. He had to get close enough to push the barrel into Jupiter's back, feel his muscles tighten with fear, relax with recognition at Archer's voice in his ear, then seize when the realization of this seemingly chance meeting's purpose sunk in.

He snaked his way through the crowd, bumping into people, stepping on their feet, finally getting close enough. Archer pulled out the gun and aimed it at the back of Jupiter's head. The thought of pulling the trigger and Jupiter's brains splattering on the man next to him made Archer reassess. He wanted it clean. He didn't want the blood on him, but he enjoyed the power of holding Jupiter's life in his hands—so close to him now, after all this time, that he could breathe on him. All Archer had to do was pull the trigger, but he didn't. He couldn't. He needed another option. He tried one more time and aimed the gun at Jupiter's head. His hand shook. A woman gasped. He lowered his pistol and walked through the crowd. People avoided him and struggled not to make eye contact. He made it back to the other side of town with the pistol still in his hand. He kept walking and eventually the pistol was gone. He had dropped it somewhere, he didn't know when.

• • •

Archer was not watching where he was going when he bumped into the man.

"If you intend to walk, at least plan to keep your eyes open," said the stranger.

"My apologies, sir—" Archer looked at the man, then took a step back. It was like looking at himself—not the Archer of now, but the

Archer of the past, before his trek across the country, before the hell of war, before the desperate need for survival.

The stranger seemed taken aback. He stared at Archer for a while. He must see it as well, thought Archer.

"No apologies necessary," said the stranger. "Why don't we go inside? Join me for a drink."

Archer agreed.

"Name's Ellis," he said over his whiskey.

"Archer."

"You're from the South. I hear it. What parts?"

"Georgia. And you?"

"North Carolina. Greyback?"

"Uh huh. You?"

Archer watched Ellis's eyes jump. "Yes."

Archer laughed. "You don't have to lie. You jumped conscription, didn't you?"

"I jumped at my best chance for survival. Can't blame a man for that."

"No," said Archer, "you can't blame a man for that. Funny thing, war is. Atrocities are bookended by the mundane. You'll watch a man lose his head in a spray of blood—a man with whom you shared bitter tobacco, stale hardtack, and a lewd story or two—and hand to heaven, you'll remember some forgotten lean-to in the distance, or the way the sunlight sends up orange over the green line of the trees. Hard to look at nature without thinking of a man dying."

Ellis took another sip of whiskey. "What are two southern boys like us doing out West, Archer? I've come to strike it rich. The high seas, that's the future. Trade with other nations across the vast oceans. Sure, this country is big, but soon it will run out of room—it will be around the globe that America finds her sustenance for the future, and I mean to take part in it."

"So you're a sailor?" asked Archer.

"Well, of sorts. Something like that. I'm a cooper."

"A cooper?"

"I make barrels," said Ellis.

They both laughed.

"You'd be surprised how often a good barrel comes in handy on a ship sailing across the ocean."

"I can imagine," said Archer.

"What about you? Why are you here?"

Archer thought for a moment, took a sip of whiskey. "I came to San Francisco to kill a man."

Ellis, lifting his drink for a sip, stopped short. He looked at Archer.

"I tracked him here, all the way from the South. I've been here for months. I finally get close to him and I couldn't even pull the trigger."

"Why's that, Archer?" Ellis asked, still frozen.

"It's hard to kill a man you grew up with. No matter what he's done." Archer stared at Ellis, then smiled.

"Oh, you're a sly one! Almost had me. Guess I deserved that. I love a good story. Cheers, to Archer."

They clinked glasses. They drank awhile. They grew warm and removed their coats.

"Archer, I've had my fill. My bladder needs to see a man about a stagecoach. I'm going 'round back."

Archer nodded.

Ellis was gone for some time before Archer realized that he wasn't coming back. Archer reached for his coat, but it was gone. Ellis had left his and taken Archer's.

Things just seemed to happen. Somehow, he was in Chinatown. He did know the phantom smell in his nose. He could not pin it down until he entered the opium den. He rested on the floor next to two very quiet men and began to board his green dragon. That is when he realized what the smell was: it smelled like home . . .

• • •

Archer's mother held his arm tightly. "Come closer to your mother, boy. I want to show you something. I want you to see truth in its rawest form. I want you to see how a man acts when he thinks no one is watching. And how that impulse to behave in such a way is in you. But you're still a boy. You have me for a mother. We can start now, and make sure it doesn't grab ahold of you, like it has so many men in the South, like it has your father. Come to the window, boy, but don't make a sound." She parted the curtains as she held Archer's young body to hers. For a moment she was breathless and still, then Archer felt her chest heave. "There," she said. "Look, but don't throw these curtains back, look through the space I have provided for you. You see there . . . that's your father . . . going into the slave shed. Do you see it? Tell your mother if you see it."

"Yes, ma'am, I see it," said Archer, not really sure if he had or if it was the phantoms of his mother's mind projected onto his own.

"You did see him, didn't you, Archer?"

"Yes, I saw him."

"*What* did you see? It's all right, you can tell your mother. Don't be afraid. Now is not the time to be worried about decorum and what is and what is not appropriate. Tell me what you saw. You're an innocent in this situation, and I promise you will still be innocent, even after speaking such abominations to your own mother."

Archer began to tremble. His young mind not fully able to grasp what was happening, only sensing the danger on an animalistic level, not knowing the plot, but knowing that he was in some kind of strange performance of double-speak and whispers that is common in the adult world. The dual-play, where the words spoken are from one performance, yet the facial expressions are from another. The kind of play that children always know is being performed, even when they cannot seize the content.

"Say what you saw." She grabbed him tightly, shook him.

"Mamma, I . . ." He was confused. He did not know if he should repeat, but he knew that whatever he said would mean trouble, for him, for his mother.

"Speak," she said.

"I saw Daddy going into the slave shed."

"There's a good boy," she said before the tears. "Such a good boy," she said into his neck. She held him so closely that Archer felt suffocated by her sobs. "I'm sorry. I'm sorry you had to see your father in that way, but now you know. Now you know the kind of man he is, and the kind of man you must not become. The kind of man that would build slave quarters right outside his wife's bedroom window. Taunting her. Begging to be spied on, debasing her, turning her into some kind of immoral voyeur. You do understand, don't you?"

"No, Mamma," Archer said to his surprise.

"You do know why your father is going into that shed, don't you, son?"

Archer shrugged his shoulders, then shook his head.

"Don't play games with your mother. Don't be like him. Do you know why your father is in that shed?"

He shook his head again.

"Oh dear God how you've learned already. Don't make me debase myself and speak the horrors that go on in that shed. It's bad enough that *I* know, but then to make me say it to my own son. He's trained you well, your father has. Hasn't he?"

"Yes—I mean I don't know, Mamma."

"Fine. This is the game we'll play. I'll say it to you, to show you that I am not afraid to remove all ambiguity from the situation, so that it is clear in your head what has occurred this night and why I've acted the way I have. But I will retain what is left of my dignity. I shall not say it aloud. Come closer to your mother, and I'll whisper it into your ear." She cupped her mouth over his ear. He could feel her hot breath and tears snake along the contours of his ear. Then she spoke, a whisper that became breathless and hurried and full of tawdry details that made Archer's ear grow physically hot. His eyes grew wide as he looked through the parted curtain, a sliver of moonlight shining through the clouds and the slave quarters casting a long shadow upon the house.

"There," she said as she finished. "Now there won't be any games between us. Now you know the kind of man you must not become. Now you know what threatens the honor of so many of our men in the South. Promise me you won't be like them, hand to heart, promise me."

"I promise you, Mamma." But even then, the lurid details went to work, tilling the soil, planting the seeds, laying foundations and erecting monuments, vivid and sensual in his young mind where none had been before. But they were there now, thanks to the brief tutelage his mother had given him. Now they were there, gilded, opulent, garish. Now his mother was asking him never to kneel at such altars. Even then he could feel the temptation rising, and he wasn't sure if it was a promise he could truly keep.

"Promise me," she said again.

"I promise."

"Heart to heart?" she took his little hand and placed it above her left bosom.

"Heart to heart," he said, pulling his hand away.

"No," she said. "Don't pull away from me in shame. There should be no shame between you and I. There should be no shame in *this* room. Down there, in those quarters, there should be the shame. There should never be any shame in this room. Heart to heart," she said, again placing his hand above her bosom.

Archer looked her in the eye. "I promise, Mamma. Heart to heart."

Maggie watched her patrons through the two-way mirror.

"Mrs. O'Connell."

She hadn't heard Clement enter. "Yes."

"I'm afraid our concerns about Jupiter are warranted."

"How so?"

"We were all set to round up men to crew some ships, and Jupiter was nowhere to be found. Had to hire muscle off the docks. We crimped two men—one from a brothel, the other from an opium den. They're down below. I went to his room and he wasn't there. But I did find this." Clement handed her a box. Inside were a deed to ten acres of land in San Joaquin, and five thousand dollars.

"Dear God. So Dalmore was right."

"Seems so, ma'am."

"Why would he betray me, Clement? Have I treated him so poorly?"

"You've been more than fair, ma'am, but it's possible that he just wanted to be free of this business. Made himself conspicuous so he'd be of no use to you. You can't do this forever."

"Where is he now?" asked Maggie.

"Word is the Scourge of Dublin just got beat by a Negro. I'm certain it's him."

"And now my shadow is famous." Maggie stared through the mirror, absently toying with her pearls. "Clement," she said without looking at him.

"Yes?"

"If Jupiter wants peace, then we should give it to him." She faced Clement. "Permanently."

"Of course, Mrs. O'Connell."

•   •   •

Sonya and the boy read the sign outside the O'Connell Hotel.

"Come on," she said to him.

"I don't think we can go in here, Mamma."

Clement stopped them at the door. "The boy's right. You can't come in here."

Sonya couldn't speak. She handed the folded poster to the man.

Clement smoothed it out and read. He looked at her, then the boy. "Wait right here."

The drunken men presented their vacant gazes. Those that didn't look at her with contempt looked at her with lust. She brought the boy closer and her coat tighter around her.

Clement reappeared. "Follow me."

He led them up brass steps, behind the bar, then to a room filled with exotic artifacts. Chinese, it seemed to Sonya.

Maggie was seated, reading a book. She marked her place and closed the edition of *Robinson Crusoe*. "Nonsense. Men are always acting like boys to prove their manhood. Why does it seem that men are always searching for adventure while we women have it thrust upon us?" She stood; well-dressed. "Hello, my name is Margaret O'Connell, but please, call me Maggie."

Sonya managed a smile.

"I see that you have brought me this poster. What is it that I can do for you?"

Sonya tried to locate her resolve and express her intentions directly to this white woman. "Ma'am, I—"

"Please, call me Maggie."

"Miss Maggie—"

"Just Maggie."

"Maggie, I am the woman on that poster."

Maggie looked at the poster. "My God, it *is* you. I must say that it does not do you justice. You are quite beautiful."

"Thank you . . . Maggie."

Maggie smiled.

"It says that a J. Smith is looking for me. I have come to see him. Before the war, the 'J' was for Jupiter. Don't know if it still means that." She felt a pain in her throat. Her voice broke. It was hard saying his name.

"Oh my dear, I know the war tore apart a great deal of families. White and Negro. Are you his sister?"

Sonya did not like the way she said sister. Too much hiss and venom in the first syllable. She felt her back straighten. Her cheeks grow warm. "I am his wife."

"Dear heavens. I didn't know he had a wife . . . still living. He spoke of a woman he loved in another life, but I had no idea that I would have the pleasure of meeting her face-to-face."

"Please . . . where can I find Jupiter?"

"Well, my dear, I hate to break this to you. It truly is hard as a woman to tell you this. But I am afraid he has left the country. He has gone on a foolish chase after some woman. To Liberia."

"Liberia? That's me that he's chasing after. He's gone already?"

"He just left a few days ago. My dear, are you telling me that he has left looking for you, gone halfway around the world to some God-forsaken country, and you are still here?"

"I knew he'd been told that I was going there, but I had no idea he'd leave so soon."

"Yes, he left very soon, as soon as he heard the news, in fact. He must really love you. I did not know you were the same woman, which is why I assumed you were his sister. Heavens, what will we do? I can't stand by and watch this. You must get to Liberia and meet him there."

"I wish that I could, but I don't have the money for passage. I was hoping that I would find him before he left."

"I see . . . Sonya, I read a lot of books, novels that help me to escape the lack of civilization in this city. I am a fool for romance, and

I would love to be your benefactor. Please let me see to it that you receive safe passage to Liberia."

"Ma'am, I couldn't do such a thing. I don't know if I will ever be able to repay you."

"It's quite all right. Jupiter left in such a hurry that I failed to pay him all of his wages I owe him." Maggie went to her desk and retrieved the money. "Here you are. That should be more than enough."

Sonya's wrist bent unexpectedly. Who knew that so many little sheets of paper could weigh so much? "Unpaid wages? What is it that Jupiter did for you?"

Maggie smiled. "Why, whatever I asked him to. Now take this and go, and promise me that you will write me when the two of you are re-united. It would please my heart so. You can write, can't you?"

"She can, but I'm helping her," said the little boy. "She's getting better every day." Sonya squeezed his shoulder hard.

"That is quite admirable. I know that Jupiter can write. I want you to insist that he fulfill my request. I know how men are about writing letters. I am sure you can assert your feminine wiles to make him complete the task. I don't want you to spare any details—from the moment your eyes meet, your first embrace, and even your first kiss."

Maggie squeezed Sonya's hand—too tightly, Sonya thought.

"I will do that." Sonya tightened her grip on Maggie's hand. "I promise you."

"You are too kind. Now go, my angel." Maggie pulled her hand away, then leaned in and kissed Sonya on the forehead.

• • •

Maggie sipped her tea, licked her lips, and registered the laudanum's brief, medicinal numb. She was a long way from the wild and painful days of the gold rush. There were men scattered across the seas who, if they knew her role in their fate, would happily slit her throat.

She was smart enough to know that she would never have the fortune of succumbing to such a dramatic demise; like the jade figurines from various places throughout the Orient, and the vibrant watercolors from Nagasaki, she would become another curio among the others, collecting dust within that opulent interior.

The drug was taking effect. She imagined all of her victims thanking her for granting them the opportunity for adventure on the high seas. They watched her. She heard their voices, though their lips did not move. She thought she heard the door to her room open. "Jupiter?" But she was alone.

15

He entered the secret tunnel that ran under Maggie's to the shore. Clement would be there. His knuckles hurt—too many beatings for one night. He had won each fight, but somehow he'd lost everything. Sonya, and now a son. The nights spent crimping for Maggie were over.

The candles on the walls were lit. Someone had been crimped. He saw two men, unconscious and slumped against the wall. The wood planks above creaked down dust on them. He felt a strange relief seeing them there. Clement and Maggie could go about their business without him. Getting out would be that much easier.

He was tired of snatching men off the street and rationalizing their abductions. These men had likely done bad things—he certainly had. One of them moaned and then mumbled something indecipherable. Jupiter could tell he had been taken from an opium den. He must have had some painful memories to run from; the smoke creates some distance but they catch up every time. Jupiter could understand that kind of sadness. In a sense, they were brothers. Jupiter knelt to get a closer look at him.

He thought the dim light played tricks on his eyes. He lifted the man's slumped head. *Archer?*

Was it real? Had he been killed fighting the Scourge and his soul was now in the underworld?

He slapped Archer and shook him. Archer opened his eyes.

"We've got to get you out of here," said Jupiter. "Can you stand?"

Archer's pupils drifted under his lids.

"Taking another confession, Father?" Clement entered with two men Jupiter had never seen before.

"You can't take this man, Clement."

"Oh, now it is *this* one that I cannot have. What, is he not corrupted enough for you?"

"I came to tell you I'm done. I'm leaving and I'm taking him with me."

"Are you telling me or asking me?"

"I'm asking, Clement. I don't have another fight in me."

"That's too bad, Jupiter. Fortunately, they do."

• • •

Archer was still in the opium haze, not sure of what he was seeing. The shadows' images bled into one another with a liquid viscosity. He asked the men on the floor next to him what was going on—did they see these apparitions too? They did not answer, but he pressed with a whisper. "What's going on?" Again, they did not answer. Finally, he mustered enough strength to give one of them a shake. The man's hat fell off. Archer was going to apologize, but then the man's head fell off. Instead of flesh and tendons, he saw only a neck full of straw and hay.

• • •

He had dutifully removed terrors of the war from his memory castle. Yet every so often they would sneak in, returning distorted and more horrific from their time without shelter.

Jupiter was the first to fall into the hole; the rest of the regiment fell in afterward. There were twenty of them in the dark, already weak and now broken by the fall. Somewhere in the darkness, a voice that did not belong to any of the enlisted men said, "You shall pay for what you have done." There was the smell of sulfur and the temperature in the darkness began to rise. Still no light, no images, nothing, only the heat. Then the smell of burning flesh. Then the screams. To the point where the smell became so intense that the screams were no longer screams but something more: bloodcurdling animal anguish. The shouting continued and Jupiter covered his ears. He did not realize it was his own muffled screams.

• • •

Jupiter felt a flare of pain in his cheek, then opened his eyes. Clement lorded over him. "Why were you so protective of that sorry sod? What's his connection to you?"

Jupiter looked at Archer slumped in a corner.

"His father was my master before the war."

Clement whistled softly. "I wish I had time for a glass of rum and *that* story."

"Rum sounds nice, and there's always time for a good story."

"Not this time, I'm afraid. I've already granted you an extension. She wanted me to kill you, you know."

"Then why didn't you?" He could not move his hands; they were tied behind him.

Clement paced and rubbed his brow. "Guilty, I suppose. She still thinks you took care of Hutchins for the Chinese."

"I told her it wasn't me."

"I know. I made sure she didn't believe you."

Jupiter nodded, although he was still confused. "Why?"

"This whole way of doing things is coming to an end—for her at least. She's above it. I never should have exposed her to the crimp. Mr. O'Connell would have had my throat slit, were he living. She deserves better. You must have seen it too—with your sudden birth of a conscience and all. Dalmore will come to her aide, and in gratitude, she'll marry him and leave this unsavory work to men like us. I had to get her away from you. I saw her coming from your room that night. She cares for you, but that would bring her a world of pain that I cannot allow. Since I am the one who brought you in, it's only right that I be the one to remove you."

Jupiter shook his head and laughed. "You think making a woman like Maggie become indebted to a man like Dalmore is helping her? You couldn't be a bigger fool."

Clement knelt to Jupiter's level. "You are not as smart as you think you are. I have been providing you with answers. How foolish can I be if I possess all the information that you desire?"

Jupiter stared.

"Your wife and son paid a visit to Maggie."

Jupiter struggled in his shackles and let out a primal scream. Clement watched with pity. When he was spent and heaving, he looked at Clement. "Did you hurt them?"

"How could you ask me that? Haven't you been listening? I am not a monster."

"Where are they?"

"We didn't have the heart to tell them what happened to you. Luckily, your wife provided a story. She's gone to find you in Liberia. Maggie was generous enough to give her the payment from Mr. Lin that I discovered in your room. Should set them up nicely in Africa, I suppose. Nothing there but huts and savages."

He thought about her waiting for him again. Alone in a foreign country, how long would it take for her to stop waiting this time? "Spare me the suspense, Clement. How does this end?"

"You know how this ends. You'll be placed on a ship. A life of adventure awaits you . . ."

16

The rocking roused him. Surprised by the soothing motion, his eyes opened with an eager flutter—his vision was blurred by the blow's lingering mist—hoping that all of the preceding events were imagined and just one of the vivid nightmares that had plagued him as of late. A dark figure leaned in rhythm with the oars sluicing the water. The other figure pointed to a ship in the distance. Jupiter knew this routine all too well. It was no dream.

He looked out beyond the edge of the skiff and saw the moon reflected in the temporary mirror of the water's surface—tormented and agitated by small torrents made by the oar. Archer, where was he? The weight on his shoulder was not his deadened arm as he thought but the slumped and unconscious Archer leaning on him.

Soon there was only moonlight and a large ship. He knew all too well what awaited him inside its hull.The lantern blinked its ominous signal to the approaching skiff. The oarsman turned to recognize it. Jupiter lunged for an oar as it rose from the water.

"Move fast, man, he's awake!" He grabbed hold of the wooden plank, but he could not turn it round and bring it hard against the oarsman's head. He was too late and there was another man behind him watching over Archer and himself. The man brought down the club against Jupiter's head, sending him back into submission as he stared into the half-open eyes of Archer, who moaned something unintelligible. They were moving farther from land, but he still heard the water as it gently kissed the shore. It was so peaceful that it scared him.

•   •   •

He saw figures unknown to him, but was keenly aware at how ef-
fortlessly he was moving. *What is happening?* thought Archer. He
observed the shadow play and thought he heard himself laugh but
was not sure; the opium was still massaging his brain. It had been so
long since he had not felt any pain in his leg, yet here he was, gliding,
flying! But to where? Even in this state he could tell that this dark
tunnel did not lead to something good. Had that been Jupiter he saw?
Or just a shadow of a phantom in the opium den? Had he tried to kill
Jupiter . . . and failed? Only to have Jupiter overtake him . . . kill him?
Was he now headed toward purgatory? If he didn't know before, he
was certain when he saw the small boat. Those silent waters must be
the river Styx.

17

The *Intono* was roughly six hundred tons, one hundred forty feet in length, twenty feet in depth, and its beam was thirty-two feet tall. Her hold had seen a variety of common cargo, from copper and molasses to guano and ice—but she was not unfamiliar with intrigue: embargoed cotton, opium, and guns had also all been welcomed aboard.

•   •   •

Jupiter looked around the ship. There were other men on board, captured like Archer and him. They were bound at the wrist and hurried over to the other bound men. Their captors conferred with each other, and two other men waited silently at the forecastle. Jupiter noticed the burliest of the men first. He had a broad chest with thinning red hair. Faint spots dotted his skin like splattered rust-water. Jupiter knew he was Irish. There was a young boy trembling in silence. There were no calluses on his hands: he had never been on a ship before. Among them was a Chinese man who did not look at Jupiter or Archer or any of the men; he did not look at anything at all, he stared without aim.

Jupiter looked at Archer, still drowsy from his beating and the opium. He continued to watch the crew as they went about the ship's business, ignoring him and the others. It was all commonplace for men aboard a ship. A well-dressed man did nothing but observe the crew as well. Jupiter assumed he was the captain by his clothes, but he only looked at Jupiter and the rest of the men in haughty silence. He turned away. As he did so, Jupiter thought he smelled the scent of rosewater.

• • •

Archer's senses were returning but not as fast as he would have liked. His eyes rolled lazily over the deck and forecastle; across the ship were the desperate faces of strangers and the menacing ones of his captors and their accomplices. Then he looked to the black water sloshing noisily in the darkness, and finally to the face of the man Archer had sworn to kill.

"Where are we?" he asked Jupiter.

"On a ship . . ."

Archer sighed. "Why, goddamn it?"

"This ship is desperate for a crew. We've been shanghaied."

"How did this happen? They just snatched me off the street?"

"It happens that way sometimes," said Jupiter. "Most of the time it's brothels, saloons"—Jupiter looked at the night sky—"and opium dens."

Archer recalled the strange visions. Hadn't he seen Jupiter in a brawl after putting a gun to his head? "How do you know all of this? Were you there?"

"I was in a fight. No one was happy about me beating a son of Ireland. They got me too."

It was hard for Archer to follow. He was still confused, but he was sharp enough to observe Jupiter and the cavalier way he spoke to him, answering every question without a hint of deference. Was it the war that had bred such confidence? Or was he masking the guilt over murdering the Colonel? Archer wasn't sure. But he could sense Jupiter was hiding something.

• • •

Jupiter was overwhelmed by the events; he acknowledged their strangeness. Why had they come together in this way? He hadn't seen Archer in years. Seven? No. Eight—just before Archer had dressed in Confederate grays, on his way to pursue glory and honor, and to protect the South and ensure that Jupiter and everyone like him remained enslaved.

Angry embers glowed in Archer's eyes. Jupiter understood, given all that had unfolded, but what it was specifically he did not know. He had so many questions, yet sat in silence. What was Archer doing in San Francisco? During the war, he had wondered more than once, as he fired his weapon, if Archer was among those white faces and gray coats. Was the look in Archer's eyes the result of defeat, or had he gone home to see the Colonel, only to discover that he was dead? An invisible hand had pushed them together. That was the only way that Jupiter could explain it.

•   •   •

No one spoke among the captured men. They watched one another, waiting for some kind, wise fellow to bestow his knowledge upon the rest of them. The crew allowed this to go on until the sound of plank boots, perfectly timed for the most dramatic effect, came moving up from beneath them.

"Salute your captain," said one of the men.

"Sir, we cannot," replied the burly redhead. "We are bound."

"What is your name?"

"Higgins."

"Then stand, Higgins," he said.

The sound of the boots continued, then Jupiter saw a man that stood well over six feet, with broad shoulders. Even outside of this intimidating context, the man would have struck an imposing figure. A windswept beard filled in his gaunt cheeks. His hair was coal-black where it wasn't bands of gray steel. His eyes were a haunting and murky sea-blue.

"Burns, untie these men," he said to the first mate, who then followed the order. "Men," said the captain. "I apologize for the theatrics and any inconveniences I have caused you by bringing you here tonight. But you will find it is well worth it"—he paused there, looking each one of the men in the eye—"for I plan to take you on an adventure. Once this is all over, I promise you shall be thanking me. You think you have been captured or kidnapped or whatever the term is, but you have been freed. What I will show you . . . you have never seen the likes of."

Higgins rubbed his wrists after being untied. "Listen to the *Grand* Captain. His *High* Benevolence. Dope us on shore and then you drag us on board and act like it's a fair fight."

"I always fight fair," said Barrett.

"Fight fair? Club in the back of heads and turn us into slaves, right, mate?" he said to Jupiter.

"Would you like to club me in the back of my head to make it even?"

"Aye, Captain, I would."

"Burns, toss the man a belaying pin."

"What, is this some sort of trick?" said Higgins. "I grab the pin, you pull a pistol?"

"No trick. You beat me and you are free to do as you wish. The pin, Burns."

Burns handed Higgins the pin. He was incredulous at first, tossing the pin from hand to hand. Barrett watched him silently. Then Higgins rushed him.

Barrett stepped aside while hitting him in the windpipe. Higgins stumbled and rushed Barrett again. Barrett threw his elbow into the man's nose. The sailor dropped the pin and grabbed his bloody geyser.

Barrett snatched the pin. "I think you should stop now."

Higgins screamed and charged Barrett. Barrett brought down the pin on his head, blow after blow, until he was unconscious. He tossed the pin back to Burns, who recoiled from it, letting it fall to the deck when he saw it was covered in blood.

Barrett used Higgins's shirt to wipe the blood from his hands. He looked at all of the men. "I think you will all learn that I am truly a fair man."

The well-dressed man looked on, unfazed, with his hands behind his back. Tall and slight, he had the soft, hairless face of a school-teacher or office clerk. His eyes barely narrowed at the sight of the bloody Higgins. There was something twisted within him.

"Is this the cooper?" he asked his man while staring at Archer.

"He is, Captain Barrett," came from behind him. Confusion conquered Archer's face. What was this talk of him being a cooper?

"Captain, sir," said Archer, relying on the posture and intonations of his days in the regiment: shoulders back, chest out, eyes straight ahead. "There must be some mistake. I am not skilled as a cooper."

Captain Barrett gave his men a hateful look, then retreated to one that was deceptively harmless as he looked back at Archer. "You are not skilled in coopering you say?"

"No, sir. I am not."

"Oh, then it seems we have made a mistake . . ."

"Aye, Captain, it does . . ."

"Well, I am quite embarrassed. In fact, I am mortified—but for you, for you I am horrified."

"Captain?"

"You can't make barrels, and you've never been on a ship. It wasn't my intention to crew my ship with idlers. Do you know nothing of the sails above you? Flying jib, topmast staysails, the royals—fore and main? Top gallants? Fore royal, main royal, fore top gallant? Main topgallant. Fore topsail. Main topsail. Main topmast staysail. Main sail. Mizzen top gallant. Mizzen topsail. Mizzen? If you cannot provide the skills I require, then what use are you?"

The crew showed their teeth in menacing half-smiles. Archer braced himself for the worst. Veiled threats came from the crew:

"Long swim back to shore. Has he got the lungs?"

"Doesn't matter if he does. The sharks'll get him 'fore he tires out."

"Nah. The cold'll get him—then the sharks."

Archer set his mind on lunging for the captain's throat if he were to order his men to come at Archer. He hoped that he would be able to force his thumb into Barrett's eye and take it with him into the after-life. At least he'd die with honor.

The men began to circle Archer. As they came closer, a voice came from behind him.

"Sir, I know something about coopering. I'd be happy to teach him." Jupiter had known the danger imminent once Archer had confessed his ignorance. That word—coopering—ignited a vivid memory. He could see one of the old avuncular slaves, his hands like weathered leather, placing a copper ring around the curved planks that would make the barrel, and Jupiter's own young hands hammering them into place. *What would go into those barrels?* asked the young Jupiter. *Anything,* was the old man's reply. That was at the forefront of their preparation.

Jupiter remembered that as he remembered most things that he wished to. It had been some time, but surely he could recall enough to suit the ship's purposes and save Archer's life.

Captain Barrett arched an eyebrow as Jupiter spoke up. "So you can cooper?"

"Yes," said Jupiter.

"And you're willing to trade your life for his, in the event you can't teach him how to cooper properly?" Jupiter could feel Archer's eyes on him, but he kept his fixed on the captain.

"Yes," said Jupiter. "I am. He can learn. I knew him on land. We have good memories."

The captain's rigid grimace softened a bit. "That doesn't surprise me one bit. One skilled darkie is worth more than ten untrained white men. Tell me, white man to white man, how does it feel to have him come to your rescue?"

Archer seethed. He had come all this way to kill Jupiter, why not now? Especially after such a humiliating reminder that he deserved it.

"World's gone topsy-turvy since the war, hasn't it?" said Barrett. "Imagine that—darkies educating." He turned back to Jupiter. "So you say you have a good memory. I named a number of sails. Repeat them to me.

Jupiter looked at him in disbelief.

"Repeat."

Jupiter closed his eyes. "The flying jib—"

"Wait," said Barrett. He revealed his pistol and placed it at Jupiter's temple. "Continue."

Jupiter repeated the sails, stumbling on the mainsail.

"Stop," said Barrett. "Impressive." Barrett turned and pointed his pistol at Archer. "Continue," Barrett ordered Archer. He trembled and closed his eyes. "Mizzen top gallant . . . mizzen topsail . . ."

"We're all waiting."

Archer remembered the last sail—the mizzen sail—but he was not sure if he wanted to say it. He wasn't sure if he wanted to survive. What would life on this ship be like with a man like Captain Barrett? Would death be a better alternative? Archer stayed silent and waited for Barrett to pull the trigger. He felt the pressure of the gun against his temple, then suddenly ease away.

"Can't we put an end to all this infernal horseplay and madness?" The dandy appeared behind the captain. "Shouldn't we be getting on with the ship's business?"

The playful nature left the captain's face. "I should remind you, Mr. Singleton, that the ship's business is our business." He motioned his head toward his men. "Leave us to it."

"Very well," said Mr. Singleton as he turned away, but stopped short of leaving. "But please do remember that our business, the ship's business, is my business. See to it that it's minded."

Barrett looked at Archer. "Impressive, nonetheless." He holstered his gun. "Like I said, I am a fair man."

• • •

Archer did not take being embarrassed in front of the other men lightly. Jupiter had killed his father and created a situation in which Archer must be his student or be killed. Archer considered foiling Jupiter's tutelage. His main purpose would be served: Jupiter would no longer be walking this earth or sailing its seas.

But that would ensure that they both would be put to death. That idea soon passed, as Archer realized that it wasn't enough to know Jupiter was dead. He would have to see it, plan it, execute it, and live to talk about it. Years from now, on a gloomy day, when his spirits were low, he would think about the man who had killed his father, and that would surely place him in a better mood. No, Jupiter had to die, and Archer had to live.

• • •

San Francisco

Clement entered her room without knocking. He watched her in bed. A half-empty bottle of laudanum rested on her night table. "Maggie . . ." She moaned, then clutched the sheets to her chest.

"It's done," said Clement.

"So my troubles are over?" she asked lazily.

"Almost, my dear." He sat next to her on the bed.

"Now that he's gone, will it appease Hutchins's men?" Her lids drooped.

"It's all been sorted," said Clement. "They seemed satisfied."

"And what of Mr. Lin and the Chinese?"

"That isn't our concern." He stroked her thigh over the sheet. "None of this should be. You should marry Dalmore and leave this behind you."

"Is that what the two of you have planned for me?"

"He's rich. And when he dies, you'll be richer. Margaret O. Dalmore has a nice ring to it."

"I could never marry a man like Dalmore," she whispered. "He doesn't realize a wolf recognizes another wolf by scent, no matter if it's in sheep's clothes. Jupiter knew that."

"You will be taken care of," said Clement.

She laughed. "And what will you do? Watch another man have me? Or have you been offered some other consolation? Haven't you wondered why Dalmore wants to marry me, so?"

Clement grabbed her arm. "Do you think I'm so blind? I've killed—and worse—for you."

Maggie took his hand. "With these?" She kissed his palm.

"Yes," Clement said before he kissed her. She brought her hands to her chest but Clement eased them away. There were no breasts—just a long scar, waxy and flat, from armpit to armpit where the breasts once were. He kissed her again, softly, down her neck, past her clavicle, and from one end of the scar to the other.

•   •   •

Maggie rose and dressed before he did. From her window, she watched the fog blanket the city. She heard Clement stir in the bed behind her.

"Clement."

"Yes, love?"

She did not turn around. "The *Prodigal Son* leaves this evening. She's a large ship. With Jupiter gone, you'll need a head start on the others."

She heard him get out of bed. "Of course, Mrs. O'Connell," he said, closing the door behind him.

•　•　•

Preston Dalmore borrowed a coat from his driver. He did not want to take the chance of being recognized in Chinatown, especially with tensions rising between the Irish and the Chinese. After his last visit, he saw no need to return to the place, but things had become complicated on a personal level. Gao Lin had summoned him—*him*, a man who, not so long ago, would have scoffed at the request.

He entered through the usual route, the hallway under the saloon, the cast-iron door guarded by a large man with long hair. Dalmore did not have to introduce himself. Another man approached him as he entered the room. "Good evening, Mr. Dalmore."

He recognized the man from a previous meeting with Gao Lin. What was he doing here? He must have looked puzzled, because the Chinese man patted him on the shoulder. "It's *Tom*, Mr. Dalmore."

"Tom. Yes, of course."

"Please, Mr. Dalmore. Be seated."

"Thank you." He sat at the large table.

Gao Lin sat across from him but remained silent.

"Gao Lin is very disappointed." Dalmore heard Tom's voice behind him. "Forgive his silence."

Dalmore searched the old man's face. Nothing. "Is there anything I can do?"

Tom paced behind Dalmore. "When you asked for Gao Lin's help, it was on the condition that there would be no reprisals. Gao Lin lost a grandson."

"I've heard," said Dalmore. "My condolences."

Gao Lin did not respond.

"He was beaten to death by an Irish mob," said Tom. "Hutchins's men."

"Are you certain?" Dalmore turned.

Tom hovered. "I am certain."

Dalmore repositioned his chair to face Tom; it made an undignified screech. "Our agreement was that I would hire more Chinese in my shipyard—which I have done. The attack on Gao Lin's grandson could easily be related to that."

Gao Lin said something in Chinese. Whatever it was, Tom did not translate it for Dalmore. "You are in this situation by your own design, Mr. Dalmore. Do not pretend to be doing us a favor or that we are friends."

"No, I would never be so presumptuous," said Dalmore.

"You were losing money long before our involvement. The only reason your ships continue to be built is that our people are willing to work twice as hard for three times as little."

"This is true," said Dalmore. "The Chinaman—" He stopped himself. "Your people are some of the most diligent workers I have ever come across."

"We are glad that you appreciate our hard work. All we wish to do is keep them working and safe from your white mobs. But if this was some ploy to have the Irish and Chinese wipe each other out, while you are left to take your pickings from the aftermath, I can assure you, Mr. Dalmore, that that is an unlikely outcome."

Dalmore felt a trickle of sweat escape his armpit and run down his side. "Of course not," he addressed Gao Lin. "I am offended by the suggestion. Lin, I have known you for over ten years. We have had dealings before. Why am I being met with such distrust now?"

The old man stood and left without ever answering Dalmore.

Tom sat next to him. "As I said earlier, we do not intend to suffer because of your troubles with money."

Dalmore was growing tired of this Tom West. "What do you know of my affairs?"

"I know about your failed adventure in gunrunning."

Dalmore's fingers tapped the table lightly. "It did not end so well."

"I also know that you cannot force your guns upon China as you did your opium."

Dalmore smiled. "Let me correct you on recent history, young Tom. It was the British that forced opium on China, not Americans."

Tom also smiled. "You are British, are you not?"

Dalmore stared. "I was once. A long time ago. But what say you of the opium you peddle here? No one has forced you to do such a thing."

"Indeed, Mr. Dalmore, there is a surplus of opium back in China. So much of it that it all cannot be sold there. A great number of my people brought their dependence on opium with them across the great ocean. We provide them with whatever they need to tolerate the harsh realities of their existence, so that they may continue to work tirelessly for respectable white men such as you."

"I've grown weary of this," said Dalmore. "What is it that you want?"

"I want to be assured that our agreement shall be honored."

"It will, I *assure* you. Satisfied?"

"Not quite," said Tom West. "Our arrangement was an investment of sorts. I think that it would be best to make it official."

"I don't follow."

"Gao Lin Imports will make an investment in the Dalmore Shipping Company. You need capital. Our money will allow you to continue building your ships—in return you shall give us a percentage of the profits and our people preference in hiring."

Dalmore thought of the *Cressida*, the ship of his dreams that had yet to be completed. Until that moment, he was not sure why he had been doing all of this. The boy in him had conceived that ship. She had to be finished.

In the cramped quarters, hammocks swayed between rows of two-tiered bunks on either side of the ship. It smelled of damp wood and men who needed a bath—stronger than one offered by sea spray. Kerosene lamps flickered, struggling to light the perpetually dark space. Among the crew of twenty men, there were none of the bonds commonly formed on a ship. Jupiter decided that, for his own safety, it must stay that way for him. He had learned that most of them, at one time or another, had been crimped.

•   •   •

It was backbreaking work. Rigging sails, scrubbing the deck—through work they fought off the seasickness within a few days. Archer faster than Jupiter: an opium eater's equilibrium is used to being assaulted. Down in the galley they ate their meals. Jupiter and Archer forced themselves to eat the slop—each horrid mouthful.

Archer threw a hateful look at Jupiter.

"Ever been crimped before?" asked a grizzly old sailor.

"What?" Archer wasn't sure if he heard him correctly.

"Crimped. They shanghaied you in 'Frisco. Ever happen before then?"

"No, thank God."

The sailor swallowed a spoonful of slop. "They snatched me off a tit in Portland—and thank heaven for it. A day longer and I would have been cut to pieces and fed to the pigs. Overstretched myself at one of their fine brothels. Ever been?"

"No. I haven't."

"Fine brothels, fine. The ladies have fire in their blood. It's enough to turn an old seadog like me into a landlubber. Best of all there's no malaria. Not like the damned African coast. Ever been?"

Archer grew uneasy. "No."

"Gibraltar?"

"No."

"Newfoundland? East Indies? Have you ever set foot on a ship before?"

"No, no, and no." Archer stared into the unctuous paste in front of him.

"What's the story 'tween you and the Negro?"

"There is no story."

"I can tell by the way you look at him, or don't look at him. Seems like he might not be with us for long if you had your way."

"I have had enough of the damned questions."

"Fine. I've grown sick of asking them." He slid his tin plate over to Jupiter's side of the table. "Feisty one, ain't he?" he said, tilting his head toward Archer. "What ports you been through?"

Jupiter thought about it. "None since the navy."

"Navy?"

"Served on a gunboat at the start of the war, then left to fight on land."

"What about your friend?"

"Why all the damn questions?"

"Oh, you're cut from the same cloth, the two of you. Not to worry, I'll figure it out. One thing on this ship we got plenty of is time."

19

Archer continued to learn coopering under Jupiter's tutelage. Each day, Archer grew more dedicated to killing Jupiter. He couldn't ignore how Jupiter acted as if nothing had happened, as if he hadn't murdered his father. It gave Archer license to remove such a monster from the earth. Of course, Negroes weren't fully men, but even a dog shows remorse after biting the hand of his master. But here was Jupiter, relishing in his new role as teacher and Archer as student, not ever mentioning the former roles they played in that old world, now so far away. Instead, he went on teaching Archer, teaching him and saving his life. It was enough goodwill to get a man killed.

After a few days, Captain Barrett approached Archer with the rest of his men in tow.

"Here's your ring. Here's your planks. Let's see how many barrels you can make from them. Remember, I want a solid barrel. No leaks. Any leaks from these barrels, and my man Burns will see to it that your gut does likewise." Burns gave Archer a menacing grin.

Jupiter nodded at Archer. "You can do it. Remember what I taught you." Some of the other men snickered, and Archer realized it was a show to undermine him. He imagined his hands around Jupiter's throat, but he instead went about the business of putting the barrels together. He stared at them blankly, waiting for those lessons to overcome the rage he felt for Jupiter. Finally, they did come. He put the barrels together—five in all—from the materials that Barrett had laid before him. A good hour had passed, much too slow for normal coopering, but the barrels were constructed nonetheless.

Barrett looked at Archer. "You've made fine replicas of barrels. Let's see how they hold." The men lifted heavy barrels of water, pouring them into the first barrel that Archer had made. Once finished, they inspected the new barrel for any leaks. There weren't any to be seen. Barrett's men stayed silent, as did Jupiter and their fellow captives. Barrett's men lifted another barrel and poured it into one that Archer had constructed, and repeated this process on the third, fourth, and finally fifth barrel. The second, third, and fourth had not leaked a drop. They waited on the fifth, running their fingers across each seam where the planks met. None showed. The man nodded at Barrett.

"Well, it seems you live to sail another day," said Barrett.

There was a spattering of applause from the crew.

Archer was overwhelmed and quite surprised by just how overwhelmed he felt. "Thank you, Captain Barrett," he found himself saying.

"It seems that it is your tutor, and not me, that you should be thanking," said Barrett.

The glee left Archer's face as he turned to Jupiter. "I do thank you kindly for all you have done for me."

20

Jupiter felt relieved when Archer was spared. He thought back to their childhood, when war was just a game that boys played—how they chased each other on the sprawling plantation, commanding their imaginary regiments like diminutive General Washingtons. Strange how quickly war became such a bloody business when they fought each other on opposite sides of the battlefield.

How would he break the news to Archer that the Colonel had gone mad and died by Jupiter's hand? He hadn't said a word about it. He hoped that the time would present itself on its own.

Jupiter hadn't spoken to Archer much; it felt strange trying to forge a friendship now, given their relationship in that previous world. But he knew they would have to depend on each other in order to stay alive, even though only a few years ago they would have killed each other on sight.

• • •

Ship labor was even beneath his duties as a slave. At least in bondage he'd been Archer's or the Colonel's valet. He'd never engaged in field hand work. However, he went about his ship duties diligently, another means to survival, once again plotting his freedom.

He thought about the day he went off to war. He had hoped to steal off in the night when no one, especially the Colonel, would see him. He'd managed to gather up his knapsack and make it past Sonya, but there, in the darkness of the road, he heard a voice speak to him from the shadows. "After all I've done for you, you can't even say good-bye before you go off to fight in a war that would end our way of life?" He could not see his face, but he knew the Colonel's voice.

"Thought it best if I disappeared in the night without making a fuss."

"For your sake or mine?"

Jupiter didn't answer.

"You've thought about what you're getting ready to do? The South is the South. The North won't win. You're liable to die fighting for those liars up north. Despite what they tell you, they don't give a possum's ass about your people. Down here, you know where you stand. There is no paradise up there."

Jupiter thought about it. He wasn't looking for paradise. He was looking for freedom. He had no illusions about freedom being a paradise, but he wanted it. Whatever hard times freedom brought, he wanted them. He wanted to experience living on his own terms, and no matter how disappointing, no matter how trying, it sounded like heaven to him. But he could never express that to the Colonel and make him understand. Instead, he offered a curt, "I know exactly what I'm doing," and began to walk off into the darkness down the road.

"I'm in my rights to shoot you! Your body is my property. You are my property. You are stealing my property!"

Jupiter kept walking, and the Colonel kept raving into the night. His anger, verbal fireballs, illuminated the darkness and shadows in which he stood. He kept walking until the ravings grew faint and could hear nothing at all— Suddenly, he could see an electric light blossom in the night. It was strange to him because he had recalled this memory before and no such light was present. Yet here was this mystifying light, and now a constriction of his lungs and throat, and the wet coldness around his ears, mouth, and eyes; the weight of it pushing him down further and further into a blackness that surrounded his entire being.

21

Archer swung the pin against the back of Jupiter's skull. He slumped and fell overboard, ever so quietly. Not even a scream or yelp. No blood anywhere, except on the end of the pin. Archer felt a sweet satisfaction in committing the act in front of all of those people, yet there were no witnesses. None. Or so he thought.

"He's down there! Man overboard!" screamed Burns, the first mate. "Man overboard!" Burns screamed again. No one moved. He did not repeat himself; instead he jumped into the murky waters, landing right on top of Jupiter. Archer and the other men ran to the edge. Both Jupiter and Burns were below the surface. Then, after what seemed like a long while, all of the men searched the water's black slick surface for a sign of Burns, but only Jupiter's face emerged.

22

All the crew stood on deck. Jupiter, soaked, angry, and Archer still touched with the look of the lunatic. No man said a word. They heard the footsteps, then saw Captain Barrett's head appear from below.

He approached them silently, taking the time to look each member of the crew in the eye. He lingered to register their response and reactions to his scrutinizing glare. He made his way to Jupiter and Archer, the boatswain keeping them apart.

"Well, Mr. Clark, tell me what has happened here," Barrett said while looking at Archer.

"Aye, Captain. It seems the Johnny Reb struck the Negro in the head with a belaying pin. The blow sent him reeling overboard. Luckily he was able to hold on to something and we pulled him back on board quickly enough."

"What was this ordeal about?"

Archer and Jupiter shared a look and held their tongues.

Barrett pointed at Archer. "Tie him to the mast."

"Aye, Captain."

•   •   •

Barrett revealed a hinged case with two clasps at the opening. Out came the whip, thick and coiled like a giant snake. He brought the whip close to Archer, who could sense the weight of it.

"I rarely put men to the whip myself," said Barrett. "It is an art I do not have the knack for. An evil art, but necessary nonetheless.

Peace must be maintained on a ship. We can't go around harming one another at the slightest whim." Barrett raised the whip as if he were about to crack it across Archer's back.

Clark wedged a splint wrapped with a rag between Archer's teeth. He clenched his jaw.

"This man will receive forty lashes for his actions. A small price to pay for attempting to kill one of us—one of your brothers for the duration of this voyage. We can't have any man breaking the cohesion of this crew—this family. Understood?"

Aye, Captain!

Barrett handed the whip to Jupiter. "Give him the forty lashes he has earned . . . and be quick about it."

Jupiter observed the whip's handle—embroidered, it had the look of snakeskin. He had never held a whip before. He was not one of those slaves who had doubled as an overseer for their master. Although during the war he had pulled enough triggers and handled enough knives, he had never held a weapon like this.

"With respect, Captain, I will have to decline." He presented the whip to Barrett.

"There is no declining. I present the rules to the ship—once she accepts them they must be followed or she'll fall apart and sink, taking us all down with her. Either you put the lash to him or we will all take turns putting the lash to you. Forty—from each of us."

Jupiter looked at the whip, then into Barrett's eyes—shrewd and dispassionate, they were all too familiar. He dropped the whip, then removed his shirt and let it fall to the deck. Arms wrapped around the mast, he positioned himself next to Archer. Some of the crew gasped.

Clark went for the whip. "You insolent black devil. I'll beat the hide off you."

Barrett looked at Jupiter's smooth, unscarred back. No whip had touched it.

"On your word, Captain," said Clark. "I'll whip a lesson into him."

Jupiter's ignorance of the whip was apparent. He stood with his arms unbound, as if once the whip made contact with his flesh, he could maintain the position and resist thrashing around like a fish snatched from the water. He had no idea how to prepare himself for the pain that was to follow. He just stood there, offering his back as if he were merely a child about to receive a spanking.

Archer spit out the gag. "What are you doing? He'll kill us both."

"You're probably right. But if I die, I don't want my last act to be whipping a man I've known all my life."

"Shall I count backward from forty, sir?" asked Clark.

"That'll be all, Mr. Clark."

"Captain?"

"Enough, Mr. Clark."

Clark lowered the whip.

Barrett walked over to Jupiter. "Put your shirt back on. If the two of you want to kill each other, have at it, but I'll have no martyrs on my ship. It's bad luck. Mr. Clark?"

"Captain."

"Untie these men, and put Archer in the holding cell for ten days."

"Aye, Captain."

"And know this—if the two of you defy me again, I won't make such a theatrical display about it. One night, when no one is watching, you'll just disappear. The crew will just assume you fell overboard, and eventually they will struggle to remember your names."

23

Since Burns died saving Jupiter, the men thought it was right that he should have whatever remained in the dead man's bunk. Alone—the rest of the crew on deck—dark, and damp, the quarters felt like a tomb. Burns did not have a cabin to himself, just a thin sheet of muslin that separated him from the rest. Jupiter eased back the sheet. The bedding felt impossibly warm. Jupiter fought the urge to lie down and rest. He untied Burns's sack and examined its contents. It was contraband, mostly: a knife, a pistol with a broken hammer, more biscuit and salt beef than he was rationed, rum, and a worn leather-bound journal.

Jupiter set aside the rest of the contents and opened the journal—the pages yellow and warped from time at sea. These first pages were not written by Burns; the name Percival Stone was crossed out, as was the text he had written:

> . . . *we were now at the base of the hill. The young man was quiet for a while. Fatigue was evident in his open mouth breathing.*
>
> *"Not long ago," he said, using the stump that once bore a hand to wipe his brow, "I could have made such a journey with ease. But with part of my lung missing, even waking is a struggle. My attempt to escape has turned my body into a prison of sorts. But I do not regret a moment. I have experienced what only a select few have survived. It is obvious what the ordeal has done to my body. I have no hand or foot, and my lungs search for that missing piece*

with every breath. But my mind," he said, tapping his stump at his temple, "my mind has grown many limbs."

Our journey continued. We trekked through the deep, green brush that covered the hillside. My young companion remained in a constant struggle with his body. There seemed no end to our quest, and I feared that exhaustion had affected the mind of my guide, and that he was leading us to a point of no return. Then, as if some demigod had intervened, we came upon some steps. Yes, they were crude: large stones ascending to, what seemed like, the heavens.

We took a moment to rest there. My guide, Manuel, began to speak. "What you will see at the top of those steps, no average man has seen. It is a sight mostly reserved for people like me: the limbless, or what your people may consider deformed or grotesque. I ask that you maintain your civility when we reach the village."

I agreed.

Many steps. We climbed so many steps: a thousand in all. At the top, a vision emerged. One that quickly shifted from fantasy to nightmare. "My home," said Manuel with a deep look of satisfaction.

And then, as if listening, they emerged. Fifty people, from children to the elderly, came out of their shacks. The sight of them dummied my senses. I could not stand to look at them nor look away. Every one of them was horribly deformed or limbless: missing legs, arms and complete sections of the jaw. It was as if God had paused during their physical design. I felt my stomach turn even though my head could not . . .

—most likely by its owner before him, but the pages that followed were truer to form:

—Capt. gave my cabin to the fop, Singleton. Paid cook to piss in his food.

—Capt. took us round the Horn. Met with angry storms. Lost six men overboard.

—Capt. took us up the S. America coast rather than tack out west. Wanted to save time. Very concerned with time. Met with fierce South-westerlies.

—Crimped two crew.

—Men sick with dysentery. Shit and vomit higher than waterline.

—Lost another man to sickness.

—Crimped another man to replace the dead. Ten in all.

From there, the pages were blank. Jupiter placed the journal back in the sack—he had overlooked something. A wood figure, carved crudely, but he could see that it was a dolphin. Small enough to keep in a pocket, it was something a boy would keep for good luck, a hidden totem to conjure up courage and wonder. He ran his fingers over the dolphin's ridged body, and squeezed it in his palm.

• • •

Jupiter struggled to maintain his balance down the narrow stairs that led into the *Intono*'s holding cell. The air was foul and damp. He felt as if it clung to him. He spotted a seething barrel of wastewater as the source of the smell; a rat broke the liquid's surface, sprang off the barrel's rim, and disappeared into the darkness. Jupiter flinched. Unmoved by the events and his surroundings, Archer sat monastically on a small bench. He looked frail and ill—his time away from opiates was revealing its toll.

Jupiter approached the cell and revealed Burns's biscuit and salt beef. "You should eat," he said.

"Keep it. Don't want your charity." Weak and distant, his voice seemed whispered from an abyss.

"It's not charity. Burns was stealing it. I found it in his sack." Jupiter held some of the food through the cell bars.

Archer hesitated, and then took the food—the cell was so small that he did not have to rise to grab it. He chewed the beef slowly, getting used to the taste of salted leather, trying to ignore the smell of shit and piss.

The lamp offered dim light. Jupiter looked around for that errant rat. "God, I hate being on a ship."

Archer laughed behind the tough meat. "And you were always so fascinated by Father's ship in a bottle."

No smile from Jupiter; he remembered the beating for touching what did not belong to him. "I remember that. It was a replica of the *Circe*, the British ship that brought the first Smiths to America."

"And we've been cursed ever since."

Jupiter nodded, then wondered if Archer had meant to include him among the cursed.

"I don't know about curses," Jupiter said, "but I can free you from the spell of opium if you're interested."

Archer grabbed the cell bars and pulled himself up. His eyes were wild and electric. "You, free *me*?" He pushed his hand through the bars, grasping for Jupiter as his forearm refused to slip through.

Jupiter moved closer to the cell, just barely out of Archer's reach. He wanted to tell Archer that the Colonel had lost his mind, and that the man had died long ago and had forgotten to take his body along with him, and that killing a man in such a situation is, truly, to free him. He wanted to say these things, but years after the incident he had not applied the same rationale to the harbors and saloons of San Francisco. He told the men he crimped that their situation was a better alternative to death. There was no case to be made for his innocence.

Archer's fingers searched, the tendons rose and twitched. Jupiter leaned in and Archer grabbed his throat. He felt the fingernails burrow into his skin, and the pressure build in his skull as his breath was cut off. He thought about the Colonel.

Archer's grip weakened, his arm purpling where the bars had interrupted the flow of his blood. Jupiter shook off Archer's hand and the foul air eased back into him. Archer winced as his nerves awakened and he eased his arm back through the bars. He leaned into the cell wall and pressed his head against it. "Tell me what happened."

Jupiter rubbed his throat. "He was sick. . . . His mind was gone long before I got there."

"Why'd you come back? To gloat?"

"No. I came back for Sonya." He answered quickly, but he was confused by the question. Was it to gloat? Did he really come back for her and not because the plantation was the only home he knew? "He was babbling nonsense, covered in sores; he hadn't bathed in God knows how long."

Archer looked up. "Clara wasn't taking care of him?"

"Said she was too scared of him. Saddened by him. He was haunting those secret passageways of his like some ghost. He didn't even recognize me at first . . ."

Archer let go of the bars and sat on the stool. "You said he babbled?"

"That's right."

"What did he say?"

"Incoherent mostly. None of it made much sense."

Archer stroked his chin. "Did he mention me?"

Jupiter paused long enough to hear that rat scurry about.

Archer looked at him. "Don't bother lying to me."

"No, Archer, he didn't mention you."

"So go on . . . how did you do it?"

"Don't do this."

"Don't do what? I am his son. You don't think I deserve to know how my father was killed?"

Long pause. "Strangled him."

Archer nodded. "You wanted to get your hands on him . . . feel his life slip away."

"It was a canteen strap."

"Did he fight much? Did he beg you not to?"

"No. He didn't fight at all. He was so compliant that I couldn't stand to look at him. I kept my eyes closed through most of it."

"You come back from the war—atrocities everywhere—and you

couldn't face the burden? Tell me, Jupiter, am I supposed to feel sorry for you?"

"You can feel however you want, as can I."

"Go on with the story."

"You've heard the story."

"No, there is always more."

"I came back to the plantation to look for my wife, only to find our father lost to madness."

"Our father," whispered Archer. "Let me tell you my side of the event. After getting shot in the chest, and in the back, and not being able to feel my legs—or much of anything except pain—for a month, I needed the laudanum to get me through the painful transition of feeling again. Even that couldn't stop the nightmares—it enhanced them. It eased the pain but did nothing to erase the sight of the man next to you spilling his brains all over your uniform. Or the sight of amputated limbs piled high under a tree. A sea of wooden boxes . . . it's still there; you know us Smiths have a hard time forgetting. After all that, after losing the war, I return home only to find my father's corpse, rotting, unmoved for days. Then I discover that he was murdered by someone he'd fed and clothed and cared for. Wasn't winning the war enough? You'd gotten your damned freedom. Did you come back to gloat, rub it in his face?"

"I don't need you to explain the hell of war. I told you why I came back, Archer."

"That's not all of it. Don't play the goddamned saint with me. *Our father*—" Archer spat in the shadows. "You knew him like I knew him. You would have killed him anyway. Maybe I would have too. My mother lost her mind and took her own life, watching the things he did with your mother. You know the type of man he was. Even if what you say is true, his being feeble-minded just made it easier."

Jupiter hoped that was not true. There is no kindness in letting a man die without dignity. People have shown wounded animals more mercy.

"I can see your mind working, Jupiter. You've had a lot of time to work on your story, but I won't let you portray yourself as a hero. I shouldn't have tried to kill you. That was a mistake. From this moment forth, I shall forever remind you of who you really are."

Jupiter lunged at the bars, rattling Archer's cage. "I don't need you to tell me who I am!"

A shaft of light came down the stairwell. "Hey, what's this?" Clark waddled down the steps. "You shouldn't be down here."

Jupiter raised a hand to shield his eyes. "We're just having a conversation, that's all."

"I don't care if you're giving him a wank. Up to the deck with you. Captain's cried 'all hands.'" Jupiter lingered, looking at Archer. "Now," said Clark.

●　●　●

Jupiter went back on deck. The door closed and the place went dark again. Opening the door had let the sea breeze in, mellowing the putrid air. Now, with the door closed, he was reminded of how foul it was. The rat scurried back into Archer's cell, sniffed around the waste bucket, then detoured under his bench where some crumbs had fallen. He let the rat finish his meal before bringing down his foot and crushing its skull.

24

Aided by the moon shining through the deck lights, Barrett sat at his desk, writing in his journal. A traditional log was not needed for this type of journey. He wrote the word *Cuba*, lifting his pen from the page as the ship rolled and the desk moved with it. He felt the rope that anchored the desk to the floor grow taut, and continued his writing. They would be expecting him. He was already behind schedule. Storms and sickness had delayed him.

It was important that the cargo be delivered. No room for error; he would never get another opportunity to redeem himself and make good on his word. He had run out of chances.

There was a knock at his door.

"Yes?"

Singleton entered. "A word, Barrett?"

He did not even bother addressing Barrett as captain on his own ship. Barrett hated the look of Singleton, with his beady eyes and doughy face. He had the look of a country doctor but possessed no such skills. Barrett nodded at the seat across from him.

"I'm worried about the progress we are making," Singleton said as he sat. "I wonder if you could push these men harder."

The ship rolled again. The desk rope went from slack to taut.

"Are you telling me how to run my ship?" asked Barrett.

Singleton smirked. "I am telling you what I need from this ship— you and your men."

"These men are not my men, they are my crew. Half these men

have never set foot on a ship before. My men—men I trusted—died of dysentery. I am well aware of our progress. I am doing what I can to make proper sailors of them."

"I understand that you feel you are doing what you can, but I'm telling you that results need to come at a faster clip."

"Well I guess that answers my question—you *are* running my ship now. These men are your doing, not mine. You didn't want to hire a proper crew; the lot of them were shanghaied. A thief can't complain if there are cracks in the china."

"And I'm sure you are quite familiar with accepting stolen goods—in whatever state they come," said Singleton.

Barrett smiled. "These are strong accusations, Singleton. I am insulted."

"Oh come off it, Barrett. I know you don't want me on this ship—and no one wants to be off this coffin more than me. But I wouldn't have to watch over you like a governess if it were not for your past incompetence."

"Something tells me you don't mind playing the governess. In fact, it suits you. Why do you insist upon prancing around this ship perfumed?"

"Have you smelled this ship? These men? I won't let this ship uncivilize me."

"A ship doesn't change you, Singleton. It only reveals who you truly are."

The desk slid and Singleton slammed it into place. The journal fell to the floor.

"These guns must make it to China," said Barrett. "And they will."

"You said that on your previous attempt."

"True, but we were attacked by pirates. You can't control their moods; they tend to be a bit mercurial. I've made this run for your employer before, and with considerable success."

"Which is why you have been given another opportunity. But pirates or no, my employer doesn't accept capriciousness as an excuse."

"I understand, and once we reach Shanghai there will be no more causes for concern. Maybe then I can tell him how much I appreciate the second chance."

"He doesn't give second chances, Barrett, only last chances. I don't care what you do to these men, break them or uplift them, just get us there faster."

Barrett nodded at Singleton as he left. He retrieved his journal and turned to a blank page. In his best script he wrote Singleton's name. He waited for the ink to dry and then drew a line through it.

25

Heavy rain came before the strong winds. They were caught by surprise. No one had heeded the seemingly innocuous warning of whistling wind. No one had watched the water for telltale disturbances. No one had searched the horizon for a witchy cloud. Once the worst of it hit, there was not a man on board who did not have rope or canvas in his hands. Barrett ordered that the sails not be shortened. He did not want to lose time. This was met with disapproval by the men, but they did as ordered.

The wind forced the *Intono* to her side; water pushed through the lower deck. The sea seemed to grab her by the stern, almost pulling her under. One of the topmasts broke, buckling the main yard. She caught less wind. This eased her up a bit and they were able to ride out the duration of the squall. One man had been lost overboard. The whole ordeal lasted no more than five minutes.

• • •

The men were drenched and miserable. They did their best to wring out and dry their clothes and bring lamps to the center of their quarters, placing them under hammocks with the clothes above them.

Higgins paced and mumbled as his clothes sloshed around him. "He works us like dogs and there was no one out there to watch for squalls, and that bastard doesn't even allow us to shorten sail. Steers us right in the middle of her, all so he can make good time for his mysterious cargo. Reckless. I know now, for certain, that he is a madman—it's not as though he isn't putting his own life at risk. How can a man value the lives of his crew if he does not value his own? What do you have to say to this?" He nudged Archer with his shoulder. "Are you as angry as I am? And you, Black Jack," he said to Jupiter. "What about the shenanigans he put on between the two of you?" The crew nodded and huddled around the lamps. "That fop on board . . . I say we do something, and there is no need to say the word, men. I think we all know what must be done."

*Aye*s came from the men. Jupiter and Archer glanced at each other.

Higgins went on. "We'll take this ship and sail it to the nearest port. Once we hit land we'll leave the ship to him—but that's if he is cooperative."

"And if he isn't?" asked Jupiter.

"Then we'll just have to sacrifice one of our boats. And he and Singleton will just have to handle things on their own out there. Something should be done. *Aye*, something should be done. Something ain't right about this ship or its captain. He's obviously of a sadistic nature. Half the men on this ship were kidnapped. Black Jack, why doesn't it infuriate you when I bring up the crimping? And here you are, enslaved once again, your life in another man's hands."

"It certainly does," answered Jupiter.

"Good. Then you can help us. You fought in the war?"

"I did."

"Then you can help us to fight for our freedom. You can teach these men what you know. Are you with me?" Higgins extended his hand. Jupiter looked at it for a moment and then clasped it in his own.

"The guillotine is prepared to fall, men. On which side of it will you be?" Higgins sidled up to Archer. "And you fought in the war as well?" he asked Archer.

"I did," Archer said, shoveling a spoonful of the horrible gruel.

"Is it safe to assume your inclusion in our group?"

"I do think I can be of some help," said Archer.

"I knew it was a grand idea to come to you. I am pleased to hear that. You see, all of us are tired of our situation, but few of us are so aptly trained to *change* our situation. We will be needing someone with a more strategic skill set, so to speak."

•   •   •

"What will we do about navigation?" said Jupiter over Archer's shoulder.

"What's that you say?" Higgins asked.

Jupiter spoke louder. "What about navigating the ship once we seize it? Who here can sail?"

Higgins grew red. "Easy, Black Jack. Let white men talk as white men must."

Jupiter only smirked in response and then returned to his gruel. Archer stared at Jupiter in silence, then returned his attention to Higgins. "He's right," Archer whispered. "Once we take the ship, who will navigate?"

"I can do it," said Higgins.

"You? You've manned a vessel?" asked Archer.

"No, but I've seen it done many, many times. It has been a while, but I am sure that I can recall enough to get us back to shore. We haven't yet gone far enough to lose our path."

"If we overtake Barrett and his men, you are certain that you can get us back?"

"Aye, I am certain. You have my word."

•   •   •

You have my word . . .

Barrett closed the cover of the brass amplifier tubing that ran from the crew's quarters to Barrett's. He went to his desk and wrote the names *Higgins*, *Jupiter*, and *Archer*. He drew a line through each of them.

The *Orpheus*. Somewhere in the Atlantic . . .

Sonya and Jacob had boarded the ship called *Orpheus*. Five other families were headed for Liberia as well. By now, Sonya was well-traveled, but she had never been on a ship. She marveled at the size of it, even though it was of modest tonnage. A woman of adventure, she had now crossed the country twice, and was about to cross an ocean for the first time. She thought about the grueling journey west with Titus and other former slaves, how they met hostility at every turn.

She thought about the letter she had received from her only friend, who had immigrated to Liberia before the war and after her master had freed her on his deathbed on the condition that she left for the new nation. It spoke of how great and brimming with opportunity the country was. America would never willingly give them this brand of liberty. For a Negro, this was the only place of true freedom. The letter was ten years old. Sonya hoped that everything in it would still hold true.

• • •

Dearest Sonya,

I hope this letter reaches you in good spirits. I am safe and happy here in Liberia. In fact, I am flourishing. There is no greater testament to the magic of this country than my ability to read and write. I did not speak these words to another soul. I write to you, Sonya, in my own hand. There is a strong moral center here. There are Christians of all sorts. They have built hospitals and schools—in which I have received my education—and they work to introduce the Natives to the teachings of Christ. And the Natives seem grateful for it. They have embraced us warmly, just as they have Jesus. The tropical climate requires some adjustment, but Liberia is a land of abundance. There is work for everyone, there is food and shelter for everyone, and there is love for everyone, as this country is free from the hate, free from the oppression of America. This country is free. Liberia is the best for the Negro, for home is always the best place. I hope that one day you will do more than visit me. I hope that you will join me.

Mary Parham,
African Colonization Society
Monrovia, Liberia

26

Jupiter, Archer, and Higgins worked to repair one of the masts that had been damaged during the squall. Higgins was more concerned with seizing the ship than repairing it.

Singleton walked the deck. Archer and Higgins dispersed when he came in earshot. He hovered over Jupiter while he worked.

Jupiter acknowledged him with a nod.

"I've noticed the men acting strangely," said Singleton.

"Have you?" Jupiter kept working.

"Yes, I have. I've also noticed that they act strangely around you, as well. Maybe I am alone in these observations. Have you noticed something . . . *off* about the ship?"

Jupiter looked around. "I've noticed that Barrett is the captain, but he is not its master."

"That's very astute of you. Is there something going on with the men that I should know about?"

"Not that I would know of—sir."

Singleton leaned over Jupiter's shoulder. Jupiter could smell his floral perfume. "I could pay you handsomely . . . find you work on any ship you'd like."

Jupiter looked at him. "I never want to see another ship as long as I live."

"Then what do you want?"

"I want to see my wife and son," said Jupiter.

"Are they still in San Francisco?"

"No. They are waiting for me in Liberia."

"Liberia?" Singleton paused for a moment and stared into the blue-gray water. "I think I can be of some assistance. My employer has ships that reach every corner of this earth. I am sure that once we arrive in Shanghai, we can find one headed to the Dark Continent. Your wife and child, what are their names?"

27

The *Orpheus*. **Somewhere in the Atlantic.**

One of the other colored passengers grabbed Jacob by the shoulders and shook him. "Where's my watch, you little thief?" Jacob struggled in the man's grip.

Sonya ran over to them. "Unhand my son!"

"This little scamp has stolen my pocket watch."

"What are you saying? My son would never . . . Jacob, do you know what this man is talking about?"

"No, Mamma, I didn't steal anything."

"He's a liar," said the man. "I saw the way he surveyed us in the cabin, assessing what we had, all of our belongings. He's a little too curious for my tastes. He was obviously seeing what could be taken."

"Sir, I can assure you that we have no need to take anything from you," said Sonya.

"My father gave me that watch on his deathbed. You think this is the kind of riffraff we should bring to the new country? One who would steal a watch from his brethren?"

"He did no such thing. If you brought the watch on board with you, it is still on board."

"Sir, maybe I can be of assistance," said one of the passengers who had come upon the scene. "Why don't you unhand the boy?" A tall man, skin like polished ebony, an easy smile, moved over to them gracefully. He placed his hand on the man's shoulder. As he did so, the man released Jacob. "Sir, it has been my understanding that when an item goes missing while on a ship, one could easily suspect the crew. Inform the boatswain or captain, and I'm sure they will perform a thorough search of the crew's quarters. Usually, the search is enough to scare the culprit, and then the missing item *mysteriously* resurfaces. These kinds of things happen when the crew is of a different *persuasion* than the passengers. They think we will be too scared to speak up. But the fearful type is not among us, am I right?"

The man nodded.

"You do see the logic in this?"

The man locked eyes with him. "Yes, I do."

"You'll go tell the captain of your missing property. You will insist that he search the crew's quarters. If nothing turns up, then we will revisit the situation and search our own quarters. Isn't that right?"

The man nodded.

"Good. Be on your way."

The man stepped away and looked as if he were unsure in which direction to head. He looked back at the stranger, who pointed in the direction of the captain's cabin.

"Thank you for your assistance," said Sonya.

"Not at all, Miss . . ."

"*Mrs.* Smith."

The man tipped his hat. "Mrs. Smith."

"This is my son, Jacob."

"Jacob? Well, Mrs. Smith and Jacob, I am Sebastian the Magnificent."

• • •

Barrett ate his supper. The spoon stopped above the bowl when he heard footsteps. "Come in," he said before a request was made. Singleton came in.

"Whenever I see you, Barrett, you are always eating in here. You never join me in the galley."

"I prefer eating alone."

"I suppose that makes sense. I can't claim to be good company."

Barrett said nothing.

Singleton sat across from Barrett. "The men are unhappy."

"Bad food, no rest, and no women—men are always unhappy on a ship."

"There is something amiss with them—the men."

Barrett stared at Singleton. "You've been talking with the men?"

"Just one."

"Just one? So you have a spy amongst the crew?"

"Spy is such an ugly word. I prefer *familiaris*."

"I have never heard that word before, but it sounds like something caused by an unwashed backside."

"As you wish, Barrett, but there is a plan afoot."

"I know." Barrett returned to his food.

"You know? Then why aren't you doing something about it?"

"I'm sailing this ship and its cargo to Shanghai. Nothing shall stop me."

"You've got a mutinous crew on your hands. We are all in danger."

"What does your man suggest we do?"

"He's not equipped to handle—"

"No, he's not equipped, nor are you."

"Barrett, what will you do?"

"I shall finish eating my supper. . . . Any man that threatens to take my ship shall get a bullet in the head or lungs full of seawater."

Singleton stared.

"And then it would just be the two of us," said Barrett. "Wouldn't that be nice? Me at the helm—I could teach you how to rig a sail. A two-man crew—no, three. I forgot about your spy. It would be a challenge—a ship this size—but I think I can whip the two of you into shape. I could turn you into a proper sailor in no time."

Singleton reached into his jacket and pulled out a straight razor. He left it clasped.

"Singleton, are you planning to shave? I wouldn't want hair in my food."

"My employer expects that this ship takes its cargo to Shanghai. As long as the cargo arrives, then he will be satisfied. There is no prerequisite that you arrive with it."

"Careful, Singleton. You think that you could align yourself with them, get rid of me, and that they would let you live?"

Singleton blinked.

"In either scenario you're a dead man. You said work them harder, and I worked them harder. I listened to you once, but not again. You're quite histrionic, Singleton, and I don't like talking to another man in these soothing tones. But not to worry, I know how to handle a ship, and I know how to handle men. I've grown tired of this conversation. Please leave."

Singleton stood.

There was a knock at the door. "Captain Barrett, it's Higgins. May I enter?"

Singleton looked at Barrett.

He nodded.

Singleton unclasped his razor.

Barrett took his pistol from the drawer, and held it under the desk. "Come in," he said.

Higgins rushed through the door. Singleton swung his razor, and Higgins dodged the swipe.

Barrett fired his pistol, barely missing Singleton's head as Higgins tackled him.

Archer ran in wielding a knife, followed by five others.

Higgins and Singleton rolled on the floor of the cabin, fighting for control of the razor. Barrett fired two shots at them indiscriminately, before Archer knocked the pistol down and brought the knife to Barrett's throat.

Barrett laughed. "It's been such a long time since I've had such soft hands near my flesh. It's been a long time at sea. A man can get lonely."

"Stop talking now," said Archer.

Higgins got the best of Singleton and took the razor.

"I can feel his hands shake. His never held a knife to a man's throat before." They led Barrett out of the quarters. They marched Barrett onto the deck for everyone to see. Archer spoke first. "All I want is to go home. We do not wish to harm anyone. If you let us do that, it will stay that way."

Barrett laughed. "And who will do that? I'd rather throw you overboard than sail you back home."

"We don't need you, Captain Barrett. I'll sail us home," said Higgins.

Barrett said, "You sail? You couldn't lead a dung beetle to shit."

"I know enough to get us back home," said Higgins. "I encourage you to keep your criticisms to yourself. 'Tis both wise and helpful for someone who wishes to stay alive."

"As you wish."

Archer secured Barrett in his quarters and bound him with ropes at his ankles and wrists.

"You know you are a fool to follow him," said Barrett.

"I just want to return home safely. I have a . . . woman and a boy," said Archer. "We both do."

"Then why aren't you leading? Why follow such an idiot. You're a born leader. I can see it in you."

"Ah, your tongue is so silver, Captain."

"Aye it is, but I am both accurate and sincere."

"If I need your advice, I will ask for it directly."

"Please do, and know that I am always here at your beck and call."

"I'll take note of that," Archer said as he tightened the ropes around Barrett.

28

"Sebastian the Magnificent?" asked Sonya. "A strange name."

"Yes, in this context, off the stage and away from an audience, it is quite strange."

"You are a performer?"

"Performer? A conjuror, an illusionist, a spectral medium, the best magician our dusky race—or any other—has to offer."

"A magician?" asked Jacob.

"That's right, a magician. Are you a follower of the dark arts?" he asked with a sly smile. "Do the spirits speak to you, offering you entry into the locked parts of the human psyche?"

Jacob shook his head.

Sonya grabbed the boy's hand. "We are a Christian family."

"Of course. I am a Christian as well. I am merely profiting from the gifts the Great Spirit has given me. I meant no offense."

"Why is a magician on a ship headed for Liberia?" asked Sonya.

"I for the same reason all of us are headed there. Opportunity. I'm sure you know all of the obstacles America has put in our way. It's even more difficult for people in my line of entertainment. Very difficult indeed. I've had my equipment damaged, assistant harmed, threats made. I am a great magician, but making that kind of hatred disappear is a trick that even I couldn't pull off. But in Liberia, we will have a need for entertainment, and escape from the burden of all that nation-building, and I intend to provide it."

"You intend to be the nation's sole entertainer?"

"Oh, I certainly hope not. But I will open a theater where I will perform, and the proceeds will go to opening a school for the arts. Hopefully, that will trigger the beginning of a scene for entertainment and culture. Little sister theaters will dot the country."

He was ambitious. Sonya liked that.

"And maybe you will be my first student," he said to a smiling Jacob. "And what about you, Mrs. Smith? What are your plans?"

"Sonya . . ."

"Sonya."

"I plan to meet my husband there."

"I see. A pioneer, is he? Already establishing stability for you and the boy. Commendable. Where in Liberia is he? What business is he in?"

Sonya looked out into the sea, as gray as the sky above it. "Honestly, I don't know. We were separated during the war. I only learned recently that he was alive and headed for Liberia."

"How sad, how fortuitous—but how exciting. You had no notion of coming to Liberia before learning of your husband?"

"Strange, but the idea of it has been in the back of my mind for some time. A friend of mine when I was in bondage was freed by her master on the condition that she left for Liberia. I received a letter from her once. She wrote of things I never thought possible."

"The Lord works in mysterious ways," said Sebastian.

"Yes, he does," said Sonya. "The greatest magician of them all."

Sebastian looked at Jacob. "So, what were you doing in the cabin? I saw you looking about. It was as if you were devouring everything with your eyes."

"Oh, I was just remembering things."

"Remembering?"

Jacob nodded.

Sebastian scratched his chin. "What was the name of the couple on the top bunk at the left of the cabin?"

"The Prices."

"How many trunks did they bring with them?"

"Four."

"What passenger brought the most trunks with them?"

"The Cooks."

"And how many did they bring?"

"Seven."

Sebastian smiled. "A *memorizationalist*. Impressive." Sebastian leaned in close to Jacob's ear. "I'm sure if you think back and remember correctly the Cooks only brought six trunks."

Jacob squinted, then nodded a moment later. "You're right. Six trunks."

"Talented boy you have here."

"He gets it from his father," said Sonya.

"What a great gift to bestow. A talent like that could be well utilized in my act."

Jacob looked at Sonya. "Mamma?"

She put her arm around Jacob and brought him closer. "I'd have to speak to my husband about it first, but I must admit it doesn't seem likely."

"Well, the trip is long; give it some thought." He tipped his hat. "It was a pleasure meeting both of you."

In front of him the sun was setting, cloaking him in shadow as he walked toward it. *He looks*, thought Sonya, *like the antique sculptures of Moors that rich white men kept in their drawing rooms.*

29

Higgins spent three hours or so getting acquainted with the wheel—
and then the next three days staring at the sails, at the maps, at the
stars. They were lost. Archer didn't have to ask; Higgins's face betrayed him.

"I thought you knew how to sail this damned ship," said Archer.

"I do . . . or did. I think my mind's gone feeble," Higgins said. "I'm
so tired. The things I thought I knew I don't know any longer. Maybe I
never knew them at all."

"What do we do now?"

"Seek Barrett's counsel."

"What, unbind him and leave him at the wheel?"

"No, leave him bound, but bring him up on deck to instruct me."

"How will we know if he advises us in truth?"

"Well, everyone's life on this ship is in danger—his included. If we
are lost, so is he."

Archer brought Barrett up and he laughed as Higgins struggled to
navigate. Archer gave him a kick to the back of the legs. "Enough with
your foolishness. Instruct Higgins," Archer said.

Everyone watched one another anxiously.

"Don't worry. We'll make it home," Archer heard himself say. He
didn't realize Jupiter stood next to him.

"Of course we will," Jupiter agreed.

Barrett continued toying with Higgins as he instructed him. Archer
watched and said nothing. What was the point in trying to save face

now? The mutiny had already fallen apart. They would all, very likely, die soon.

Barrett was having a good time—almost sputtering on himself as he prodded Higgins. Higgins looked at Archer as if to say, "Can't you give him a poke to back him off?" Archer pretended not to receive the intended message. It didn't matter anyway, for when he looked back at Barrett all that was jovial had left his face. The humor ceased, the jibing stopped.

"What is it?" asked Higgins.

Barrett kept silent, staring out past the bow onto the seam of the sea and sky. This too irritated Archer. "Speak up," he demanded of Barrett. Still nothing. Archer looked at Barrett's men. They too had a similar look on their faces. Singleton's face, normally inscrutable, was now an artist's palette of emotive colors.

"You don't see it?" asked Barrett finally. "How flat the sky and sea are? The pale gray and violet hue to them, like the lips of a corpse."

Archer did see it; the sea and sky looked like two planks or a flat rendering from an unskilled artist's hands, removing all dimension from his subject.

"Storm's coming," Barrett whispered.

"Surely, you've sailed through storms before," said Higgins.

"I have, but this one could be something else. This one will test everything I have ever learned."

30

Jupiter watched as rain fell on the *Intono*. The wind was fierce and relentless. "Untie me," he heard Barrett call out to Archer. "Untie me, goddamn it!"

"Just continue to instruct us," Archer responded.

"I can't continue to yell over the storm. Soon, every time I speak I'll end up with a mouthful of sea. We all will."

Archer thought for a moment. "How do I know this isn't just a summer squall, and you're using our ignorance to your advantage?"

"Is that a chance you'd like to take? Does this seem like a summer squall to you?"

Jupiter had had enough of this. He had tolerated the mutineers and their foolish undertaking primarily because they were white and he was black, and therefore he was outnumbered. It had gone far enough. Jupiter pushed his way through the wind, up the deck, and behind Barrett. He brought out his knife and cut the ropes that bound Barrett's wrists and ankles.

Archer pointed his gun at Jupiter as Barrett rushed past him and pushed Higgins aside. "He was meant to remain bound," Archer said to Jupiter.

"Let him steer," said Jupiter. "Be smart about it."

"You dare to tell me to be smart?" Archer's jaw clenched, a vein in his neck becoming visible. "The nerve of you."

"There will be time enough for fighting . . . hopefully," Barrett called out. "I'll need for you to untie my men, as well. We'll be needing all hands on deck for this one. The likes of it I've never seen."

The anchors were secured to the deck. The life buoys were repositioned to the deep-sea line. In that weather, should a man go overboard no boat would be sent for him. The wheel was double manned, lifelines were rigged, weather-cloth spread. The wind and the sea seemed to scream, making it almost impossible to hear orders from the man next to you.

They watched Barrett. His calm command of the ship in its crisis instilled in them the same calm and confidence. His mouth moved, his hands gestured; they could not hear him, yet they responded to his pantomimed orders intuitively, communicating through the silent link of crew and captain. Barrett motioned to Jupiter and Archer to assist him at the wheel. They tethered themselves to the base.

"Don't look back at the sea!" Barrett yelled to Jupiter through the wind.

The ocean roared, Jupiter misunderstood the noise and looked back; the sight of the water, mountains of waves, made him shudder.

Barrett grabbed Jupiter by his rain- and sea-soaked collar and pointed to the mainmast. "Watch!" he shouted in his ear.

●　●　●

The winds were unbearable. Mountains of water rose and fell on the ship. The sails billowed like an assaulted flag—lightning even struck one of them. Barrett stood at the helm like a regal figure at his throne, leading the tiny nation of the *Intono* through the battle with nature. A merciless wave shoved the ship to her side, sending Archer some six feet in the air, and likely overboard, had he not had the presence of mind to hold on to the railing. He hung on as the ship swayed relentlessly. His eyes pleaded with Jupiter. Jupiter ran over to Archer but the wetness of everything weakened his grip. Archer held on, clawing into the ship's wood as blood dripped from his cracked fingernails. As the ship bobbed and bounced, so did Archer, slamming his face into the ship.

Again, Jupiter tried to grab him, but there was too much movement.

"Somebody help me!" Three men came up behind him, each one anchoring the other as the first man held on to Jupiter's waist. With all his might, he pulled Archer back on deck. They both lay on the deck, gasping for air. Jupiter almost asked if matters were settled between them, but thought better of it. The storm wasn't over. There was still a chance that they might die.

•   •   •

The first mate plodded up the deck, battling the barrage of wind and water to get within earshot of Barrett. "Keep that main topsail set! We'll keep a handle on her, even in this wind."

"What about those storms sails, Captain?"

"Don't bother. They're not high enough to keep the ship from rolling about."

One of the men was already furling the sail. He did not hear the order and fell to the deck. The wind and sea were so loud that no one heard his screams as he fell, or the horrific sound of impact.

Jupiter looked over to see Barrett screaming at the storm like some mad king. "You won't defeat me! You can't win!" The storm raged on for hours; each hour more difficult and frightening than the next, each seeming to make a promise that the *Intono* would be buried at the bottom of the sea. However, their determination was rewarded, and the men of the *Intono* were allowed to let their skin rise in gooseflesh as the wind stopped its continual assault and softened into a gentle whisper of a breeze.

31

"I am happy to report that my watch has been located," said Mr. Cook. "I apologize to your son, ma'am."

Sonya looked at Jacob, then at Mr. Cook. "We accept. But let this be a lesson not to judge in such haste."

"Of course. Again, my apologies."

"Feels good, doesn't it?" Sebastian said as he watched Mr. Cook walk away. He sidled up to her.

He seemed to appear out of the mist. "What does?" she asked.

"Watching an old man eat crow." He gave Jacob a pat on the back and smiled at him. "Let's say I show you a trick. Are you ready to learn?"

Jacob nodded. Sebastian revealed a deck of cards and asked him to pick one and place it back in the deck. "I will now tell you what card you picked." Sebastian showed him the ace of spades. "Is this your card?"

Jacob reached for a card. "This card is mine. But I know how you did it."

Sebastian smiled. "Go ahead, and tell me."

"I picked the card, but when I gave it back to you, you bent it a little so it felt different from the others." Jacob showed him the subtle bend in the card.

Sebastian looked dumbfounded.

Sonya stifled a laugh. "My, my . . . Sebastian the Magnificent. You're right, it does feel good. Watching an old man eat crow, that is."

Sebastian managed a smile and turned to Jacob. "That was an easy one. There are others more suited to your impressive talents. Would you like me to teach you?"

Jacob nodded.

32

After the storm

"He still living?" Jupiter asked.

"Yes," said Archer. The boy was still unconscious. Archer turned his head carefully, revealing a pulpy wound stretching from his ear to what should have been his temple.

"Is he in pain?" someone asked.

"Yes and no," answered Archer. "He can feel but can't communicate, or he is completely unaware."

"Can't you give him something?"

"No laudanum on board. Maybe there's rum."

"Wouldn't matter. He's in no shape to swallow."

"We can't just let him suffer." Archer looked at Jupiter. "Why don't you all rest," he said. "I'll watch him through the night and we will see how he does."

• • •

That night Archer watched the boy. He remembered the first time he saw him, trembling in fear after being shanghaied. His chest rose and fell, his fingers twitched under the blankets, but he was essentially dead. Sea life was full of superstitions—wasn't there one about keeping a mortally wounded man on a ship? He did not know. He leaned over the boy and adjusted his pillow. He should be comfortable. *Comfortable*. He wanted to laugh at the absurdity of it, but he had already put the pillow over the boy's face, bearing down with all of his weight.

33

The *Intono* gathered to hear Captain Barrett speak. "All is forgiven, men. All is forgiven. You've suffered punishment enough, these last few hours. You've learned that nature—the seas—can be more ruthless, more merciless than any man. While nature gave birth to us, she is not like us. She strikes without warning, or rhyme or reason, but we as men can rise above it. You men have risen above it. Never mind what has come before. Never mind the differences that separated us. Never mind what titles we gave one another before now. On this day, the next, and all that follow, we shall regard one another as brothers." A loud cheer came from them. Jupiter and Archer shared a look, but stayed quiet.

• • •

Calm weather gave the *Intono* a respite. Some of the men formed a circle and sang old songs. Jupiter and Archer recognized some of them from camps during the war. One of the men danced an Irish jig as the onlookers slapped a rhythm on wooden spoons.

"Enough of this singing and dancing, lads. It's time to hear your stories." Barrett went around one by one. Some men came from as far away as Russia. Some men had wandered in from the plains, tired of boring farm life and drawn to the adventurous one that the West promised. Some were prospectors, fooled by the promise of El Dorado. But they all were like Jupiter and Archer, in search of something that they couldn't find.

"Your turn," Barrett said to Archer.

Archer looked away. "No story to tell."

Barrett laughed. "Of course there is a story to tell. You end up on this ship, drugged and beaten, yet within a matter of weeks, you've put a knife to my throat and attempted to take my ship. Am I supposed to believe that before these incidents that I have mentioned, nothing has happened to you?" The men laughed. "Forgive me if I find that hard to believe. What's the connection between you two?"

Archer said nothing. Jupiter spoke up. "I was bound on the plantation his father owned."

Barrett raised an eyebrow. "Slave and slave master, on the same ship?"

"Former," Archer and Jupiter said simultaneously.

"And how is it that you both have ended up on my ship?" asked Barrett.

"I followed him here . . . to seek retribution for my father."

"Meaning what?" asked Barrett.

"Meaning he killed my father."

Everyone's eyes ran to Jupiter like tiny insects.

"He killed your father?" Barrett asked, still looking at Jupiter.

"That's right," said Archer, gauging the mood. "This man killed my father."

"Is this true, Jupiter?"

"In a way, but—"

Barrett put up his hand. "You say this man killed your father. That's hard and terrible stuff, but Archer . . . can you blame him?"

Archer's eyes widened.

"Your father kept a man as chattel for all of his life. Preventing him from seeing all this world has to offer, making him believe that he was less than a man, denying him all the natural rights of a man—family, property, discovery of his true nature and spirit. Why, if a man did that to me, the least he would deserve is a bullet in the head."

Archer began to tremble.

Aye, aye, said the men behind Barrett.

"Surely, you must understand Jupiter's situation. I mean, here you were, bound against your will for a matter of days, yet you felt that was justification to put a knife to my throat."

Aye, said Barrett's men.

Archer remained silent, but his eyes revealed his rage.

"That's very hypocritical of you, Archer." Barrett turned to Jupiter. "Did it happen as he says?"

"It's true I took his life," said Jupiter, "but he was suffering from madness."

"Madness, you say?"

"Yes."

"He seemed to be syphilitic," said Jupiter.

"*Syphilitic*, you say?"

"Yes, he seemed to be suffering from the symptoms."

"*Symptoms?* Jupiter, are you learned?"

Jupiter was aware of their sudden anticipation. "Not as well as I should be, but I've picked up a few things."

"Where, might I ask, did you pick these things up?"

"On the plantation. The Colonel . . . Archer's father allowed me to use the books in his library."

"You don't say. How rare, indeed. I spent a lot of time in the South, and there were few, if any, Southern gentlemen who would allow their slaves to be educated, to borrow books, or even he himself touch a book that a slave had touched. Rare indeed."

"Yes, the Colonel was a rare man," said Jupiter.

"So you come back to your former plantation and find your master wormed through by madness, and you decide to take his life and usher him along, because you cared for him in a way and it pained you to see him suffer?"

"Yes, it was difficult."

"I can see that, Jupiter, I can. He was kind to you, but he was still your master. You could not have come and gone as you pleased, could you?"

"No."

"I'm sure some of your family members were sold off." Barrett turned to his men. "'Twas a common practice in the South." They nodded.

"Yes, that did happen." Jupiter thought of his mother, how her family was scattered throughout the South until her arrangement with the Colonel kept them together.

"And yet you were compassionate enough to end his life only to end his suffering."

"That's right."

"Well, some of it's right, not all of it," said Barrett.

"How do you mean?"

"Well, this man sold your family, kept you bound, and to ease his conscience, every now and then he'd let you read a book, exposing you to worlds you'd never know as long as you were his. A strange kind of torture, isn't it?"

Aye, it is, came from someone in the group.

"Jupiter, you want us to believe that as you— How did you do it?"

"Do what?"

"Kill Archer's father."

Jaw still trembling, Archer stared at Jupiter.

"Strangled him," said Jupiter finally.

"Bare hands?" Barrett asked.

"Canteen strap," said Jupiter.

"Canteen strap. Good way to kill a man," Barrett said.

Aye.

"And you want us to believe that as you strangled him there wasn't a hint of satisfaction?"

Jupiter said nothing.

Barrett smiled grimly, then promptly changed his demeanor and addressed Jupiter and Archer. "What's done is done, men. It's in the past. Everything you thought mattered belongs to the old world. We are entering a new world now. Leave the corpses in their graves."

Archer and Jupiter were locked in a gaze, not saying anything. The other men tried their best to gauge what was happening.

"Look over yonder," said a sailor holding a spyglass. "What is it?"
Barrett went over and peered through the lens. "'Tis a ship."
"Ship? Naval vessel?"
"Possibly," said Barrett. "Or worse."
"Worse?"
"Pirates."

34

Jupiter and Archer were still locked in their gaze, but Jupiter's mind was not on the present tension, or on the deck of that creaking ship; it was back on the plantation, years ago, before the war, when Jupiter and Archer were still children. Jupiter could see himself in that smoke-filled drawing room full of the other cigar-smoking, brandy-drinking plantation owners. The Colonel had allowed Jupiter to learn to read and borrow books from his library; in fact he'd encouraged it. He often quizzed Jupiter on the materials that he had read.

"I don't believe that violence is the best way to train them," the Colonel said, as he sipped his brandy.

"Well, did you hear about that nigger that ran off from Johnson's plantation?" asked Mr. Banks. "Stole four chickens from surrounding farms, and even caught him trying to scale the walls into the bedroom of a white woman down the road. They cut his foot off so that he wouldn't run again. That's the kind of lesson a nigger won't forget."

"I disagree with that," said the Colonel. He waved Jupiter over to him and held out his glass. Jupiter poured the brown amber liquid into it. "I disagree with that wholeheartedly. Not only for their sake do I not think it effective, but I am more concerned with what it does to us."

"To us?" asked Banks. "Why, it keeps our property in the proper context, and keeps them from running off."

"Yes, that's one outcome, but there's the other. What does it do to us?"

"Colonel, what do mean?"

"It diminishes us, this slavery business, is what I mean."

There were laughs and puffs of cigar smoke all around. Jupiter's eyes danced between the white men as they drew in smoke.

"I believe it sullies our spirit," said the Colonel. "It lowers us. Debases us. Takes us down from rational beings to beasts dominating other beasts."

"Well, man *is* an animal."

"No, man is *more*. Man is rational. And white men are the most rational of all men."

"And you, sir," said Banks, "obviously are the most rational white man of us all, for I have no idea what you are talking about."

"Well, we fool ourselves into treating the Negro as if he were just one step up from a beast in a farm or in a stable—this isn't true. The Negroes are men . . . as we are men."

There were gasps all around.

"Hear me out, gentlemen. Hear me out. The Negro is a man as we are men, but through education, culture, and history, we have cultivated our intellect and traditions. The Negro is raw. He needs our influence, not our scorn. We are superior because history has proven so. There is no need to enforce this through violence."

Banks interrupted the Colonel. "So you are saying that if one of your slaves ran off, you wouldn't put the lash to him?"

The Colonel sipped his brandy with leisure. "One of my Negroes would never run off. Do you see any shackles around here, or whips? You see how well behaved my Negroes are? I challenge you to name any other plantation where you were surrounded with such an atmosphere of culture and cultivation from the master to the servants, down from the big house to the slave house. Sirs, I challenge you; I defy you."

None of the men responded.

"This is because I allow my Negroes to see the world as it is. To see the hierarchy that nature and history have established. And I do that by using the rationale that nature has provided all men that inherent ability to see things that nature has gifted in us. My point is that if you allow a Negro to live up to his capacity, you will learn that, yes, they have a fixed capacity. It may not be much, but it is enough to see that by nature, he is below a white man. If you treat him benevolently, with magnanimity, even though he knows that you can harm him, if you teach him benevolently, it only reinforces his inferiority and the white man's superiority, and he becomes grateful to you for not using the power and strength that nature has given you. In other words, he will be grateful and loyal for your magnanimity."

There were laughs all around.

"Good God," said Banks. "Colonel, you give the Negro too much credit. First of all, I don't think the Negro enjoys the sort of intellectual complexity that understands all that you have said."

Jupiter poured the rest of the brandy, then stood in a shadowed corner of the drawing room so as to not be seen or influence the conversation.

"Of course they do," said the Colonel. "They can understand it—we can just understand more. White men aren't living up to their potential like we used to. We are diminishing our potential by handing out beatings and romping about in the slave house with our wenches and Negresses. Brute force is so unnecessary. There is plenty enough intellect for the Negro to understand magnanimity and gratitude."

"Well, I haven't seen it."

"Jupiter, come here," said the Colonel. He came over. "Now do you remember that book I gave you to read?"

Jupiter looked at the other men. All of them seemed to look at him with menace.

"It's fine, Jupiter," said the Colonel. "They won't harm you."

"Yes, Colonel. I remember."

"You remember the name, don't you?"

Of course Jupiter remembered. "It was Cicero's discourse on rhetoric."

"That's correct." The Colonel beamed.

"Why, he's nothing more than a parrot," said Banks. "And even a parrot can recite Shakespeare if you read it to him long enough."

The Colonel looked at Banks and allowed his cigar ash to turn bright red. "Archer, come in here," yelled the Colonel. A young Archer entered the drawing room. Jupiter watched him as the Colonel placed his hand on the boy's shoulder. "Come here, the two of you. Do you remember that book I had you read?" he asked Archer.

"Cicero, Father."

"That's right. Now what is Cicero's basic thesis on rhetoric?"

Archer recited the premises and the aspects.

"Now, Jupiter, what do you think? Is Archer correct?"

Jupiter had already seen the flaws in Archer's analysis, but he was hesitant to say so.

"It's fine, go ahead."

He revealed the flaws that Archer had stated.

"This is reprehensible," said Banks. "Embarrassing your own flesh and blood with one of your slaves!"

Archer looked down.

"I am just presenting facts to you, Mr. Banks."

"Facts?" Banks made some quip about facts in Latin.

Jupiter immediately recognized the quote from one of the Colonel's books. Jupiter corrected Banks.

"What was that, boy?" Banks flared.

"You should use the masculine suffix."

Banks stood up, gulped his brandy, walked over to Jupiter, and smacked him across the face. The Colonel stood up, grabbed Banks by the throat, and held his still lit cigar less than an inch from Banks's face.

"You let your niggers talk to your guests like that?" Sweat formed on Banks's brow.

"Correct, sir, you are a guest. This is Jupiter's home. Wrong is wrong. It knows no color. If your Latin is inferior, his being a Negro doesn't make your inferior Latin any better." The Colonel let him go.

"I think we've seen enough here," Banks said as he walked out with the other white men in tow.

• • •

Archer, still on the other end of Jupiter's gaze, was having the same memory. Archer remembered the fever he'd felt around his collar, hot as coals. The eyes of all those white men in the room, seared into his forehead. He could feel the weight of their expectations on his shoulders. A strange and desperate telepathy emerged in his mind: Don't embarrass us by letting a nigger embarrass you. You are a white man; act accordingly. But Archer had already felt defeated. Cicero wasn't his strong suit. He knew that, and so did his father. But could he challenge his father?

The Colonel had asked Archer the same question in privacy days earlier. The situation played itself out just the same, but the Colonel had placed a comforting hand on Archer's shoulder and instructed him to duplicate his responses at the upcoming party. *I want to prove a point to my guests. Especially that blowhard, Banks.* The Colonel chose to embarrass Archer to prove a point. Archer played along—he always played along, even while the Colonel claimed to be so virtuous, and Archer knew his secrets; he didn't want to disappoint his father under any circumstances. But this had been the first time that Archer, looking into his father's eyes as he put his arm around Jupiter, truly wanted to kill him.

35

That night in Sebastian's cabin, the necessary materials for effective conjuring were scattered throughout: cards, *Les Tours de Cartes*, Witgeest's *The Book of Natural Magic*, Antoine's *Theory of Chemical Trickery*, and Balsamo's *The Rise of the Conjurer.*

"They say a magician never shares his secrets. But if one can decipher a trick on his own, well then that is another thing altogether. Are you excited about being reunited with your father?"

Jacob shrugged his shoulders. "I've never met him."

"Never?"

"Mamma says the war tore them apart before I was born."

"Your mother never took another husband in all that time?"

"There was Uncle Titus, but I don't think Mamma really liked him that much. She knew him from the plantation."

"I see. Is your mother excited to see your father?"

"I don't know. She doesn't talk about him much."

"I see. Well, this is still an exciting time for such a young man. Are you afraid?"

Jacob shook his head.

"If you are, I can teach you a spell that will ward off fear so that you are never afraid again." Sebastian leaned in and whispered ancient words in Jacob's ear—words in a language long thought dead, but still living in secret in the hearts and minds of powerful men. Jacob had never heard the language, yet he felt he understood, and his eyes grew wide.

36

"What can you make of it?" Barrett asked his man with the spyglass.

"She's a naval vessel all right."

"But she can still be manned by buccaneers," Barrett said.

Time passed and they continued to watch. The watchman gasped as Jupiter was in earshot.

"What is it?" Barrett asked.

"Why . . . she's unfurling the Union Jack."

Singleton approached Barrett. "What does this mean, Barrett?"

"The British vessel is close to seizing upon us."

"Should we worry?" Singleton asked.

"We have few items of contraband other than those we have indentured to sustain the ship. If they remain quiet, then nothing should happen. Our true business lies elsewhere, as you know. We must keep them from searching the hold at all costs."

"Indeed. But what if the men do talk?" All eyes fell on Jupiter.

"Of the men that talk," said Barrett, "we shall kill them first. And I mean upon the first word uttered shall death commence, stunning the naval officers into immobility with our sudden mercilessness."

"My God, man, you are insane. Splendid," said Singleton.

"Indeed, sir, I am serious. I don't know if she still uses that Tower, but I have no intention of spending my last days in an English prison."

"We are in agreement on that point," said Singleton.

"'Tis a grisly business," Barrett said, "but it is something we must do." He looked at Jupiter as he addressed Singleton.

Jupiter grew uncomfortable and left them to join the other men. He questioned whether to say anything to the others. Who knew how they would act after the failed mutiny. Would now be the time to repeat another? Would the other men even trust what Jupiter had heard?

Jupiter watched Archer as he went below. Jupiter felt the strange urge to confide in only him. Despite all that they had been through, he would understand. The two of them would figure out what to do. He sat next to Archer and waited for the other men to be distracted.

Archer edged away from Jupiter as he sat down.

"They've spotted a ship on deck," said Jupiter.

Archer glanced at Jupiter. "So?"

"She's naval." Jupiter could hear Archer's heart pounding, the soft gasps he tried to conceal.

"Naval, you say?"

"Yes, and British."

"British?" The optimism left Archer's face.

"What's wrong? You think they won't hear our story?"

"It won't matter. Usually other countries—especially Britain—tend to stay out of these things. For all intents and purposes, the *Intono* is a sovereign ship. She may as well leave us be."

"That could be," said Jupiter, "but she's gaining on us mighty fast. She has some intention. What it is, we don't yet know."

Archer only nodded.

"All hands on deck!" they heard.

The men scrambled on deck to find Barrett looking through his spyglass. "All right, men," Barrett said, "prepare the ship and do be on your best behavior, hospitable and such."

"What is it?" asked Archer.

"She's raised her white flag," said Barrett. "Looks like we'll be having guests."

37

Somewhere in the Atlantic

The storm passed. Sonya reflected on how impressively Sebastian had handled himself during the storm. Watching the way Sebastian was with the boy—holding him steady as he pointed to something in the distance at the edge of the horizon, laughing in that way that men laugh with each other, a secret language that she never understood, finding humor in the strangest places. It warmed her heart seeing him like this, but she felt guilty for not providing it sooner. Anxiety. Fear. What was she to face in Liberia? What kind of man had Jupiter become? What kind of husband or father would he be? Would there be other moments like this for Jacob, or would this be the last time she saw him happy?

38

They watched the uniformed skeletons fall out of the naval vessel and into the skiff. There seemed to be about eight of them. The crew pulled them up to the *Intono*, and by the sight of them as they neared, it was as if they had reached into eight graves and retrieved eight corpses. They all wore the uniforms of the Queen's Navy, but they may as well have been patriotic sacks—so gaunt and emaciated they were. Their leader introduced himself as Captain Quincy, and his first mate as Matthews.

Barrett introduced himself as well. "Well, Captain Quincy, please join me in my quarters. There you can tell me of your ordeal. In the meantime, your men will be fed."

"Thank you," said Quincy.

Archer noticed something strange about him. Quincy seemed weak and small and feeble, but no less weak and small than the ticks that had spread the black plague.

Gruel was prepared for them. The crew sat silently as they ate. Until the spoons began to scrape the bottoms of the wooden bowls. They ate ravenously. Archer thought of animals feeding on a carcass. He had to look away to keep his stomach from turning.

"Tell us your story, Captain Quincy," Barrett said as they finished.

Quincy leaned back, wiping his mouth with the sleeve of his uniform. "'Twas a horrible ordeal, Captain Barrett. We were on Her Majesty's *Provencia*, transporting prisoners to Norfolk. It seems one of our first mates was corrupted and was able to free the prisoners. The prisoners overtook the ship—killed so many of our men, what you see is what remains. We fought them off, but it was weeks before we could. They exhausted our rations. We killed every last one of them. We were hit by a squall and drifted off course, our minds weak from fatigue and all, but then we saw you and followed, hoping that you would be kind enough to grant us some hospitality. And you have, sir. You have indeed. But to continue our journey we need some of your rations to get home."

Archer didn't like Quincy's story. There was nothing of the honor befitting an officer in Her Majesty's service in the story. The fact that he was asking for rations, never questioning Barrett's intent or the *Intono*'s destination, seemed odd.

"Forgive my manners, Captain Barrett," said Matthews, "but we didn't come empty handed." He revealed a small brown sack. "A bit of tea. Not much, but it's damn fine tea."

Barrett held up his hand. "That isn't necessary, Matthews. But might I offer you a cigar? Or perhaps you'd prefer something hand-rolled from Mr. Clark?"

Matthews smiled. "That sounds tempting." Quincy looked at him. "But I think I shall decline."

"Very well," said Barrett. "We'll discuss rations later. Continue your story. So you say you were caught unexpected by a squall?"

"That's right," said Quincy.

"And it took you off course?"

"I confess we were a bit unprepared. There was an incident on-board—a distraction that sent my attention elsewhere. An unfortunate mistake."

Barrett nodded. "I would say so. Unprepared . . . and you had all sails set, of course."

"Yes . . . yes, of course."

"And you clewed up the flying jib and hauled down the royals and top gallants?"

"Correct. We did all of those things."

"I see." Barrett leaned forward. He spoke slowly. "And then you brought down the mainsail and hauled up the mizzen topsail?"

"We—"

"And when you got ahead of the wind, did you haul out the topsail yards and the reef tackles?"

The Brit swallowed.

Barrett stared. "You spent time on ship, but you are no officer. Your story's a captivating one. Intriguing. I haven't heard such captivating tales since I was a boy. Norfolk hasn't been operated as a prison in over a decade." Barrett laughed.

Quincy did not. "As far as civilians are concerned, she's closed—but the monsters of the world are still sent there in secrecy . . ."

"I do thank you for your tale, but I think a tale such as that only deserves the meal we have already given you—nothing more."

A deadly glow seemed to rise in Quincy's eyes. "Why, Captain Barrett, you've seemed so hospitable till now. Why do I get the feeling that your hospitality is ending?"

"As I said, I am sorry for this situation, but any navy man worth his salt would have known that you were near Tikopia. You should have gone there. You're some miles off course, but I'm sure you can make it. You all seem the resilient type. Our rations are allocated precisely for the demands of our trip. We have none to spare. Seek out the island I've told you about. You should have gone there. Despite your situation, I cannot reward stupidity."

"Captain Barrett, I implore you. Have you no heart?" Quincy's teeth showed like fangs.

Barrett's eyes held Quincy's. "Are we through with this masquerade?"

"Aye, Captain. We are. Forgive us for deceiving you, but the sea, she's humbled us, made us desperate. We wanted to be polite. We didn't want to come on your ship slashing throats and spilling blood. We wanted you to feel comfortable. Forgive us, Captain Barrett, we are sensitive souls. But our agenda has not changed. We will still be needing everything you got."

"I sympathize with your dilemma, I truly do, but had you come aboard as yourselves, we would have embraced you. We are all rogues here. With the exception of one or two, none of us has aristocratic pretentions."

"Well, that is good to hear, Captain. You rarely meet such an accommodating man at the helm."

"You misunderstand me, sir. That was then; this is now. Now I am offended. Once I have been offended it is very difficult to get back into my good graces. We lost a bag of grain to a rat that broke through the sack. The rat is not inside—he ate his fill and ran off—but his shit remains throughout. You and your men are welcome to it."

Quincy sighed. "I'll have that cigar now."

"By all means."

He lit his cigar with the lamp flame. Matthews stood and reached for the tea that he'd offered.

"Shall I put on a kettle for your tea as well?" Barrett asked.

Matthews held the sack. "It is not tea. It is gunpowder. I'll blow up the lot of you if you don't give us what we ask."

"Men, I understand your desperate situation, but you'll take this ship down, all of us, if you ignite that. You won't be just killing us, you'll be killing yourselves too. We all will die."

Quincy said nothing. His clawlike hand reached into his jacket; out came his pistol. He pointed it at Barrett. "Sir, I have asked you nicely. I shan't ask again. Now I am telling you. All of your rations are ours. In fact this ship is ours."

Barrett laughed.

Quincy aimed his pistol at one of Barrett's men and shot him. Quincy's skeleton crew drew their arms as well. "Now here's the situation. This ship is ours. You can have the naval vessel or you can have the sea. Take your pick."

Barrett held up his hands. "I understand. Just don't hurt my men," he said while inching closer.

"Don't come any closer, Barrett." Quincy stood up. As he did so, Barrett rushed over to him and stepped on the bottom of his dragging coat. Quincy fired his pistol, but it only grazed Barrett's shoulder. Barrett grabbed Quincy by the throat, squeezed, then took the gun from him.

Quincy's men tried to fire their weapons, but Barrett's men were already upon them. Barrett lifted the pistol and pulled the trigger under Quincy's jaw—which removed it entirely. Matthews threw down his gun and surrendered. "They weren't loaded! They weren't loaded!" he said, but it was a ruse. He put the sack of gunpowder in the kerosene lamp and threw it at Archer. Archer leapt out of the way before the lamp exploded on the wall behind him.

The blast sent everyone reeling. The quarterdeck was now aflame.

Jupiter rushed Quincy's man, pinned him, then twisted his neck until he heard it snap. Quincy was dead, but the flames raged on. The fighting took so long it spread to the entire ship. There was no saving her. Jupiter saw Archer on the floor, still dazed. He grabbed him by the arms and dragged him through the fire.

"Head to the skiff and retreat to the British vessel," Barrett told Jupiter.

They grabbed what they could. Some men were caught in the flames. It did not take long for the *Intono* to light up the night sky and dark waters like a Roman candle. Jupiter, Barrett, and Archer all retreated to the skiff. There were bodies in the water. The blast had made a few of them islands of fire. They passed one, and a charred hand reached from the water and grabbed the boat. A scorched head surfaced. "Barrett . . ." it said. "Barrett . . ." Barrett leaned over the edge and held the scorched head under the water until it let go of the boat. Jupiter and Archer looked on in shock. "No sense in letting him suffer," said Barrett.

39

Somewhere in the Atlantic

"Ladies and gentlemen, gather 'round," Sebastian called out to the other passengers. "You will now witness the amazing illusions of Sebastian the Magnificent and Jacob the Great."

The crowd that had gathered clapped lazily.

Sebastian thought that it would be a good idea to increase the morale after the storm's threat. Possibly, if pleased with his abilities, they would provide some word-of-mouth once they reached shore. "You will now witness the astonishing illusion, 'Boy on the Mast.'" Sebastian waved his hands with flair and covered Jacob with a blanket. The audience could see him twitching underneath it.

Sonya ran her fingers across her neck. After some moments, Sebastian snatched back the tarp, and there was nothing there. Sonya gasped. "Jacob? Jacob? My son!" She spun around the deck, then stopped on Sebastian. Who was this man? She knew nothing about him. Had she been foolish enough to let him use her boy in his dark experiments? The other passengers picked up on her fear. "Jacob," they called out. "Don't worry—we'll find him."

"Everyone, there is no need to worry," said Sebastian. "Jacob is still with us."

"What have you done with my son?"

"He is with us, but above us. Behold."

From the top mast, Jacob waved. "Here I am."

The other passengers gasped—then clapped.

"Get him down from there." She grabbed Sebastian's collar. "Now."

"He's fine, be assured." Sebastian grabbed her wrists, looked into her eyes. "He's fine. I promise you. I'd never do anything to hurt him, or to you."

Jacob shimmied down the rope with the agility of an acrobat. "Did you like the trick, Mamma?"

Sebastian let go of her wrists. She grabbed Jacob. "Yes, you are truly great."

40

San Francisco

The day was cold and clear, and the *Cressida Pacific* loomed proudly over the harbor, ready to embark on her maiden voyage. Dalmore could taste the salt in the air. Through flash and smoke, a photographer from the newspaper immortalized her image. Upon the dais, Dalmore posed with the mayor and governor. The crowd applauded when he was introduced.

"When we aim to describe a man or define him, we often do so by the use of one word—he was not *this*, he was *that*. This is unfair to the man being described. I am many things, not just one thing. For instance, I am a fighter and a dreamer, but most important, I am a *builder*. I speak not just of ships and railroads. As this world continues to expand at breakneck speed, it is important that we remain connected to one another. I am a builder of connections. I contract the vast spaces of time and distance. I close the gaps that separate us.

"And how does all of this start? Ships are built. Track is laid. Empires rise. Wealth is created, men are enslaved, and it seems to us to come out of nowhere, like the product of some dark alchemy. However, it is no sorcerer's trick, it is a spell we cast on ourselves (and then we cast on others). All of this happens because some man somewhere was told *No!* and he refused to listen. He was denied something, and with every fiber of his being he refused to listen, and he sought it out, and he obtained what he sought. But there were others watching—there are always others watching—and they took that as a lesson on how to achieve their own desires and their own aims. That is how it continues. As long as there are people who want something that they can't immediately possess, the size of the want grows, the scope widens, swells, and becomes exaggerated. It becomes a grotesque caricature of the original desire, a monstrosity enlarged and swollen. But then their monster becomes normal. A little boy who dreams of crossing oceans, making tiny boats out of paper, his circumstances, his environment tell him *No!*. Then years pass, and before anyone has realized it that paper boat has become a behemoth with vast sails, or a dragon spewing coal smoke and steam, and requires a hundred men working in its belly to feed its fire—to fuel it. That is how it happens. It never ends. It never will.

"Despite all of that, I knew I had amazing gifts to offer this world, but I needed a country big and brash enough to handle someone like me. It is strange how I am more British in America than I was as an orphan on the streets of London. . . . I was such a sad, desperate boy then—but dedicated to survival. . . . The things I did for food and shelter . . . picked pockets, robbed a grave or two, I even let those perverted aristocrats fondle me for a few shillings—but I was never buggered, mind you. . . . I stowed away on a ship and was adopted by the captain and owner of the line. . . . He was a horrible man . . . beat me mercilessly. . . . I laughed when he died. . . . I took his name only to prove that I could do more with it than he ever did. . . . I don't even remember my old name. . . . Did I have one? My mother was a whore . . . but here I am . . . I grabbed this country by the hair, spread her legs, and gave her a proper fucking . . ."

A crash—

Cymbals? There's a band?

A scream—

Cheers? Laughter? Where is the crowd?

The maid stood over a tray of broken china, her hand trembling over her mouth.

"Mr. Dalmore?" she managed to whimper.

He saw her and himself—naked and shriveled. There was no crowd, no harbor, just home. He collapsed clutching a sketchbook of lewd drawings, but it was the half-finished ship, bare and vulnerable, that was last on his mind.

41

They watched from the boat. Edged by darkness, a mountain of fire on the water, the burning *Intono* lit up the sky like a night-sun. Barrett stared into the blaze, never blinking. A roaring ocean, gasping flames, the screams of drowning men—invisible in the black water. Barrett's lips trembled and mouthed words, but no sound came forth. He looked at Jupiter and Archer with a wicked smile. "Men, it is now . . . *us*. I sense apprehension; this is understandable, but know this—we are moving forward. The past is no more. You see, everything that you have learned of me . . . my actions had their purpose. That's all in the past. The past," Barrett pointed at the fire, "is on that ship. Soon it will be on the bottom of the ocean, forgotten."

Jupiter and Archer said nothing.

"I am upset, men. I am truly upset. And not for the reason that you may think. Yes, I loved the *Intono*; I sailed her to every corner of the earth. I became a man on that ship. But it's her cargo that concerns me. I have kept you in the dark long enough. I can admit now, with humility, that I need the two of you. I need your help. There were guns on my ship, meant to supply the Chinese armory, and now they are on the bottom of the ocean. My assignment was to circumvent the embargo that the English had placed on the Chinese after the Opium Wars. They don't sell them modern-day weapons, mind you."

Jupiter and Archer backed away from Barrett as if he were a wild animal and they unsure of his next move.

"I see," said Barrett, "you men need more reason to trust. I understand, and I am willing to earn it. But know that I too need to feel as though I can trust you. For I am inviting you to participate in something bold and grand. While I know that the two of you are quite capable, I need to be certain of your dedication."

"Dedication to what?" asked Jupiter.

"Ahh, the most important question, *dedication to what?* To fairness, to shaking the yoke from one's own neck, and to presenting others with the opportunity to do the same."

"I don't follow," said Archer.

"Nor should you," said Barrett. "*Lead*. I am asking you to lead. You two—others just like you—shoot at each other while around the world cotton prices soar. The same with tobacco. Britain steps in to fill the void, and new kings are made throughout North Africa and the Indies. All because of cotton grown on plantations like the one on which you were bound. All the while, men like you and Archer die on the battlefield. The war ends and it's back to business as usual. Cotton prices soar and a revolution breaks out. It's all connected. There are no coincidences, only convergences. We are puppets. When our strings are pulled by the same master occasionally they cross. They told you it was your war, but it's their war. All wars are their wars. They pin your race to your back, and they create myths to dull and distract you. Don't believe them. I've been in those smoke-filled rooms where these things are planned. It is a bloody business. You lose your appetite when you see their fangs up close.

"Haven't you ever wondered why it's always these poor, sad, and honest men who die in wars? And when the world shakes from the violence, in its aftermath it is always the same people who remain in power—who seem to become even more powerful."

"Like the rich," said Archer.

"The rich?" Barrett smiled. "I wish it were so simple. No, I am speaking of a very select few—wealth is part of it, but these men are more powerful, more cunning than a bunch of misers pinching every penny. These men are far more powerful than that. I have seen them in their smoke-filled rooms, turning ideas, thoughts, and whims into power and money with the flick of an ash. They turn one thing into another, they can turn blood into gold—they are alchemists of a different sort. I've seen it done. They have hired me to do their dirty work. There was a time when I thought myself privileged to be considered useful to them. But I was just one of their minions. Then I realized my own power. If they were alchemists, then what was I? A master of the waves who knows every corner of this earth like a carriage driver knows his way around London. I can slip through any blockade like a shadow. So if they are alchemists, sorcerers, then what are we? If powerful men need men like us, then isn't it we who are truly powerful? Shouldn't we remind those who think themselves weak just how powerful they truly are?"

"And how do we do that?" asked Jupiter.

"Haven't you been listening?" said Barrett. "Guns, my dear boy. Guns."

•   •   •

The smell was the first thing that they noticed. There were decomposed bodies . . . that looked as if something had feasted upon them.

"These must have been the British officers," Barrett said. "The first thing we must do is rid this ship of the dead."

They tossed the dead overboard. Looking at each other, Archer and Jupiter both had the same thought—though they did not express it—of tossing their fellow soldiers into shallow graves after a battle. This was no war, and even though these men were from another country, it was no less horrible.

After scouring the ship, they found little food, but they did find a good set of maps. By candlelight, Barrett surveyed them, tracing his finger along the latitudinal, then longitudinal lines. He tapped his finger on a spot with no visible land, just ocean. "This is where we head."

"Help! Help!" they heard someone cry. It came from the ship's belly. Jupiter grabbed the candle and they went down to investigate. It was dark. It was fetid. "Come out," Barrett demanded.

"I can't," the shadows pleaded. "I've been bound."

The candle failed to sufficiently cut the darkness, but a bound figure became visible. "Thank God," it said. "The things they've done to me. . . . Please tell me they are all dead."

"Aye, they are," said Barrett.

"Who said that?"

Barrett held the candle closer to his face. "I did."

There was silence, then a breathy rattle, then laughter. "Why, it is such sweet news to hear that they are dead, but even sweeter to hear it from your lips—Captain Barrett."

42

Somewhere in the Atlantic

Sonya and Sebastian were alone on deck.

"You seem to have recovered from the thrills of the day," said Sebastian.

"I have."

"I apologize for giving you a fright."

Sonya nodded. "He's taken quite a liking to it. I've never seen him this way."

"It's the adventure. Boys need it—men do too. I guess it brings out the man in a boy, the boy in the man."

Sonya smiled.

"That amuses you?"

"I once heard someone say something similar."

He moved closer. "And what does adventure bring out in a woman?"

Her lips parted. Her tongue tasted salty air.

"You seem to be a woman who would know," said Sebastian.

"I have endured a lot, because I had to. I would not call them adventures. Survival. Necessities. Burdens."

"And never an ounce of enjoyment in all that time?"

"I'm married, Sebastian."

"I know, Mrs. Smith. But if your husband isn't there—God forbid it—or if something has happened to him . . . That land is known for giving the fever to even the acclimated—if something like that was to happen I'd be there for you and Jacob. I'd make sure that you didn't mourn long. Mrs. Smith, I would see to it that that day would be your last day of sadness."

"Don't. Don't call me that or say those things." She closed her eyes. The ocean howled like wind through a canyon. She thought of those days on the plantation. Jupiter leaving. Her mother sold off and later dying. Colonel Smith's descent into madness, terrorizing the slaves that remained. She opened her eyes. Sebastian was smiling. "My last day of sadness," she whispered. "How could anyone be foolish enough to promise such a thing?"

"I have been known to make miracles happen."

43

"Madam, I was devastated to hear of your husband's passing. My condolences."

Maggie stared at the small man. She thought she detected a bit of insincerity. "Yes, Mr. Dalmore was a fine man. A fine man with a keen mind. So sad indeed, but people die from strokes every day."

The accountant looked at her. "It is good that you are maintaining the proper perspective."

She nodded. "I appreciate your concern, but I think there is the matter of Mr. Dalmore's estate to discuss."

"Yes, of course, Mr. Dalmore's estate . . . well, I am afraid that a second offering of condolences may be necessary."

She felt hot. "How do you mean?"

"I mean that as far as Mr. Dalmore's assets are concerned, there are hardly *any*. None, practically."

She felt the presence of something lurking behind her, then a chill raised her flesh. She had been in this situation once before, when Mr. O'Connell had died, leaving her nothing but his name; and rather than admit that as his widow she was just as poor as that young girl he had taken in, she went to Miss Ellen for help. And now, after all she had done to amass her small fortune, there was nothing left.

"It seems," said the accountant, "that Mr. Dalmore owed a lot of money. He was quite over-leveraged."

"Are you saying there is nothing left? Not even the money that I brought into the marriage?"

"No. I am afraid not. All that is left is what has been completed of the *Cressida*."

That damned ship. "The *Cressida*, is she near completion?"

"Yes, I believe so. Madam, if I may be so bold as to offer a suggestion? You could try to sell the *Cressida* upon its completion, but I fear that few would offer anything more than an insulting price, given your situation . . ."

"Why didn't my husband's creditors seize the ship instead of his other assets?"

"Most lenders prefer cash over unfinished ships—but that leads me back to my point—you could run the ship yourself. Transporting cargo across the Pacific can be very lucrative. Even with one ship. I understand that there are passenger quarters. You could find a crew right here on the docks. I'm sure there would be plenty of men eager for the work."

"I thank you for your input, but I know something about crewing a ship."

"Of course you do, madam. My apologies."

●　　●　　●

She thought she would never be in this position again. She thought back a few months prior—to the earthquake that shook the young city and sent a flash of terror through it like a tyrannical parent. Her place was left in shambles. It was remarkable that she had survived—the same could not be said of Clement and the men who worked the tunnel that led from her place to the harbor. They were crushed under the saloon's collapsed floors—sealing them in. She had survived again. Aside from a few fires, the city was undamaged. She thought about the biblical Sodom and Gomorrah, how San Francisco was possibly an improvement upon it. No matter how many times God pushed her down, the bitch kept getting back up. She did not want to believe in signs, but in this case, she could not help it. Before he died, Clement suggested that it was time for her to get out of the horrible business she was in and get involved with a man who was not afraid to get his hands dirty, yet still see the bigger picture.

But then he'd suffered a stroke. She thought she was protecting herself by combining her assets with his, but, in fact, he was broke. He'd used her money to build the ship he had dreamed of since he was a boy.

•   •   •

The heat was so oppressive inland. She couldn't remember the last time she had left San Francisco. She needed the fog and sea breeze. She looked over the land—isolated and sun-scorched—why would anyone want to live here? It wasn't much, but it would be enough to borrow against and finish the *Cressida*. She noticed a weathered shack in the distance. It was run-down and neglected by time, but if he had just told her about it, then maybe the two of them could have made something of it. A place where they could have been together—free from the judgment of prying eyes. It would have been nice.

She wiped the sweat from her brow and it stung. It was too hot. She fanned herself with the deed to Jupiter's land.

44

"Well, Barrett, are you just going to stare at me or are you going to untie me?" the bound man asked. It was the first time Jupiter had seen Barrett appear surprised.

"Murphy?" asked Barrett.

"Well it sure ain't Davy Crockett. Get these damn ropes off me." Barrett untied him. Jupiter noticed that this *Murphy* wore the same uniforms as the prisoners had worn.

"What are you doing down here?" Barrett asked him.

"Prisoners overtook the ship. I wasn't for it," Murphy said.

"You weren't for it, Murphy?"

"It didn't make a damn bit of sense—and in case you haven't noticed, I'm not as spry as I used to be," Murphy said. "So they kept me bound. I heard them talk about seizing a ship they passed. Plundering its rations. Now that I see you, I can be certain of what's come to them."

"Aye," said Barrett. "You can be certain. Our priority should be to get this ship to land—and shed those damn Union Jacks. They only draw attention rather than give us coverage."

Murphy looked at Barrett. "I said the same thing to them . . . but they didn't listen."

"We should head to Tikopia Island," Barrett said.

Jupiter noticed a look of relief and exasperation come over Murphy's face. "Of course," Murphy said. "Tikopia Island. That makes perfect sense."

"Then it's settled. Murphy, let's get you situated."

• • •

Barrett knew Murphy from his smuggling days during the war. The Brits had steadily smuggled contraband to the Confederate South. Seems one of Murphy's deals had gone bad and he'd tried to go it alone. Tried to kill one of his debtors rather than pay what he owed, which is how he'd found himself headed toward the prisoners' island.

In the days that followed, Jupiter noticed a change in Barrett brought on by Murphy's presence. The two of them always seemed huddled together conspiratorially, and Barrett seemed to separate from his men.

"When this is over," Jupiter overheard Murphy say, "let's do a thing of our own. There is work to be done, fortunes to be had in Cuba."

"Cuba, you say?" asked Barrett. "I believe I heard something of it." Barrett's eyes went from Murphy's desperate grin to Jupiter's face. Barrett's look did not change.

45

An uncharted island somewhere in the Pacific

They docked on the south side of the island. It was good that it was
night: he did not have the energy to fight the heat. Jupiter's legs felt
unsteady as he walked on shore. Strange, he thought, how accustomed
he had become to life on a ship. On a ship, these men were dependent
upon his survival. What would happen now that they were on land
again? Would this island bring him closer to finding Sonya and the boy,
or was it just another detour?

There was dense jungle up ahead. "I'm surprised you didn't head
to the island yourself, Murphy," he heard Barrett say. "A man with as
much seawater in your bones should have known better."

"Aye, maybe I'm getting dull in my old age," said Murphy.

"No, sharp as a blade you are, Murphy. Sharp as a blade."

•   •   •

Archer had never been there before, yet it seemed familiar to him—
possibly from all of those books he'd read as a child of adventures and
sea voyages. But this was no boy's story. Already, Archer's instincts
had failed him so many times. All of his presumptions would have to
be abandoned. In every situation that he seemed prepared for, he was
proven wrong. It was then that he had the heartbreaking realization
that he needed these men. As long as they lived, he lived. He was dependent upon a man he wanted to kill.

Where did that leave him? What use was he—or Jupiter for that matter—now that they were back on land? Those trees ahead looked ominous. He could disappear into the brush and be claimed by nature, never to be seen again.

• • •

They started a fire and waited.

Barrett warmed his hands over the fire and then lit a prison-ship cigar in the flame. "Do you have any children?"

Jupiter stared into the fire. The roar of the waves grew louder. "I have a son."

Barrett took a long draw from his cigar. "What does he think of all this crimping business?"

"He doesn't know, but if he did I can't imagine he'd take too much pride in it."

"How old is the boy?"

Jupiter watched a crab's shell make its way into the fire's circle of light. "Seven."

"Seven? You do not seem certain."

"I had to think for a moment. I didn't know he existed until a few days before we were put on your ship."

Another long draw from his cigar. Tobacco smoke mingled with the smell of burning wood. "Father and son meeting for the first time, interrupted by such a tragedy. My apologies to you, Jupiter."

"Just get me to Liberia."

"Liberia . . . I know it, somewhat. Remind me, why are they there?" Barrett asked.

"They received some false information that I was there looking for them."

"From where did this false information come?"

"Another slave from the old plantation. One of my rivals for Sonya's affection."

"And this man was close when you found your wife and son?"

"Yes. He'd been taking care of them since I left for the South. Thought I died in the war."

Barrett looked at Jupiter. "And you know for certain that the boy is yours?"

"Yes, I am certain. And I know the boy is not his, if that's what you mean."

"Your wife confirmed this?"

"No, we haven't spoken."

"I thought you found her and the boy just before our paths crossed."

"No. I only saw my boy and the slave I just mentioned. Saw them in the street when I went looking for their mother."

"And you said not one word to them?"

"No. I was too shaken. When I managed the nerve to find them, my journey ended with a club to the back of my head and not the antici- pated embrace from my son."

"You have never spoken a word to this boy, never spoken to the mother about him, how are you certain the child is yours?"

The fire flared from a strong gust of wind.

"I know because I saw myself in him. One look and I knew he was mine. Blood can recognize blood. If you can quiet your mind, remain still, you can hear the blood in their veins whisper to the blood in your veins. Maybe it's something a slave learns, families being broken up and all. You had to recognize kinship on sight. See that the blood flow- ing in that stranger's veins is your own. I knew he was blood, just as I knew it was Archer even in that darkened room."

"Archer?" Barrett looked over at the sleeping former Confederate soldier. "I see . . . Oh, I see." Another puff from the cigar. "I presume he was obviously mulatto, or a quadroon; that's how you put it to- gether. Strange thing to rest upon. It's as if you think there can be only one quadroon or mulatto in all of San Francisco."

46

They walked silently except for the sound of footsteps, shoulder to shoulder in a flanklike fashion. There was a sound. Barrett held up his hand for them to stop. They heard the sound again, an echo of footsteps. There was nothing but darkness and shadows and the sound growing louder. The bushes rustled. A breeze? Their senses tingled as the bushes began to move. Two women, dressed like men, emerged from the bushes, with the twenty or so men behind them.

"Good to see you are still alive," said Barrett.

She wore the ragged jacket of a sea captain with a scabbard at her side. The younger woman remained silent.

"It has been a long time, Barrett," she said.

"Aye, it has."

She looked over Barrett and his tattered crew. "By the looks of things you need another favor." Her accent was English and islander, skin like sandalwood, bright green eyes.

"Always so observant. We do. We have a line on selling that cargo that you have been holding for us."

Jupiter and Archer looked at each other.

"And I assume you have come with the payment?"

"No, I haven't—but soon. We'll sell the cargo to our contact in Shanghai. Where's Dunham?"

Kalana sighed. "Dunham is no more."

"Dead? What happened to him?"

"Yerby happened to him."

"Yerby? Who is Yerby?"

"That's not as important as what he has done," said Kalana. "He's a pirate hunter. He chases down stolen cargo and sells it back to the owners for a profit. He was some kind of British official, but he was relieved of his duty for disrespecting one of the natives and causing tension for the British. He hunts us down and takes what he can get. Contraband of all sorts, including people."

"People?"

"Sells them off as coolies for the guano trade."

Barrett stared into the fire.

"If you are thinking of going after him, don't. It is too dangerous."

Barrett looked at her. "Very dangerous indeed, if you are frightened."

She leaned in, the fire almost nipping at her long hair. "I never said I was scared, Barrett. I am just not a fool."

"How many men does he have?"

"Ten. Twenty. Could be more. His usual crew, as well as natives that he has armed."

"Good. With us, the men you have left, and the men that have joined me, I think we have a chance."

"These men?" She scowled at Archer. "Who are they?"

"These gentlemen are warriors all the way from America."

Her sister laughed. Kalana spat into the fire. "Warriors . . ."

"Aye. America was at war with itself. It was very bloody. These two men fought on opposite sides of it."

Kalana studied Jupiter's face. "You were on the side that was victorious?"

He heard Archer swallow. "So they say," said Jupiter.

"Fine. We will help you, but you free our men being held by Yerby—and we want a share of his cargo when you sell it."

"That's fair," said Barrett.

"In addition to what I am already owed."

"Always a shrewd one . . ."

"I have to be. These are complicated times on this simple island. We still have a crate of weapons. They are old and not reliable at all, but they should be enough." She looked at Jupiter and Archer. "This evening, send the smart one to me. My sister can have the dumb one."

Barrett put his hand on Jupiter's shoulder. "Looks like your social schedule is booked. Try not to disappoint her."

" 'The dumb one'?" asked Archer.

• • •

"The last time I saw you, Barrett, I gave you rations, you set sail to retrieve my payment, and left your man here for collateral."

"I know, Kalana."

"He grew ill. He cried for you. But you never came. Strange how if you can live long enough, all wishes come true.

"He would scream for you every night and pour out the dark parts of his soul. I did not know your tongue then as I do now, but even then, his cries haunted me as I slept. Now I know your tongue. What he said still haunts me in these painful waking hours as I approach the long sleep. I know your tongue well enough, Barrett. . . . I could be better, but now that I know it, I do not like you as I once did. The last white man that asked for our help made agreement with us, took our food and resources. They had our men load their ships, then killed our men, my brother with them, and left without payment," said Kalana.

"My heart aches for your loss, as you can see," said Barrett.

"Those men I spoke of called themselves the Black Hands. They had their bodies marked with the sign of a clenched fist. Have your men remove their clothing. We will inspect your bodies. If any of you bear this mark, this night will be your last."

"Of course." Barrett nodded to Jupiter and Archer, and they began to undress.

"This is ridiculous," said Murphy.

"Your man is not undressing," Kalana said, pointing at Murphy.

"Go ahead, Murphy," Barrett said.

"I know that we are desperate, but are we desperate enough to embarrass ourselves for the entertainment of savages?"

"Savages?" In a breath, Barrett revealed his knife and had it at Murphy's throat. Kalana lunged, but then she put up her hand to stop them.

"You have the nerve to call them savages after you have your men take my ship, kill my men while you wait on deck, and watch my ship burn?"

"Barrett, I didn't know . . ." pleaded Murphy.

"Oh, you knew," said Barrett. "You knew the *Intono* well. You could recognize it from a distance. There was no other ship like it. You knew to stay on the British naval vessel, because I would have recognized you instantly. You couldn't face me. You thought I would be overwhelmed."

"No, I swear that isn't it."

"Well, I do not believe you. Although, I'll concede it is possible that you are not guilty of the crime of which I speak, however—" Barrett ripped open Murphy's shirt, revealing the balled black fist tattooed on his chest. "You are guilty of the crime against these people."

"Barrett, please . . ."

Barrett let him plead a bit longer, and then he let his knife open Murphy's throat. Blood spewed forth, onto Barrett, some onto Jupiter, as Murphy fell to the ground holding his throat, gurgling in the darkness. Barrett dipped his hand in Murphy's blood and showed his bloody palm to Kalana. "I offer his blood to you, as well as my allegiance. Please grant me that honor."

Without emotion, she spoke. "You will have what you need," Kalana said. "What do I care? Maybe now that you have returned, Dunham's ghost will leave me."

•　•　•

Barrett held the skewered *bêche-de-mer* over the fire. Jupiter and Archer stared at him in silence.

"You boys seem at a loss for words."

"You killed him without a second thought," said Archer.

"I killed a man who burned my ship. A man who killed our host's brother. A man I knew well. A man who deserved to die. How many anonymous men have the two of you put down for much less? Brothers you *are*. The two of you love to believe in lies. But I'll be sure to fix all that. They put a gun in your hand and told you to kill white men. How many white men did you kill?"

Jupiter did not answer, but thought, *Too many . . . maybe not enough.*

"Who is your man? Whose familiar face did you project onto those soldiers as you aimed your rifle?"

47

Liberia

The *Orpheus* arrived at the coast. Eager men from the Kru tribe carried the belongings of the new arrivals to the dock. Excited by all she saw, Sonya struggled to take a deep breath. The air was as thick as cotton. It seemed like home in a way. There was a strange sensation of peering through the looking glass: an upside-down re-creation of the South. Black men walked around with obvious wealth, although overdressed for the oppressive heat. The houses, with their wide porches and tall Greek columns, looked so much like the homes on plantations that she shuddered at the sight of them.

They were led to an immigration office. Weary, unfriendly clerks took their information and showed them to the dormitories that they would be staying in until their sponsors arrived.

Sonya told them her situation. They told her she could stay for a month until a proper sponsor arrived. Money was the bottom line. Just like at home—just like the world over.

●   ●   ●

The hardest thing to stand was the smell. Too many people packed into such a small space. That heat, that humidity—it was oppressive, suffocating, enough to make her choke.

They had been there long enough to almost exhaust the grace period, and still no word of Jupiter. She began to wonder if he'd ever make it there. She hadn't realized what a long journey it was—half a world away—ample time for anything to happen. She had not found Mary. Maybe she was gone too; maybe she had married, changed her name, and died. She had only received one letter from the woman in that entire time, and none of the beautiful descriptions in that letter matched what Sonya saw. There were loads of promises, so why wouldn't they be broken.

She'd refused Sebastian's offer; she knew what that would mean. That kind of hospitality could never be repaid.

"Could you please check again," she said to the clerk.

"I have checked, ma'am, and the result is still the same. I think it's time to accept the reality of your situation. The good news is that you are here. Liberia is the only place in the world for a Negro to enjoy the fruits of liberty. However, we will have to find other lodgings for you and your son. Six months is the limit or I am afraid you will have to return to America. We cannot expect you to wander the streets. We do not allow émigré vagrancy. A woman with your background and complexion might be able to work in the homes of some of our merchants. On the serving staff, of course."

She didn't like the haughtiness of his accent, the condescension in his voice as he spoke to her. After coming so far, the thought of becoming a servant again turned her stomach.

"No. I'm sure I should wait."

The clerk sighed. "The cost of your lodging will be deducted from your future earnings. Isn't there anyone else?"

There was someone. She showed the clerk the letter. "This was her first name. She was going by Parham as her last name the last time I saw her."

"Parham . . . I don't know of any Parhams in Monrovia. I shall check the records. Maybe she married under this name."

Sonya managed a smile.

"Mamma . . . how long are we going to be here?" asked Jacob.

"Not much longer."

"Should we have gone with Sebastian?"

No, she thought, *I don't trust him. I don't trust myself with him.* He knew too many tricks. The biggest one being turning a heart of stone into flesh and blood. Where did he learn such a thing? What type of pact with the devil did he make to get that kind of power? She shook her head. "No," she said, "we couldn't go with him." He had warmed places that were cooled by shadow and neglect. She stroked Jacob's cheek and forehead. He felt like a coal plucked from the fire.

48

Jupiter bathed in a hot spring, resting, thinking of Sonya, thinking of a way out. He tried to see a way forward but it looked murky.

"You cannot trust Barrett," said a voice behind him. Kalana stood in the shadows. A candle illuminated her face. How long had she been there?

"I don't have to trust him. I just need his skills."

"Why? You don't seem to be the smuggling type."

"I need to get to Liberia. My family is waiting there for me."

"Liberia . . . Where is Liberia?"

Jupiter thought a moment. He wasn't sure himself. "It's in Africa."

"Are you from there?"

"No, I was born in America. But some Negroes have left the States to start a new life in Liberia. They think being amongst their own people will give themselves a better chance at freedom and prosperity."

"It will never work," whispered Kalana.

"Why not?"

"You have been away too long. It is not your home anymore. No one will recognize you. If you come home and no one recognizes you, then you are a stranger. It's simple. That's why we are on this island and not with our people. My sister, my brother, we all had different fathers. The English sailors impregnated our native mothers. The offspring were scattered about, sold as slaves, as whores. Those of us who came back to our islands wore the white man's clothes, spoke his language—our own language ruined—our accents, our tone is different. The way we see things . . . Even though we miss home, it's foreign to us. We are strangers to them. It is not such a bad thing."

The truth of what she said silenced Jupiter. "You don't miss being part of a tribe?"

"We are a tribe—a tribe of pirates. A tribe is just a group of people that agree on what to remember. How long has it been since you have seen her?"

Jupiter picked up a pebble worn smooth by time. "Seven years."

"That is a long time. Have you had other women?"

Jupiter's cheeks felt hot.

"You shouldn't be embarrassed. She has certainly been with other men. A beautiful woman alone . . . not sure if you are alive or dead. She has needs."

"How do you know that she's beautiful? I never said that."

"She is very beautiful. You have traveled around the world to find her. She is a goddess. I have been told by a few men that I am beautiful."

Jupiter took in the strangeness of her appearance—a captain's jacket and a man's shirt revealing the curve of her bosom. Wild hair that mimicked the untamed growth of the surrounding jungle. She was definitely beautiful. She kissed Jupiter hard and forced his hand between her legs, but he pushed her away when he thought of the last woman who had kissed him with such passion.

"I'm sorry. Now that I know she's alive, and that she's out there looking for me . . . I can't."

Kalana stood. "Do not apologize. I am not offended. But if a man can be with a woman before a battle, it is a good idea that he do so. He may not survive."

"I know I'll survive," said Jupiter. "I am not a perfect man, by any means, but I want to be able to look my son in the eye when I see him again. I want him to know that ever since I learned that he was on this earth, I have tried to make the right choices."

"You didn't do what you thought was right before you learned of him?"

"I did," said Jupiter, "but I was wrong most of the time."

"I understand how complicated fathers can be, but you should not have to be perfect to look your son in the eye. You should be man enough to look him in the eye and admit that you are not perfect. Otherwise, you are of no use to him."

49

They advanced through the brush with Kalana and her sister in front. Barrett hacked his way through the unyielding foliage with his machete.

"We'll have to get free of him," Jupiter said to Archer. "You see that now."

Archer nodded with hesitation. "But how will we get back? We've no money, nothing to barter with, and we look and smell like shit. Should we go to one of these merchants and tell them our story? They'd laugh in our faces. Which one of them hasn't crimped a sailor or two for their vessels?"

"You're right," said Jupiter, "it is foolish, but either we die by the madness of Barrett's plan, or we live by the foolish pursuit of our own. By the way things stand, I'd bet on us."

Archer looked at him and stayed silent. "Stop," Kalana said. "I hear something." Gunfire seemed to come at them from all directions. Some of the men retreated into the jungle. Jupiter and Archer dropped to their bellies, searching the foliage for the shooters.

Barrett pointed to two men in trees. Archer took down both of them, and then tried to reload. Nothing moved. "Damn."

A screaming man emerged from the trees and ran at them. Jupiter did not trust the range of these weapons. He let the man get closer and pretended to struggle with his gun. The man fired two shots and missed. Jupiter raised his gun and pulled the trigger. The man held his stomach and fell to the ground. He wasn't dead. He clawed his way toward Jupiter until Archer stood over him and fired. "We'll have to let them get close. These things have less range than a slingshot."

They stayed low and looked for Barrett. They found him on his knees at the edge of a small blood-tinted pond. He held Kalana's body.

Jupiter did not approach them. They watched his body rise and fall. They wanted to tell him to keep moving, but they did not have the chance—they felt guns in their backs, and then were told to drop their weapons.

50

"Here they are, Captain Yerby." The cave was littered with extravagant contraband, ornaments made of precious metals, crates of spices, and exotic flora and fauna: all the fruits—in some form or another—of piracy. But the strangest items were the medical curiosities: shrunken heads in jars, miniature men, deformed animals with two heads, or humans with four arms.

A man sat hunched over a makeshift desk of discarded tea crates of the East India Company, as he scribbled something on parchment. He stroked his bald head as he wrote.

"Are you pirates?" he asked no one in particular.

Jupiter looked at Barrett, as did Archer. The three men were on their knees with their hands bound behind their backs.

Yerby's man nudged Barrett with the butt of his rifle. "No, we are not pirates," he said.

Yerby kept his back to them. "You are not pirates, yet you arrived here on a stolen British ship."

"We arrived here on a British ship, but it is not *we* who stole it."

"I know it's stolen. I supplied it with a few of its prisoners not too long ago. Now the ship has returned, yet none of its prisoners remain."

"Are you claiming we stole prisoners? For what purpose?"

"Sold them into bondage, perhaps. They'd fetch a hefty sum working the guano trade. I'm sure most of them would prefer an eternity of digging for dung to a few years on the colony."

"Not a bad idea," Barrett whispered.

Yerby turned around. His face was weathered. One eye was milky. He had the look of an aristocrat gone mad. "Do you see? I am a subject of Her Majesty's Royal Navy. I am only here at Her Majesty's pleasure. I supply the ship with prisoners intended for the colony, and it returns to me without none of said prisoners on board. What would happen if such a thing got back to Britain?"

Not a word from the three men.

"Answer me!"

"It would not be a good thing, I suppose," said Jupiter.

"No, it would not be a good thing. The British are not keen to embarrassment. I know this from personal experience. I represented Britain in its dealings with China. I made certain our merchants were treated fairly, and most importantly, that our opium continued to reach their shores without impediment. But one of the Hong merchants became impudent, and I put the bastard in his place. His Hong cohort demanded that I apologize. I refused. A riot—a small one, mind you— broke out in the port town's square. This compromised trade. In a way, I was exiled. But I guess you could say it was a good thing, because I was allowed to roam free and discover who I am. Free to help Her Majesty in the best way as I see fit—like hunting pirates. I track them down and return the cargoes they have stolen to the rightful owners— for a percentage of their value."

"A finder's fee," said Barrett.

"Should I not be compensated for my efforts?"

Barrett liked him. If it were not apparent that they would be dying soon, he might have smiled. "I believe I've heard that story. Was the man you mentioned named Xiao Pei?"

"Possibly. All their names sound like the screeches of vultures to me."

"No one knew what became of him."

"I know *exactly* what became of him."

"Was he here?" asked Barrett.

Yerby smirked. "Not was, *is*."

Barrett glanced at the cabinet and its gruesome jars.

"What are your names?" Yerby asked, looking at Barrett.

"My name is Captain Barrett, formerly of the *Intono*."

"And now a captain of a British prison ship? Funny, you don't sound British. American, I presume?"

"The sea is my country," Barrett said.

Yerby laughed. "How charming you are, Captain Barrett. How did you come to be in possession of our ship? You seem like a man that does not let go of things too easily. So how did you lose your ship and come into possession of the inmates?"

"My ship was overtaken by the men who overtook your officers and stole the Queen's ship. They had wandered out to sea. They were sick and without rations. They spotted my ship and boarded as British officers. Obviously, we are friends of the Queen, so we let them on board when we saw their uniforms, but it wasn't long before they showed their true colors."

Yerby seemed to mull over Barrett's statement. "And where are these men—these prisoners—who overtook our men?"

"Well," said Barrett, "they are tending to my ship at the bottom of the sea."

Yerby laughed. "I see. No survivors?"

"No. I killed the last one not but one hour ago."

"Sir, are you saying that you killed a British prisoner?"

"Like I said, Captain. He overtook my ship and we were forced aboard the British vessel."

"So, this man you killed, he overtook your ship and you brought him back to our vessel? You didn't kill him once he tried to seize your ship?"

Barrett seemed confused to Jupiter. "No. He was on your ship when we boarded. He was bound. He claimed he was bound by the other prisoners. We untied him and sailed to the island."

"But you killed him?"

"Aye, I found him to be false."

"You found him to be false? My God, Captain Barrett, you are an interesting fellow. Judge and jury, you are."

"He—"

"Go ahead, Barrett."

"I knew him in a previous life. It seems he spotted my ship, planned to overtake me, but stayed on board so that I would not recognize him. He'd hoped his fellows would do a fine job of ridding the world of me."

"I see. So this man that you have killed—who was a prisoner—was a friend of yours, but through this ordeal, you found him to be false and you did away with him? My, there truly is no honor among thieves."

"No, there is not," said Barrett.

"Well, I am sorry for the loss of your ship, Captain Barrett. I know how hard that can be. But the reality is that you were on a stolen vessel. It docked here, on the south side of the island. You could have easily brought it to our ports on the north side, waved the white flag and so forth, and told us of your ordeal. However, my men say they found you in the jungle, with naked savages carrying rations to ship. So one could assume you intended to set sail *again* with the property of the Queen. So what am I to do with your story? How am I to take it? It's quite entertaining, but it lacks the necessary ingredients to be convincing."

"I see your point," said Barrett. "I've put you in a difficult situation. Do what you must."

Archer stepped forward. "Barrett, don't—"

"Who is this man?" the British captain asked.

Archer looked at Jupiter, who shook his head cautiously. "Sir, we were kidnapped by this man," Archer said, pointing to Barrett. "Crimped and shanghaied from the port of San Francisco some weeks ago."

"My, you are a busy fellow, Barrett. Stealing men and ships." He turned to Archer. "So you are claiming that Captain Barrett abducted you?"

"Yes," said Archer. "We have done what he demands in hope of one day returning home."

"*Us* you say? You and the Negro?"

Archer looked at Jupiter. "That is right, sir."

"Your name?" the British captain said to Jupiter.

"My name is Jupiter, sir."

"Jupiter? How pretentious. You have given me a fascinating tale, but even you two did not act as kidnapped men. You were carrying rations, and spoke of nothing when my men stopped you. You did nothing to free yourselves when this other man was killed. I do not know if your story is true, but if you were not prisoners aboard this ship, you will be now. If you were not criminals then, you are certainly criminals now."

"No," Archer screamed. "I am American! You cannot do this!"

"Easy, Archer," Barrett said. "Don't give them the satisfaction. Just another obstacle life tends to put in front of us."

"You shut your mouth, you maggoty pile of cow shit."

"Oh, this is becoming quite entertaining," the British captain said.

"Your life was shit long before you met me," said Barrett. "Isn't that right, Jupiter?"

Jupiter stayed quiet.

"Take them to the cavern," the British captain said. "They'll be dealt with properly."

"You can't do this," said Archer. "We are American. We deserve a proper trial."

"Proper trial," said Yerby. "My good man, you are lucky. I could kill you right now. I could bury you on this godforsaken island and no one would miss you. You should be grateful that I am a just man."

Barrett stared. "What now?"

"We have just met and you are already a problem for me. I knew our paths would cross one day, but not quite under these circumstances."

"So you know of me?" asked Barrett.

"I've grown tired of this game. The Dunham spoke highly of you. He said that you were the most cunning man he had ever known."

"The feeling was mutual," said Barrett.

"But he lived in constant fear that you were double-crossing him somehow. Which is why he decided to shift allegiances and partner with me."

"And you are a man to be trusted? That doesn't sound like the man I knew," said Barrett.

"He feared that you would turn him in and your employer's men would arrive on the shore at any moment."

"I've never known him to be so impatient," said Barrett.

"Well, it's obvious that you did not know him as well as you thought."

"Obviously."

"Yet here you are. You have kept your word to him. You came back for your weapons."

"I am glad that you agree that they are my weapons."

Yerby laughed. "Well, now that you mention it—they are mine. It's funny how easily weapons can change ownership."

"If that were so," Barrett said, "then you wouldn't still have them. You would have sold them already."

Yerby stared. "Tell me about your connection in Shanghai."

"There is not much to tell. He is a man who needs weapons and has the means to pay for them. Too bad for him that he'll never get them."

"That's a sad story," said Yerby. "Think of another ending."

"There is no other ending. He's expecting me."

"What if I told you that I already know who he is?"

"First of all, I would not believe you, and second, it would not matter if you did."

"Why is that?"

"Because he is beyond your reach."

"And what makes you think that anything is beyond my reach?"

"Well, you still have the weapons. You could have sold them to any of the pirate gangs, but you are a pirate hunter, and it would be foolish for you to arm your enemies. You wouldn't try to sell them to the British—they would only seize them—and then sell them. Those that you can trust don't have the means to offer you a price that would be attractive. And for some reason, you do not have any connections in Shanghai. So it seems that all you have is me."

"That's good, Barrett. Very good. I'm glad that we can work together."

"No. I only work with men that I can trust. Right now, these two are the only men I can trust."

"You can trust me, Barrett. You can trust that if you do not tell me what I want to know then I will kill these two men and feed you slices of their corpses." Yerby nodded at his man.

"Greil, take Barrett away. Maybe he will be more forthcoming if the two of you are alone."

"Of course," said Greil. "I am sure he will open up to me in one way or another."

51

Days passed and still no sign of Barrett. They grew anxious whenever footsteps were heard, hoping, this time, the sound would signal their release. Maybe Barrett would return with some news.

"He's not coming back, is he?" asked Jupiter.

Archer sat huddled in a dark corner facing the wall

"No, he's not." Archer faced him. "Once he stepped out, we should have known he'd never return. We didn't want to see it. I know I didn't. But it happened because Barrett is who he is, and I am who I am. Maybe what has happened is the best outcome, and I must learn to accept it. Maybe it is best that we rot here; maybe the world is better with us in here, where we can't do any harm."

"Where *we* can't do harm?" said Jupiter.

"Yes, we," said Archer. "We hurt, we kill, and in your case, we profit from the hurt and the killed. Maybe this is our punishment. Maybe we should entertain the possibility that this all might be deserved."

A scream, horrific, came from one of the cells in that vast place. Jupiter couldn't say from which one.

"I don't deserve this," said Jupiter. He saw Archer's shoulders move, then he heard Archer laugh.

"You don't deserve this?" he said. "If anyone deserves this, it's you. Who knows how many men you've crimped. How many of them have ended up in places like this?"

"I know none of them have ended up in places like this. The men

I've crimped weren't exactly the best humanity had to offer. Yeah, they were forced to work against their will, but at least they got paid something for their work. There's plenty of people that haven't been so lucky."

"There it is," said Archer. "There's that anger. It wasn't enough for you to have your freedom by tearing the country apart—you want the power too. You wanted your freedom, but you wanted to take the freedom of everyone in the South—take theirs, take Father's, take mine."

"That's shit you're talking," said Jupiter. "I've never taken a damn thing from you."

Archer stood. "You've taken everything from me," Archer said.

Jupiter stared at him a long time. He knew this would end badly if he pursued it. No one was thinking rationally. The two of them had nothing left to lose. That's a dangerous place to be.

"I didn't take your father from you. The South took him from you. That way of life, the expectations of a proper Southern gentleman, the war took him from you, disease took him from you, but I didn't. He was already gone when I found him. A shadow of himself, babbling—it would've broken your heart to see him. I did the man a favor."

"That's how you see it?" said Archer. "You did me a favor by killing my father? Doing the world a favor by shanghaiing men? Well, you've got a deadly interpretation of favors."

"You don't think it was hard? He was my father too."

"Don't remind me. How often I was jealous of you—the way he would look at you, the way he'd take you into the house, teach you things, make me sit next to you while he tutored you—tutored 'us.' But then, when he thought I wasn't looking, I saw the two of you in some conspiratorial whisper . . . teaching you things, things that remain a mystery to me. I can only guess what they were. But I look at you now, and knowing what I now know, and seeing what I've seen, it must have been some secret for survival, because you just won't go away. Whatever he whispered to you, he must have been pouring some of himself into you, because when I look at you now I see so much of him, even more than I see in myself, and it makes me sick."

"What?" asked Jupiter. "You want the little black boy who sat next to his master's son while being tutored and taught how to read—with every word becoming more and more aware of his inferiority—you want that little boy to apologize to you? You, the boy who had everything? The boy who could have done anything, still can do anything, even after the war you supposedly lost? The war I supposedly won? I should apologize to you because your daddy, for his own sake, shared some information with me? I should apologize to you for the type of father he was, and what you saw? What did *I* see? Him creeping into my mother's shed on hot afternoons? And on those hot afternoons, the way your mother would look at me, as if I had somehow coaxed him to go in there and lay with my mother. Or the way your mother would look at me with disgust, while the rest of the slaves she didn't bother to even look at. That little boy is supposed to apologize to you?"

"No," said Archer, "I don't expect an apology from that little boy, but I expect more from the man he became."

52

Barrett had not been heard from in days. Or was it weeks? They did not know how long. The time in confinement, the hopelessness, began to twist Archer's mind. "Help us!" he screamed, knowing that no one would answer or come to their rescue.

"No one will help you. No one will help us." The voice echoed in the cavern. Jupiter ran to the cell bars, pressed his face against them, and tried to locate the source of the voice.

"This is where we will die. The sooner you accept it, the sooner the pain will go away." There was darkness, except a thin curve of light coming from a candle on an adjacent wall.

"Hello," said Jupiter.

There was no response.

"Let us out. Help us. We'll make it worth your while. We'll give you . . ." Jupiter searched the bare coffers of his mind. "We'll give you . . ."

"Give me what?" asked the voice. "You have nothing, and I have nothing . . . I do not want more of what I already have."

"Please, I have a wife and child," said Jupiter.

"I have three wives and twelve children."

"Good, then you understand what it means for a man to be separated from his family. Help us."

"You can help me to see my family again?"

"I can." Jupiter did not know how, but he meant it.

"Good," said the voice. "I believe you."

"Then you will help us?"

"Yes, I will help you, but I cannot let you out of the cell."

Jupiter pressed his head against the bars. "Why not?"

"Because I am in the cell next to yours."

Jupiter heard the sound of something metal run across the bars. The sound reverberating through the dark space.

• • •

Yerby approached their cell. He held a burlap sack. Blood had pooled on its bottom. He dropped it in front of the cell. "Gentlemen, I am afraid Captain Barrett is no longer with us."

Jupiter stared at the sack.

"I am sorry for your loss, but we still have business at hand. Who is Barrett's contact in Shanghai?" Yerby's eyes bounced between Jupiter and Archer.

"We don't know," answered Jupiter.

"Come now, is this how you choose to honor Barrett's memory—with deceit?"

"We know nothing of Barrett's dealings in Shanghai," said Archer. "He hardly mentioned the place."

"I understand," said Yerby. "You are lost without your leader. Shall you consult him one last time?" Yerby reached into the sack. He lifted the severed head by its black hair. They looked away before seeing the face that would haunt them forever.

"Stop," said Jupiter. "Put it away."

"As you wish." Yerby dropped the head into the sack.

"Maybe Barrett told us something that we are forgetting," said Jupiter. Archer looked at him. "Give us some time to recall something that may be of use."

"Very well." Yerby looked around. "This place has been here for a very long time. It is a perfect place to wait."

• • •

"Yerby is a violent man," said the voice in the other cell. "Something is broken inside him. He does not forgive."

Jupiter slid to the floor of the cell.

"I made the mistake of embarrassing him. Years ago—I do not know how long—but before the wars with the British over opium, the Emperor assigned me to rid the ports of foreign opium. It was weakening our people. I seized many crates of opium, Yerby's among them. He was the criminal he is now; he was one of the governors of the port. When he tried to get me to return the opium, I refused and told him that I had burned it all. He became enraged and beat me publicly for all to see—including my subordinates. To save face, I had him imprisoned. Eventually, the war ended and we lost control of our own ports. Opium continued to flood our country, drown our people. We could no longer punish a foreigner—British, Europeans, or Americans—for breaking our rules. When Yerby was released, he had his men track me down and beat me savagely. The Emperor complained to the British on my behalf. The treaty was still new, and they did not want to jeopardize it, so the English exiled Yerby. Although he intervened, the Emperor was not pleased with me. He considered me a failure for not ridding the ports of opium as he had asked of me. I too was exiled. Unfortunately, I was found by Yerby again. Without the Emperor's protection, I was doomed."

• • •

"You asked me if there was a way to escape this place. I have just remembered there is one."

"What is it?" asked Jupiter.

"I once shared my cell with someone. He showed me how to escape. They pushed the man into the cell. His hair was long, as was his beard. He'd been lost for some time. I did not know what to make of him. I watched him, huddled in the corner on his floor mat. For what seemed like days, all he did was sleep.

"Then one day he sprang up, alert. Every morning thereafter, he did a series of rituals, of poses, each one in slow motion. There were other strange things as well. He would save the gruel that was served as a meal in this horrible place. He let the gruel dry and rolled it into little balls until he had made a dozen or so.

"I watched all of this. But something about the man made me more curious than nervous or fearful, no matter how strange his actions seemed. He would look out the cell window for hours. Mountain. Sea. Beautiful from a distance, but deadly from this height.

"He placed the dried ball of food on the edge of the cell window and waited. A bird flew by, then landed at the edge and pecked the dried balls of gruel. The man watched the bird, inspecting, it seemed to me.

" 'Yes, this one will do,' the man said aloud. He snatched the bird by his neck, so fast that I wasn't sure if the bird hadn't been tied to an invisible string attached to the man's hand. He slowly brought the bird into the cell, soothing it, mimicking the bird's sounds, making a cooing noise. The bird stopped its frantic fluttering. The man put food in his palm, and the bird began to eat out of it.

" 'My name is Xiao Pei,' he said. 'You can tell me your name if you want, but you will have to hurry. I won't be here for long.' "

"What happened to him?" Jupiter asked. "Did he escape?"

"Well," the voice continued. "Xiao Pei ripped a piece of fabric from the bottom of his pant leg, and divided that piece into two. He took a strip of cloth over to the bars and pressed his head against them to see if any guards were approaching. He put the fabric in the torch adjacent to the cell. He brought the flaming fabric back in the cell and stamped it out. All that was left was a pile of soot. Xiao Pei spat in the soot, mixing it together with his fingers. With his blackened fingers, he drew Mandarin characters on the other piece of fabric. When he had finished writing, he beckoned for the bird. It came readily. He spoke to the bird in soft tones. He would not allow me to hear. It seemed to me that he was building up the bird's confidence before going into battle.

"Xiao Pei wrapped the fabric around the bird's foot and cinched it with the remaining string. He put the bird back on the window, and pushed it through the bars so that its wings could spread. 'Fly now,' he said to it. It soared away from the cell, disappearing in the horizon."

Archer and Jupiter looked at each other. "All of that for a bird?" asked Archer.

"No, he was not finished. 'You have just seen the beginning of your freedom—at least the beginning of mine,' said Xiao Pei. 'When that bird delivers the message it carries, I will be free.' "

Jupiter and Archer were silent.

"'It is fine. You don't have to believe,' said Xiao Pei. 'I believe. It is strange, but life has a way of making strange things come. Here I am, a boy born in the country, taught to speak English by missionaries, which allowed me to move freely in the West. Such a gift for me, but then those same English oppress my country, and I am thrown in a jail.'"

He paused in his story. "You are American, are you not? Not African?"

Jupiter looked around the cell. "You can see us?"

"Of course," said the voice. "A piece of polished glass was left in my cell. It reflects nicely. I have it angled at your cell."

A light twinkled in the darkness. "I am American," Jupiter said eventually.

"And the other one," the voice said to Archer. "You look like the son of money. What are you doing here?"

Archer looked at Jupiter. "Wrong place, wrong time."

The voice laughed. "I like that. 'Wrong place, wrong time.' I suppose we can all say that. But how did you two get here?"

They told him their story. Talking all through the night, interrupting each other on points of disagreement.

The voice put an end to the bickering. "You sound like brothers. In my country we believe that there are Five Great Relationships—ruler and subject, father and son, husband and wife, elder brother and younger brother, friend and friend. A fortunate man can experience all five. Save your fighting energy. It will seem trivial if you do not make it out of here. Save it for the day that we will need it."

"What happened to the man in your cell?" asked Jupiter. "Go on with the story."

"Oh yes, the story . . . One day we were interrupted by the return of the bird. Xiao Pei closed its wings and pulled it gently through the bars. It carried a different message bound to its leg. Xiao Pei smiled. 'We will be leaving very soon,' he said to me."

•　•　•

Archer had a strange dream that night . . .

"You two, up." Guards unlocked the cell and led Jupiter and Archer out, down a long corridor.

Archer's heart beat loud and fast. There was a shaft of light, an opening at the end of the hallway looking out onto a large courtyard where three empty nooses waited to be filled.

Archer stopped, dragging his heels.

"Move," said the guard, as he jabbed Archer in the side with his club.

Jupiter moved in front of the guard, but they hit Archer again.

"Move now."

The guards pushed Archer and Jupiter forward. The nooses grew closer. Closer.

"Here." The guards pushed them to the left of the opening, which led to another hallway with smooth steps and gilded wall panels with jade inlays. They were led up the step and into a room bursting with colors that dazzled the mind with hundreds of Oriental cartoons depicting events, of which they did not know, but which must have been of importance.

"On your knees." They did as instructed.

A man sat in an ornate wooden chair. He wore long silk robes and smoked from a long, thin pipe. Archer recognized the smoke instantly. His mouth began to water.

"You men fought wars?" asked the seated man.

"Answer him."

"Yes," said Archer.

"Did the two of you fight on the same side of the war?"

Jupiter glanced at Archer.

"No," said Archer. "We did not fight on the same side."

"You," the man said to Jupiter. "Your side won, did it not?"

Jupiter looked down. "Yes."

"And now you are free."

All of his men laughed.

"You," he said to Archer, "were on the losing side."

Archer nodded.

"And you have to live with it every day. I know what that is like. We too must live with losing every day. Looking at the men who beat us in the war, reminded of it every time we see them. It eats at the soul. But you know this, all too well."

Archer looked up, met eyes with the man.

"Yes," said Archer.

"Did you lead men? Either of you?"

They were silent.

The man clapped his hands. Two men carried in a large crate, and placed it in front of the seated man. He motioned Archer and Jupiter over to the crate—a mess of what could have once been called weapons, but now was wood and corroded metal, a bunch of loose and unassociated parts.

"This," said the man, "is what the British sold to us. We had to buy this useless heap. Why? Because after our defeat, we are not allowed to arm ourselves with the best that modern weaponry has to offer. They sell us the garbage of western wars."

Archer took a closer look at the weapons. Some of them were used by the South. One gun had the letters CSA—Confederate States Army—crudely carved into the butt.

"You men are familiar with these weapons?" asked the robed man.

"We are," answered Jupiter.

"Good. I need you to repair these weapons. Once you have repaired them, you will teach my men how to use them."

Jupiter looked at the weapons again. There were plenty of loose parts to put something together, maybe a makeshift pistol.

Archer spoke up. "Sir, we are not engineers."

Jupiter nudged him. "We will gladly do our best."

"Good," said the robed man. "I think you have made the right decision."

The dream advanced as Archer and Jupiter went about repairing the guns the best they could. Jupiter cobbled together spare parts that he hoped to make into a weapon for his own use. Those that they did manage to salvage, they used to secretly teach the men ways to improve their aim. But a man that Archer did not recognize was displeased with this.

"You are training them," said the man, "but for what? Didn't I tell you we would be freed from this place? I never said it would be easy. It may get ugly. You are training these men to be better—to be better at preventing our escape."

Archer then realized who the man was. "Listen," said Archer, "that was a nice trick with the bird and all. You send it out, it comes back, we get our hopes up thinking there's some savior out there. This is the best plan we have. We have our hands on weapons every day, and when the time is right, we'll use those weapons. Yeah, we are training them how to shoot, but we are not training them well."

"I see," said the man. "I guess we all will see."

The dream continued, advancing rapidly as dreams tend to do.

Archer and Jupiter huddled.

"I think the weak point is here." Jupiter drew a figure in the dirt floor. "Now if we can go around here," he drew a semicircle, "I think the men coming at us have a blind spot, and we can take out a lot of them before they have time to come around here," he drew an arc in reverse, "and come at us from behind."

"That's good, but if we can manage to get above this, we can have at least a one-hundred-eighty-degree view," Archer made an arc of his own, "and we could see either side—whoever's approaching—and pick them off that way."

Jupiter looked at his plan, then looked at Archer's. He had to smile. "How'd you boys ever lose?"

. . . Archer awoke in the cell, excited about the possibility of escape. He looked around the cell, at Jupiter still asleep, and at the bare floor where a plan should have been. Nothing was there. Reality set in, the excitement faded, and Archer went back to sleep.

•   •   •

Jupiter and Archer were slapped awake and snatched from their cell. Yerby's men led them through the jungle. They were silent until they reached a clearing. They walked to the edge of a precipice and looked down: hundreds of sun-bleached bones. They heard Yerby approach them. "Who is Barrett's connection in Shanghai?"

Jupiter felt something cold and hard press against the back of his neck. It was a strange relief from the island sun. "I don't know," said Jupiter.

The gun went off, triggered deafness, and then a ringing in his ears. He must have been shot. Jupiter waited for the world to go black. When it did not, he checked himself for injuries—there were none. He looked at Archer, kneeling over the savage boneyard; he hadn't been shot.

"Who is Barrett's contact?" Yerby asked again.

"I do not know." Jupiter's head jerked back. Yerby stood over him. The gun barrel came into view and pressed against his forehead.

"I won't ask again," said Yerby.

"I—"

"Not you." Yerby looked at Archer. "Tell me or I will pull the trigger."

"We don't know," said Archer.

Jupiter closed his eyes.

Yerby pressed the barrel harder. A bead of sweat fell from his brow and met with Jupiter's. He pulled the gun away. A ringed island of raised flesh appeared. Yerby knelt and kissed him on it. "I believe you."

• • •

Yerby's men tossed them back into their cell.

"You are still alive," said the voice in the other cell. "I was not worried. I am just reminding you."

Jupiter and Archer remained silent.

"I can finish my story now," said the voice.

"No one's in the mood for stories," said Jupiter.

"No, you need to hear this. One night, Xiao Pei woke me. 'Did you hear that?' he asked. I heard nothing at first, and then the drums. 'It is time,' said Xiao Pei. For what? I asked. The drums grew louder. For what? I asked again. The drums grew louder still, and then the cell wall was blown open. 'For that,' said Xiao Pei. There was smoke and dust from the cannon fire.

"When the smoke and dust settled, I could see out into the night air, the silhouette of mountains, the glimmering sea. 'Down here,' Xiao Pei said. I looked out over the edge. A lone figure was twirling something on a rope. He let it go—it soared, and caught the edge of the cell. It was a grappling hook. 'Come, let us be like the bird,' Xiao Pei said as he went down. . . . That was the last I ever saw of him."

"That's it?" said Archer. "That's your story of escape—a fairy tale?"

"It all happened as I say," said the voice.

"Then why are you still here?" said Jupiter.

"Because at the time I believed escape was impossible—even when the chance to be free presented itself, I did not believe it. I hesitated and these walls rebuilt themselves before me. Xiao Pei was free forever, while I remained imprisoned."

Jupiter rested his head in his hands. "Escape is impossible. You were right."

"I knew that before his story," said Archer.

"No, do not say that. You said you would help free me. It was improbable, but not impossible. I need you to see that if we are ever to escape this place."

53

Liberia

Sebastian neared the end of his routine. They were dazzled by his sleight of hand when he started, but now he could sense that they had grown weary. "Is this your card?" he asked the young woman in the front row. She nodded, and everyone clapped politely. To close the show he needed something astounding. He would display the powers of telepathy through mind reading and mentalism. This was usually done by the manipulation of language and the validation of what the person already believed, but as he looked at the stoic faces of the audience, he was unsure if he had overstayed his welcome.

The most beautiful woman in the house sat in the first row. He already knew her name. Mary. It was no accident that she was there. He walked over to her and stared in her eyes. "May I call you Mary?"

"Yes," she whispered. The audience was silent.

He held her wrists gently. "Mary, have we ever met before?"

She looked at the vigilant mulatto in the corner. "No." She was truthful.

"Mary, I am receiving a message from beyond. I am going to tell you details about your life. Are you willing to listen?"

"Yes."

"Good, Mary." He closed his eyes and brought her hand to his temple, the audience stirring a bit as he did so. His eyes danced under their lids as he received the song from Beyond. "You came here after slavery."

"Didn't we *all*?" someone joked.

"No," continued Sebastian. "You were freed on a man's deathbed. The conditions were that you leave and come to this new Paradise of the Negro."

Mary gasped. "Yes." He felt her fingers tense.

"Lucky guess," said the same heckler.

"You don't miss the pain of slavery, but you do miss the sweet smell of Georgia air. You dream of peaches, do you not?"

"Yes."

"And you dream of the red clay beneath your feet. The friendships you had there, you wonder what happened to the people that were dearest to you. You wonder, especially, about one person in particular, don't you, Mary?"

"Yes. Yes, I do."

"You wonder, Mary, you wonder whatever happened to Sonya."

Her eyes welled up. The tall mulatto approached and placed a hand on her shoulder. "Darling, do you want me to stop this?"

"Sir," Sebastian interrupted. "Do not interrupt my concentration. It could be very dangerous. We are in communication with the Other World. Our minds, your wife and I, are linked. Mary, shall I continue?"

Mary nodded.

"You wonder if she survived, if she made it through the hell of war. Did her mind break free of the shackles of slavery, you wonder. Is she forgotten in some unmarked ditch?"

Mary began to tremble.

"You wonder, Mary, why you have been so fortunate. You wonder, why you and not her. You wonder if she ever thought of you after you left."

Mary sobbed. "It's true. It's all true."

The crowd grumbled.

"I do wonder. I do."

Mary's husband snatched her hand away from Sebastian. "Sir, I demand that you stop this madness at once."

"It's all right, Robert," she said, stroking his face.

"Madam," said Sebastian, "I now know why I was drawn to you, why I felt such a pull. I have no control over the information sent to me from the Other Side. It merely materializes when the connection is made with the mind of the other person." He stared at her husband as he reached for Mary's hands.

His posture stiffened, but the husband looked on.

"I hate to see you in such a state, but I can only reveal what is true, not what is easy or convenient."

"It was such a long time ago," said Mary as she brushed away a tear. "But I do think of her often."

"I know that you do. I can tell you from experience, Mary, that thoughts are not just thoughts—thoughts are *wishes*, thoughts are *real*. They are very powerful and they have protected her. Sonya is alive and she is here."

"What?" Mary looked around the room.

"No, Mary, not here in this room, but in this country. It is true."

Previously, on the *Orpheus* . . .

Sebastian listened at the door. No one approached. He opened Sonya's bag and looked through it. The first objective in magic, and in seduction, is to gather information. In order to cast the appropriate spell, he needed to seem to know more about her than she was willing to reveal. Clothes, money, a book of poems by Phillis Wheatley, a wooden soldier for the boy, a locket . . . and letters.

Sebastian read them. A clearer image of Sonya emerged. He learned of the manumission of and separation from her friend Mary. He learned about Jupiter and the truth about Jacob.

"Will you teach me another trick?" Jacob asked him, later that evening.

Sebastian rolled over in his bed. "I think I've taught you enough tricks. It's time for you to seek out things on your own—the same way I did."

"But you said—"

"I know what I said, and I have kept my promise. I taught you some things that others would die to know. Now you go out and add to the knowledge I've given you."

"But—"

"I can't teach you everything I know—it's not my job to. I'm not your father. If you want to learn some new tricks then go ask your mother. She's quite good at crafting illusions."

Those were the last words Sebastian said to Jacob before leaving the *Orpheus*. He hoped for a chance to not have those words weigh upon his conscience.

• • •

"That was quite a show you put on at my house the other evening." Robert was one of Liberia's wealthy merchants, the son of a Dutch merchant and a Negro woman. He had connections that most of the Negroes in Liberia did not have.

"I hope there are no hard feelings," said Sebastian. "I was only doing my best to showcase my talents."

"And you succeeded," said Robert. "I am sure that some members in the audience were persuaded to invest in your playhouse."

Sebastian thought he detected a smirk under the dense brush that was Robert's mustache. "Well, whatever becomes of it, I thank you for allowing me to perform in your home, and providing me an audience with Liberia's finest."

"Don't mention it. I am sure something will come of it. My wife was quite taken with you—and she is adored by some of Monrovia's most respected families. But surely, you must have known that."

"How so?" asked Sebastian.

"Well, by your performance of . . . *mind reading*. You knew things that my wife has only confessed to me in darkness and the warmth of our bed."

Sebastian became aware of how hot it was. He swallowed. "It was merely a trick, Robert. Nothing more."

"Don't feign modesty. It was certainly more than a trick. However,

I'm sure that whatever becomes of your ambitions, Liberia will find a use for your talents."

There was a long silence between them. Uniformed men marched past Sebastian and the merchant as they strolled along the town's main road. "Liberia's armed forces," Robert said to Sebastian. The troops stopped in the plaza and continued their exercises. They lacked cohesion, thought Sebastian, and they were a motley group ranging in age from sixteen to sixty. "Mind you, it's all for show," continued the merchant. "All designed to make us feel safe. Who knows what we would do if another skirmish were to erupt right now. They may be holding the entirety of our arms. The armory is as bare as a pauper's pockets."

Sebastian looked confused. "We have no weapons?"

"Not many, but we have debt. You'd be surprised to know how difficult it is for a black republic to buy weapons though the legitimate channels. It's all very convenient, mind you. It was not that long ago that we found French naval officers trying to make deals with the native chiefs along the coast. They plied them with all sorts of temptations and bribes—iron, rum, and, of course, guns. When we appealed to our fathers and uncles in Washington and London, the French eased. But why did they do it? They were looking to claim most of Liberia for themselves—the precious bays and coves—and they will make deals with the natives to get what they want."

"You can't be suggesting that we fight the French—or any country in Europe," Sebastian said. "We've lost that war before it's begun."

"No, they would never fight us directly, that would be too much of an international embarrassment. They would just arm the Grebo and set them against us, and then call it a civil war. All of Europe would claim what's left in the aftermath."

"That does not sound like a very promising future, yet you continue to do business here."

The merchant smiled. "And you have not run away and hopped aboard the first ship bound for America. We all believe there is something here worth dying for. Do we not?"

Sebastian thought it was funny how easily the man talked about war though he had never fought in one. The last thing Sebastian wanted to think about was fighting in a war, but Sebastian hadn't fought in a war, Shadrach had—and he never wanted to bring that sad figure back to life.

"Fortunately, there are other ways to obtain arms. Cuba is in the midst of a revolution. Once the War Between the States ended, tobacco and cotton prices stabilized. This was a heavy blow to their economy, and the turbulence that followed set the stage for their rebellion against Spain. Smugglers are making their way to the Caribbean to supply the insurgents with weapons in exchange for cash crops."

"What does Cuba have to do with us?" asked Sebastian.

"Cuba is a small island. There are only so many guns one can sell there, and America has a surplus as well. All the guns are floating around the Atlantic. They shall find their way to Africa soon enough."

• • •

The day after the performance at Mary's home, he went looking for Sonya in the city. She wasn't at the ACS boarding facility, but he learned of Jacob's condition. He found them at the hospice, but did not make his presence known. He recognized Jacob's condition at once: the telltale signs of malaria. He peered in at them and left. He had to leave; it had been a long time since he'd been around death and sickness. He did not miss it. He covered his mouth with his handkerchief and hurried out of the hospice. He struggled to breathe in the humid air. A memory of war had begun. He undid his collar and rested his hands on his knees. He took in deep, hurried breaths as the memory unfolded. The voices spoke to him from Beyond and he listened. When they had finished, he gathered himself and went back into the hospice.

• • •

Hunching his shoulders, halving his long body so as not to make an easy target for the Confederate soldiers. He was back there in those woods—as they existed in his memory. The most frightened he had ever been, and he was alone, separated from his regiment. No sense in fighting his way back.

He heard a moan in the darkness. A wounded animal? No, a wounded man. He crawled toward the sound. It was hard to see in the moonlight, but it did well enough to reveal the Union blue of the man's uniform. It could be a trap. He scanned the dark for immediate threats. The man had been shot in the leg, in the back, and stabbed in the left cheek. The bullet had passed through the leg. A bullet still remained close to his rib. Sebastian had managed to keep his medic bag: rags, forceps, but no more of the laudanum or alcohol, just herbs he had gathered. He broke off bitter leaves and placed them in the man's mouth, had him chew when he could. Sebastian felt around the wound, the bullet forming a round hill of flesh. The man winced. "You'll have to be quiet. I can see it's painful, but I don't want to learn from experience." The man nodded. Sebastian put the forceps into the wound and fished around for the bullet. The man thrashed like a hooked fish. The wound made a wet, popping sound as Sebastian withdrew the bullet. All of this under moonlight. He put a rag, stained with the blood of ten other men, to the wound. "At sunrise we'll make a better compress. This should do 'til then. Are you feeling better?" The man nodded. "What is your name?" Sebastian could tell that the man wanted to lie, but was too weak to be dishonest.

"Archer," the man said.

"You just rest, Archer. We'll take better care of this at sun-up."

The sunrise woke Sebastian. He had drifted off, despite his promise to hold vigil. He went to check on Archer, but he was gone. Archer may have wandered off and died in the tall grass. He stayed low and crawled around the area. He found a body, but it was not the white Yankee he had helped the night before. It was a colored soldier. He still wore his pants, but his shoes, shirt, and cap had been taken. His eyes were open. There was a gash in his throat. He stared at the morning sun. Sebastian closed the dead man's eyes.

54

Yerby's Cave

"Captain Yerby?"

A voice came from the darkness. Yerby turned. One of his men walked slowly from the shadows. As he came into the light, there was a knife at his neck. A man dressed in black held the weapon. Other men armed with guns rushed the cavern like ants. Two of them ran up to Yerby and forced him to kneel with his hands raised. A call was shouted outside the cave. A man entered, dressed in the same fashion as the others, but there was something regal and frightening about him. "Do you know who I am, Captain Yerby?"

Yerby nodded. "I believe so. Ten Dragons."

"Good. Then you realize it would be pointless for you not to cooperate. The outcome will be the same."

"You can have the weapons," said Yerby.

"I know I can have the weapons, Captain Yerby. But that is not the only reason that I have come here. You have something else that I want." He motioned to one of his men to retrieve the man from his cell. Now in the light, all could see the horrific things that Yerby had done to him. He had no nose, no ears, waxy scars where his eyebrows should have been. Three fingers were missing from his right hand. Everyone tried to suppress their disgust. "Did Yerby do this to you?"

The man nodded.

The leader placed a knife in the man's good hand. "Make him pay."

He looked at the knife. "I cannot. He must live with what he has done. That is punishment enough. I do not want my soul burdened with his death."

"That is very admirable. I envy you, but I am not so enlightened."

"I am sure you believe revenge is the answer. But he has been humiliated—a strong punishment for someone who has believed himself invincible for all these years. Let him live to remember this defeat."

"Wise words, friend. Tell me, what is your name?"

"My name—"

"Wait, is it Xiao Pei?"

The disfigured man nodded.

"I thought it was you. Let me tell you a story. When the Emperor ordered that all stores of opium be destroyed, his men came to my village. They found a small warehouse on the water. They entered and found one crate of opium. *One*. My father and four brothers were inside that warehouse. They were tied up. The opium and the warehouse were burned with them inside. Five men for one crate. You oversaw ridding the Empire of opium. All that happened because of you. Do you deny it?"

"No, I do not deny it. I was a different person then. My time here has changed me. I have the name of the man you seek, but I am not the same man."

"I understand how this place must have changed you, but while your soul has been lightened, mine remains heavy." A breeze came into the cavern, candles flickered, and blood spurted from Xiao Pei's neck.

Yerby screamed as Xiao Pei fell. "I was not finished with him yet!"

The leader placed a comforting hand on Yerby's shoulder. "He wasn't yours to kill. Whatever he did to incur your wrath was petty compared to what he did to my family." He walked away and gave a signal to one of his men. When he had left the cavern, his man pulled the trigger. Yerby collapsed in a pool of Xiao Pei's blood.

Jupiter and Archer's cell opened. Barrett appeared before them. "You two look surprised to see me. I'll explain in due course." He clapped sharply. "Quickly, now, chop-chop. Let's load those guns."

Stunned, Jupiter and Archer followed quietly.

Barrett stopped at Yerby's collection of jarred curiosities. A severed head floated in a large glass container. It seemed strangely at peace. He tapped the glass gently. "Sleep well, Greil," said Barrett.

•   •   •

Now free from Yerby's cave, Jupiter and Archer pressed Barrett for the details of his escape. Barrett obliged, but kept some things to himself. . . .

His arms were tied behind his back. Greil followed with his rifle pointed at him.

They walked deeper into Yerby's cave, into darkness and a narrow passageway of cold wet stone. Barrett saw torchlight up ahead and five cells, all of them empty except one. A disfigured face and hand came to the bars as he passed. Barrett stared. *Xiao Pei*, he felt compelled to say, but didn't.

The prisoner retreated to the shadows of his cell.

"Your work?" he asked Greil.

"You'll learn soon enough. *Move*." Greil jabbed Barrett's shoulder with the weapon. Barrett continued to walk until the cave opened up to a blue sky.

Sunlight flickered through the trees as they walked. Insects buzzed and birds chirped, rustling the leaves as they flew from branch to branch. Barrett heard the ocean—the sounds of waves that had circled the earth and come back again. It had just stopped raining. Barrett ducked wet, low-hanging vines, and walked carefully over the muddy and rocky terrain. It was hard to manage with his arms tied behind him, but as all his muscles strained for balance, Barrett noticed that the binds at his wrists were starting to loosen.

"What tribe do you belong to?" asked Barrett.

Greil didn't answer.

Barrett tried to force his wrists apart as Greil remained silent. "There's something about your hair and your skin—not fully European. It's hard to place you, but you look like one of your forbearers might have been from Papua. Am I right? Yes. I have heard my share of chilling tales about them. Supposedly they are fearsome warriors, but they fuck their daughters and eat their young." Barrett laughed and flexed his wrists. Nothing came from Greil. They went down a slope and through a stream. Barrett stepped clumsily around the muddy banks and fell on his back. Something sharp—an unseen rock—tore into his forearm. He winced, and felt the cool gray mud on his wrists, then he realized that his binds were caught on the stone. He shifted his weight and worked the ropes against the rock. He felt his hands slipping through. "I hear the men of your tribe fuck their sons too," said Barrett from the ground.

Greil laughed.

"I hear they make the old men watch."

Greil laughed harder.

Barrett laughed too. "You think it's funny that Papuans eat men and fuck children?"

Greil stopped laughing. "Yes. I am not Papuan. My grandmother was Maori—so I'm told."

Barrett laughed.

"I'm glad that you're feeling talkative. I won't have to hurt you as long." Greil poked Barrett with the rifle. "Up."

Barrett slipped his hand from the bind and knocked the rifle away from him. Greil pulled the trigger, barely missing Barrett as the rifle slipped from his hands. Greil pounced on Barrett, sending a flurry of fists at him, and then lunged for the rifle that had fallen nearby. They fought for it. Barrett scrambled and managed to grab it as well. Both men gripped the barrel with two hands. Greil rolled and shifted his weight so that he was on top of Barrett and pressed the rifle down onto Barrett's neck. "Ever think you'd die in a mud pit, old man?"

Barrett tasted sweat and blood. He heard waves crash against the shore as his throat fought to bring in air. Greil's face—inches above Barrett's—began to ripple like a reflection on water. Greil laughed again. Barrett opened his mouth and bit into the lip of the other man. He bit until he tasted the blood and saliva of the other. His jaw clenched until he felt the flesh tear away.

Greil screamed and let go of the rifle. Barrett rolled over, gasping. The torn half of Greil's lip dangled. He brought his hand to his mouth, the blood dripping through his fingers. He looked away from his bloody hands to the rifle in the stream. Barrett was already crawling toward it. Greil lunged for the rifle, but only managed to grab the barrel. Barrett seized the butt, and then found the trigger. The bullet tore through Greil's neck. He fell to his knees, his head barely attached by the remaining sinews.

· · ·

He returned to Kalana's camp and watched as they burned her on the pyre. The ocean roared as the fire took her. He had lost a ship and a daughter too close together. It was not a good omen. He thought of her mother, the young native girl who brought joy to a weary sailor trading sugar and sandalwood. How she brought his hand to her rounding belly and named the child inside. *Kalana.* A man of the sea journeys everywhere and is rarely there when he needs to be. He was not there when she was strangled by a sailor whose advances she refused. A part of him was grateful that she had not lived to see their child die. How Kalana must have screamed when she was left to fend for herself. He was not there to hear it. No matter. A man cannot let the screams of his child go unanswered.

With the fire dying behind him, Barrett took three of Kalana's men and slipped away on her two-masted schooner. While on a ship, it was bad luck to speak of the recently departed, so they mourned and sailed in silence.

· · ·

To get Yerby, Barrett needed to lure the dragon out of his cave. Ten Dragons and his men ran the underworld in Shanghai—and few people knew it. To do business with Ten Dragons, one must have displayed a zeal for discretion and corruption. He armed and financed warlords and the most secret of secret societies. When the Small Swords seized Shanghai during the Taiping Rebellion, they sought out Ten Dragons for weapons—weapons sold to him by Barrett.

Barrett walked past the brothels, opium dens, and gambling halls, and entered a small shop. A sign that read *George and Ascalon Tea Trading Co.* hung above its door.

There was no aroma of tea in the air, but there was an elderly clerk who barely bowed at Barrett. Barrett returned the bow and addressed the clerk in Chinese, *Power is sent by heaven. The strength to use it is heaven-sent.*

The clerk stared at Barrett and then ushered him to a wall of crates that obscured a door. Barrett entered, then raised his hands.

He stared at the slight man with a cherubic face, flanked by three muscular men on each side. "Barrett," said Ten Dragons. "The last time I saw you, you were selling guns to the imperial army. I swore I'd kill you if I ever saw you again. Many people died because of those guns."

"You have a good memory, Ten Dragons, you always did. But I remember selling guns to your men as well—much cheaper than I sold them to the Emperor's men, I might add."

"Lower your hands, Barrett. It makes you look suspicious."

Barrett did as instructed.

"What do you want, Barrett?"

"I need your help."

"That is obvious." He took in Barrett's woeful appearance.

"I have a treasure and I need your help in retrieving it."

Ten Dragons laughed. "Why should I help you retrieve your treasure? I hope you never find it."

"I didn't say it was mine. It's yours if you will help me."

Ten Dragons took a moment. "What is it?"

"Guns."

"This is Shanghai. I only need to stroll along the Whangpu."

"You know as well as I do that your stroll would garner you nothing but broken promises."

"I do not know that. However, I know you, and helping you is dangerous. Why should I risk my life for your guns?"

"Not just guns," Barrett smiled, "but Xiao Pei as well."

55

Liberia

Jacob was soaked with sweat. He had not said a word in days.

"Ma'am," the doctor addressed Sonya, "though it pains me to say this . . . I think it's time that you prepare for the worst."

Prepare for the worst, she thought, isn't that what she had mastered all of these years?

"The fever affects some differently than others," the doctor continued. "We have done all we can do. At this point, it is up to the boy to decide how badly he wants to live."

Up to the boy to decide? Weren't they in a Christian hospital? And yet there was no talk of the Almighty giving the innocent child any assistance. It was up to that weak boy, his blood ravaged by parasites, to muster the strength, while wavering in and out of consciousness, to decide his own fate.

He didn't have to say it. She knew how desperately he wanted to be in this world. The unlikely event of his conception, how he endured inside her womb, while she endured a host of external traumas. A mother can tell how badly a baby wants to enter the world while it's inside her. Some babies don't want it as badly. Maybe it's those sounds it hears, muffled, mysterious, and ominous, that scares them. Maybe it scares away their strength to endure. Sonya knew from experience.

There was still no word of Jupiter. A ship that he could have been on had docked without a sign from him. Maybe it was for the best. This was a horrible way to be reunited.

"How is he?"

She heard the voice, then saw Sebastian's face.

"I came looking for you. They told me what had happened."

She started to speak, but her lip trembled. He put his arms around her. She sobbed into his chest. It was a while before she spoke again. She took another attempt at the sentence she began upon seeing Sebastian. "The doctor says it's likely that he won't survive . . . but I don't believe it."

"Then you shouldn't," said Sebastian. He looked at the boy, then squeezed her arms. "You shouldn't." He let go of her, knelt, and touched the boy's cheeks. He muttered something to himself that Sonya couldn't hear. He pulled back the blanket and lifted Jacob's shirt, noticed the ghoulish play of light and shadow made on the boy's emaciated body. Sebastian nodded as he stood. "I'll be back shortly."

"What is it?"

"I'll tell you when I return."

56

San Francisco

Maggie found a cargo for the *Cressida*. Mail and parcels, dirty laundry, and a few passengers. Nothing as lucrative or exciting as opium and guns. How strange it was that she was now running a shipping line—if one ship can be called a line. She had grown accustomed to the role of crimper and shanghaier.

She sat at her desk. The Dalmore Shipping Company was profitable—no thanks to its namesake. She had rescued it. She had done what Dalmore could not do. She had done for herself what the late Mr. O'Connell would not do.

"Mrs. Dalmore?" A small, well-dressed man with thinning dark hair stood in her office. He startled her. How long had he been there?

She composed herself. "Yes."

"This is quite the establishment you have here. The business is being run impressively. Congratulations."

"How may I help you, sir?"

The man walked around the office. "You are more adept at this than your late husband."

"You knew him?"

He looked at her. "Yes and no."

"Is that an answer?"

"I was sorry to hear of his passing."

"Yes," said Maggie. "It was a terrible tragedy."

The man smiled. "You seem to be the kind of woman that recovers quickly."

"I shan't say how you seem to me, sir."

The man continued to smile. "You are very beautiful. May I sit?" He did not wait for Maggie to respond, and sat across from her. "Please, Mrs. Dalmore, join me in a conversation."

"You say you knew my husband. You had dealings with him?"

"Yes."

"What kind of dealings? And don't be coy—I do not like this game."

"Your husband's ships were to transport my guns to various places around the world. During our first endeavor the vessel was raided by pirates, the cargo stolen. Rather than receive payment for shipping my cargo, he decided that he wanted to be my partner. Partnerships require capital, of which he had very little . . ."

"And so he gave you a percentage of his company as collateral."

"Correct. He assumed the proceeds from the sale of the weapons would be enough—and they would have been. It was a calculated risk, but the gods can be mercurial. You don't seem at all surprised."

Maggie did not respond.

He smiled. "You have an adventurous spirit, don't you Mrs. Dalmore?"

"Why are you here, sir? To tell me a history lesson on my late husband?"

"Mrs. Dalmore, I thought we agreed to not be coy with one another. I have kept my end of the bargain, and so should you . . . and so should your late husband. You and I are partners. Unless you intend to purchase my shares. But that is unlikely. Anyway, I am not sure I would want that."

"What do you want?"

"I need things shipped. You have a ship. It will be lucrative for the both of us. I did not intend for things to turn out this way, but life is a mystery to be lived, not a problem to be solved. The late Mr. Dalmore and I were partners. Can you and I be partners, Mrs. Dalmore?" Two men, with tailored suits and terrifying faces, appeared in the doorway.

Maggie gasped.

"Don't look at them, Mrs. Dalmore. Look at me. Don't mind them. This isn't *that*. This is just a conversation between two business people."

Maggie gathered herself. "Well, I must say, sir, that you are quite persuasive. However, I am not concerned with any agreement you had with the dead man I married. I will ship your weapons—I like this idea—but I want my money up front." One of the men in the doorway sniggered.

"I'm willing to give back a percentage of the company—increase your shares."

"I don't want what you think my dead husband deserved. I am here and he is not. I want what I deserve. I want my money up front. A third of the anticipated sale. Dalmore ships are sound and trustworthy. Your cargo—whatever you decide to ship—will arrive at its intended destination safely. I won't be beholden to the uncertainty of your business, sir. My business has enough of its own risks. I won't wait for you to sell your weapons to get my money."

The man put on his hat and stood. He was so short and impish-looking. "I knew transporting parcels and foreigners would eventually bore a woman like you, Mrs. Dalmore. We have a deal. We'll discuss the details of the shipment tomorrow." He bowed to her slightly and left the office, the two men lingering before they followed.

Maggie took a deep breath, and then the fear became exhilaration. She had held her own with her new partner. It was a good deal. Her value was recognized. He needed her more than she needed him. In her mind, she was already spending the proceeds of her new partnership.

Her partner . . . She hadn't even asked for his name.

57

Shanghai

They docked in the old port—up the coast and used less frequently—
then entered the city through a decaying wall, a remnant of when the
city was still a citadel protected from outsiders.

The city buzzed with business. Merchants negotiating with the
Hongs, both parties trying to find favorable terms for their goods—
silks, salts, spices. The coolies followed agents of the European merchant houses, pandering obsequiously in their pidgin English. Flower
girls bloomed outside brothels. The sun turned away from the blackened windows of the opium dens.

They walked for a long time along the shore, leaving the chaos of
the port city behind, until they came upon an impressive compound.

Jupiter marveled at the statues, the beautiful gardens, and ornate
architecture—techniques that went back a thousand years—it was all
so intimidating and seductive. He had never been in the presence of
such skill and opulence. He looked over at Archer, who was in awe too.
Jupiter became aware of his clothes, his appearance. He felt dirty.

They were met by guards at the entrance of the compound. Barrett
said something to them in Chinese, placed his hand over his heart and
said his own name, nodded at Archer and Jupiter, then addressed the
guards once more in Chinese. The guard stepped aside and whispered
in the other guard's ear. "Come," he said. The three of them followed
him inside.

Upon the divan sat a man in beautiful silk robes decorated with a thousand different figures and settings. They seemed to tell a story in color and glyph. He rose to greet them.

"Captain Barrett. It is good to see you. It has been too long."

"Indeed, Wu Ping, it has," said Barrett.

"The days have not been good to you? You do not look well."

Barrett smiled. "Any day that I rise is a good day for me."

"Barrett, I apologize for my rudeness, but it has been so long since we have turned a wheel together. Please forgive me. You are my guests. Follow me."

They sat at a large wooden table, made entirely of one solid slab. "I do not know why I took such issue with your appearance, Barrett. You look better than when I saw you last."

"Yes, during the war. I suppose my position in the world has improved."

"What brings you back to Shanghai?"

"Actually, Wu, the same thing that brought me here the first time."

Wu shook his head and sucked his teeth. "I cannot help you in that way, Barrett. Not at this time."

"I didn't ask for your help."

Wu Ping stared.

"Forgive me, I do need your help, but not in *that* matter. My men and I need a place to stay while we wait to get word to our contact."

Wu leaned back in his chair. "Tell me your contact's name. Maybe I know him. I can invite him here and we can dine together, and you can provide me with the details."

"I am sorry, Wu, but I can't do that. He insists on anonymity."

"You ask for my hospitality yet you keep secrets from me?"

"Forgive me, Wu. I didn't mean to be rude. I do mean to repay you for your hospitality, but I trust that I can do so without offering too many details."

Wu Ping nodded, then studied the faces of Jupiter and Archer. He stared at Archer. "It is strange," Wu said to Barrett, "how much he looks like him."

"Who?" asked Barrett.

"Like Hua, the White God. Have you not noticed?"

Barrett did not answer.

"Of course you have. I am sure his resemblance to Hua has something to do with your meeting." He turned to Archer and smiled. "Have you brought guns into China? That is a very dangerous business. We are told that we can only purchase weapons from the British. They are the only ones who can sell us guns. Unfair, I say. What do you say?"

"Doesn't sound right at all," said Archer.

"The British . . . what they sell us . . . useless. Rusted. Some fire, some do not. Those that do fire would not harm a fly. Barrett, however, always had good guns. Not the sort the British would sell to us. But they are the kind of guns the Emperor's army should have."

"It is unfortunate," said Barrett, "but that is what happens when you lose a war. Twice."

"This is true. But we have friends. Thank the heavens for crooks and Americans."

Barrett stroked his beard.

"I am certain that by now you have learned that Captain Barrett is a man like no other." Wu Ping looked at his guests. "But did you know that he once associated with a god?" He waited for a reaction. Barrett let him continue. "That's right. A white god. Brave and strong and fair, he traveled across the sea from a faraway land called America." Wu Ping smiled. "But when he arrived in Shanghai, he was not a god yet. No, he was just a boy from Minnesota."

"Massachusetts," corrected Barrett.

"*Massachusetts*," Wu Ping said slowly. "At the time, China was immersed in a very bloody war with itself. A group who called themselves Tai-Pings wanted to replace the imperial government with their Heavenly Kingdom. Their leader claimed to be related to your Jesus. The White God—we called him *Hua*—arrived here with no money, no honor, and yet he fought the Tai-Pings valiantly to save our country. The Emperor called Hua's men The Ever Victorious Army, and was so impressed with his bravery in battle that he made Hua one of us, a true Chinese subject. He was allowed to socialize among the mandarin merchant class—and even wear the peacock feather in his cap. What, you may ask, did he do to deserve all of these privileges? He took our soldiers, woefully unprepared and moored in the past, and showed them how the old could exist with the new. He led a Chinese army against a Chinese army, a feat unmatched before or since by a Westerner. How was all of this possible? What was so special about Hua? Maybe a great deal, maybe nothing. You must understand that in China, we have only recently embraced modern warfare. The access to modern weapons was denied us after the Opium Wars. Hua's victories against the rebels all coincided with the arrival of modern weapons perfected in your country during its war with itself and then smuggled onto our shores. He became associated with all of those things, a symbol of our good fortune, and, eventually, a god responsible for that good fortune. Yes, he may have been brave, but as far as I know, he was no weapons smuggler. Am I correct, Barrett?"

"Indeed," said Barrett.

"No, he was not a smuggler, but no smuggler, if he is any good, will have his visage made into a shrine."

"That's an interesting story, but what does this have to do with me?" asked Archer.

Wu Ping smiled at Barrett and then addressed Archer. "I never said that it did. It may or may not. But you do look a great deal like him—the scar on your cheek a mirror image of the one on Hua's. If you wanted to do business in Shanghai, Archer, a man like you could do very well. Especially, if that man looked like Hua and was interested in selling guns. Of course, it would have to be among the right people. Not everyone in China is persuaded by tales of the White God." Wu turned to Barrett. "You are meeting with someone from the imperial government, are you not?"

"Now, Wu," said Barrett. "If I was, you would already know it. Such a thing would never get past you."

Wu Ping smiled. "We were friends once, Barrett. We shared a great deal."

"We are still friends, Wu. But we shared only when it was necessary."

"Very well, Barrett, then let me share this with you. The rumors have already started circling. Something is brewing between you and Clinkscales. The merchants in Shanghai believe that you are here to cause trouble. They are choosing not to choose sides, but they do not want anything to do with you. Why should I ignore this trend?"

Jupiter and Archer, their eyes bounced between Barrett and Wu.

Barrett leaned back. "I can think of a number of reasons, Wu. During the war in the States, I gave your cotton shipments priority over that of many a fine Englishman—and I never questioned how you obtained said cotton. There are many other reasons, but the most important one being that when Ward—Hua, the great White God—had served his purpose to Peking, and when the Emperor's minions became suspicious of Ward and wondered if he would use his newfound popularity to become a warlord in the hinterlands, they thought he was being financed by some enterprising merchants. They suspected that you were among them. I remember smuggling you away on my ship until the danger subsided. You were given fine accommodations once at sea, if I remember correctly. I am not saying that you owe me anything, Wu. I am just telling a tale of a sailor's hospitality."

●　●　●

The flower girls entertained the men who came from every corner of the world to experience their charms. It reminded Jupiter of Maggie's place. He wondered if she was still alive, if she would be inspired by such a place, or if such a place was her inspiration. A flower girl led them to a table. Some men eyed them as they passed.

They sat in comfortable chairs.

"It shouldn't be too long, now," said Barrett.

They waited for a long while, resisting the temptation to have their mouths and laps warmed by drinks and girls. Their desire must have been apparent. "Be patient," Barrett said to them.

"Don't worry, chaps, I'll sort them out." A tall, gangly man with too many teeth in his smile approached their table.

"What was that?" asked Barrett.

"Don't worry, I said I'll sort them out. You gents can relax. Have some drinks and some girls on me. Well, not *on* me, but gratis, you see."

Barrett looked confused. "What do you mean?"

"Well, you're making a spectacle of yourself, man, for God's sake. Shanghai is a cosmopolitan place, but some of the lads in here carry a bit of provincialism with them."

Barrett looked at Jupiter.

"I mean having a Negro interacting with us so casually still puts some people off. But I have sorted them out. You can thank me later."

Jupiter shifted in his seat.

"And whom should I thank?" asked Barrett.

"What, you can't take a joke, Barrett? You hurt me, you truly do."

Barrett squinted. "I know you?"

"Don't hold that last bit against me, Barrett. It's been far too long."

Barrett said nothing.

The man showed his teeth. "*Liverpool,*" he offered.

"Your name or the place?" Barrett asked.

The man laughed. "As you wish, Barrett. It is good to see that you are doing well."

"Why shouldn't I be?"

"Indeed you should. But there has been a great deal of talk of Clinkscales and his Shanghai endeavors."

Barrett ran a finger across his whiskers. "I know nothing of Clinkscales or his endeavors."

Liverpool touched his right nostril gently. "Of course you don't, Barrett, of course you don't. However, in case you are interested in portside gossip, smugglers in Shanghai are scrambling to pick up every bit of business, every little crumb, that he hasn't tidied up. And now I find you here with such . . . *exotic* company, and I think that those eager fools had better watch out. But then I think again that a more enterprising man had better align himself with the best smuggler on the seas."

"I think you think too much," said Barrett. "I am not the best smuggler on the seas."

"Surely, you are being modest."

Barrett did not like the looks of Liverpool. Large ears and head, beady eyes and too many teeth, he looked liked the product of royal incest. "I am not being modest. I cannot be the best smuggler on the seas, because if I were, a moron such as yourself would not know of me."

Liverpool stared at Barrett . . . and then laughed. "You almost had me, old man."

Barrett laughed. "I always had you, Edmond. It works every time."

"Yes it does, I confess. But in all seriousness, Barrett, I am surprised to see you. What are you doing in Shanghai?"

"I am here with my sons." Barrett nodded at Jupiter and Archer. "They are late bloomers and have yet to bed a woman. No better training than the girls in Shanghai."

"I don't like that answer, Barrett."

"I am not too fond of the question."

"Seriously, Barrett, I am surprised to see that you are still seeking your fortune in Shanghai. A man of your talents seems to be needed in Cuba."

Barrett arched an eyebrow.

"Oh, haven't you heard?" asked Liverpool. "The place has erupted. Sugar, coffee, and tobacco plantations all set ablaze." Liverpool closed his eyes. "Imagine the aroma. It seems that they are fighting for their independence from mother Spain, but there is a variable—the black rebels—some slaves armed with nothing but machetes, and scaring both their allies and their enemies. Imagine what they could do with proper weapons."

"I like to be paid with money. I have no plantations, no fields to be tended. What use is a slave to me?"

"Why, Barrett, have you gone soft? I've laid it all out for you. They are raiding *sugar* plantations, *coffee* plantations, and *tobacco* plantations. All of which can be traded for weapons and sold elsewhere." Liverpool's eyes seemed to gleam.

Barrett was silent for a moment. "It's a fantasy. We are a world away from Cuba. I doubt your facts are truly facts. Besides, I am no longer an adventurer. I've mellowed in my old age."

"Oh, have you?"

"Indeed. I am not as dangerous as I used to be."

Edmond's face lost its joviality. "So be it. If it is women that you are looking for, then you have come to the right place, but I do not see any women with you."

"We're selective," said Barrett.

"Very well, then let me provide the initiation." Edmond scanned the room, then motioned to a large man waiting at the top of the stairs. He acknowledged Edmond, then turned and knocked on the door behind him. The door cracked, he said some words through it, and then a dream emerged. A beautiful girl with hair like a dark cloud haloed by moonlight slinked down the steps and made her way to their table.

"Gentlemen," said Edmond, "allow me to introduce you to Mei."

She bowed and let her gaze linger upon Archer.

Hua, Archer thought he heard her say. Archer could not look away from her. He recognized a kinship; dilated pupils, heavy lids, she indulged in the same vices as he.

Edmond placed his hand on the small of her back. She brushed it away as it drifted to her rear. "This is not a whorehouse," she said with a smile and English accent. "Despite your best efforts to make it so."

Edmond raised his hand. "Forgive me, Mei. Sometimes I forget the rules. There are so many rules."

She addressed the others. "Gentlemen, you are not keeping appropriate company." She smirked. "You do not see anything to your liking?"

"We do indeed," said Barrett. "But we are here on business."

She frowned and glanced at Edmond.

"No, not with him," said Barrett.

Edmond stiffened. "You embarrass me, Barrett."

"As I see it, you were doing a fine job of it on your own." Barrett turned to Mei. "We are waiting for someone."

"Perhaps you can tell me his name and I can provide you with some information regarding his whereabouts?"

Barrett stared at her and did not respond.

Mei touched Edmond on the shoulder. "Perhaps you should come with me, Edmond, and leave these gentlemen to their business."

Edmond jerked away. "This is my old friend. I am looking forward to catching up with him. Very much so."

Mei bent over and squeezed Edmond's face. "Come," she said. He smiled and showed his big teeth. Edmond stood. "Barrett, where are you staying? We shall have to meet and—"

"Now, Edmond," said Mei.

Again, they waited for a long while. After some time, a man with glasses approached Barrett and then whispered something in his ear. When he left, Barrett stood. "We're leaving."

"What's wrong?" asked Jupiter.

"Our meeting has been moved."

•   •   •

They entered an unassuming tavern in an American section of the city.

"What now?" asked Jupiter.

"We wait," said Barrett. "We make our presence known and our intentions secret. They will find us."

Hours later, a man came to their table and sat down without asking. He was Chinese and dressed in the Western fashion of suit and tie. He waved to the waiter and a pot of tea appeared. He took a long sip, then smiled. "The tea leaf is an amazing thing, is it not? It's funny, China has given the West silk and tea, and in return the West has given us disease and opium. And now, because of the way things are, guns. An ugly trade-off, don't you think?"

The three of them were expressionless.

"You don't find my observation persuasive?"

"No, on the contrary," said Barrett. "It's just that I have pointed out those details to them already. Upon hearing, the white one maintained a similar expression, but the black one seemed to nod knowingly. Overall, I think they got the gist of it."

"You are a funny man, Captain Barrett. I like a man who can get the *gist* of things." The man stared at Archer and then looked at Barrett. "I see that you have a flair for theatrics, Barrett. His resemblance to Ward is uncanny."

Barrett smiled and nodded. "Just a reminder that I was once very useful and can continue to be so."

The man pushed aside his tea, then interlaced his fingers.

"So, Captain Barrett . . . I was expecting you months ago."

"Aye, you have my apologies, Mr. Tseng, but the sea—she makes her own schedules."

Tseng returned the bows of two silk-robed men, Hongs, or members of the imperial court. "This is true, Captain, but the sea is subservient to the heavens . . . and the Emperor is ruler of the heavens. He sets all schedules."

"Yet, despite our tardiness, here you sit."

Tseng nodded. "I apologize for the secrecy, Captain Barrett."

"No need. I am sure you have reason to be cautious."

"Indeed. There is a disagreement within the imperial government."

"A common problem, I'm sure," said Barrett.

Tseng smiled. "We are currently disagreeing about how to agree. Everyone agrees that we need to enhance our arsenal. This was made clear after our losses to the West and suppression of the rebel uprising. However, there is a faction that wants to manufacture these modern weapons here. There are people within the government that believe we should supply our arsenals domestically—build huge plants where guns are made—but we do not have the necessary industrial resources. However, our foreign friends in the West are more than willing to help us build these things—but how do we pay for it?"

"You could always borrow the money from your new friends in the West," said Barrett. "And then they will charge you fees—so many fees—for licensing the patents on their weapons."

"I do agree with them to an extent, but at this moment, it does not seem expedient. It just creates another profligate bureaucracy through which an elite few can line their pockets."

Barrett and Tseng stared at each other while the statement hung in silence. They both laughed.

"It is not such a bad idea, but building takes time. Buying is much faster."

"The same thing is happening to the Turks," said Barrett.

"Yes, but I do not think the arrangement will end well for the Turks—even worse for us. The French are helping us build ships, the British are helping us with manufacturing, and the Americans are teaching us how to properly despise the British and French."

Barrett smiled.

"These countries were our enemies in war. Now we should trust them to help us make weapons for our own defense?"

"War is between enemies," said Barrett. "But peace is between friends you can't trust."

Tseng smiled. "Can I trust you, Captain Barrett?"

"You can trust me to trust myself."

"I do not know what that means. Our prior meeting was based on the understanding that you had something that I wanted. Since you are brave enough to show your face here—after I suffered many embarrassments for vouching for you—you must have something special. Your employer wrote to me that if you did not arrive in Shanghai within a reasonable timeframe, I should expect that you were lost at sea or had absconded with the cargo. I should inform you that he suspects the latter. Now it is many months later, and here we are."

Jupiter and Archer shared a look over the long silence.

Mr. Tseng sipped his tea. "Your turn, Captain Barrett."

"I absconded with nothing. The ship was met with a few of the many hazards of sailing."

"I have not come here to question your honor, Captain. I am here to question your value."

"The ship . . . and its cargo are no more. However, in the past months, I acquired something that will be profitable for the both of us."

Mr. Tseng arched an eyebrow.

"Remingtons."

"And what of your former employer?"

"I am not concerned about my former employer. Although it can't match the lost profits, I'm sure the insurance has already reimbursed him for whatever he lied about being in the cargo."

Mr. Tseng smiled. "I studied in your country. Yale. I learned a great deal there. I like you Americans. So much more industrious than the British. You always find a way to come out ahead. But you could also learn a great deal from China. Time is of the essence. We still have enemies amongst our own people. They will not wait for the completion of a weapons factory to strike again. I am inclined to continue to do business with the gun traders—even if they do continue to charge exorbitant prices." Tseng smiled. "However, there are some very powerful people who are against this à la carte approach. It seems that the both of us have made some very dangerous enemies. I appreciate you coming all this way, Barrett. But I have already made my purchases."

"Why do you mean? Purchased from who?"

"From your employer, Captain Barrett."

Barrett leaned back in his chair. "When?"

"I'd say close to a month ago."

"From *my* employer?"

"Yes, and everything was in order."

Barrett's mind went to work. Was he lying? Was some other cargo sent to Shanghai in the event that he failed?

"Forgive me, Barrett, but I find it very curious that you would have a shipment so close to the previous one. I may be interested in what you have to offer, but I feel compelled to warn you that your employer is very angry with you."

"How angry?"

"He has placed a bounty on your head—a very enticing bounty. Dead or alive, I might add."

"How enticing?"

"Enough that you should leave Shanghai soon. It is high tide and the sharks are close to the shore. While I sympathize with your situation, doing any formal business with you might alienate your employer—or should I say *former* employer."

•   •   •

They left the tavern and discussed what they had learned from Tseng as they walked along the Bund. "How could a replacement shipment arrive so quickly?" asked Jupiter. "Unless he anticipated your failure because there were no weapons on board the *Intono*."

"There must have been," said Archer. "He just sent two shipments."

"Possibly," said Barrett. "Jupiter could be right. Maybe one or two crates were real, but he knew I wouldn't check every one of them. Why would I? He knew I would never suspect him of stealing from *me*."

"But what about Singleton?" asked Archer. "Did he know?"

"No," said Jupiter before Barrett could answer. "His job was to kill Barrett in either scenario. If we ever did arrive in Shanghai and those empty crates were unloaded, it would have been an embarrassment. Singleton would have claimed ignorance."

"And he would have killed me on the spot," Barrett added. "Clink-scales had already laid seeds of doubt with Tseng before I had even set sail. I guess there was no accounting for being lost at sea. Yes, either way I was a dead man."

Jupiter nudged him. "You're not dead yet, so we'd best get moving. We're being watched."

58

Sebastian returned with the shrub branches; white-pink flowers and gray bark, shoots of an herb with long, looping tendrils, and small green berries. The shaman that returned with Sebastian prepared the herbs in a concoction. He said words in his native language that the Americans did not understand, and made Jacob sip the preparation. He returned two more times and delivered a similar dose. The boy seemed to improve. Sebastian had bartered for the concoction by impressing him with one of his illusions—essentially trading one magic trick for another.

The shaman's presence irritated the hospital staff. "What is he doing here?" asked the doctor as he watched a half-naked native force-feed his patient.

The shaman again said words to the doctor that no one understood, though the way he looked at the doctor was translation enough. He finished administering the remaining liquid to Jacob, gathered his things, and left.

"Why did you bring him in here?" asked the doctor.

Sebastian walked over to him. "To save this boy's life, which you seemed determined to fail at."

"Ludicrous. He is improving, is he not? And you attribute that to the work of a witch doctor and not science. That charlatan gathers some weeds from the brush, puts them together, and you think that is what saved him? Not my treating him for the ten days prior to that savage's arrival?"

"Doctor, this was no magic trick. There is not a trick that has fooled me—not one that I haven't seen through—in my life. You or the shaman—it doesn't matter. The boy is alive."

• • •

Sonya held Jacob and swayed, just as she did when he was a baby. Just as she did the baby girl born a year before Jacob. She had rocked that baby slowly too. Its beauty in lifelessness a haunting, macabre combination. There was no explanation for what had happened. The baby was there and then it wasn't. Those things happened all the time, especially on a plantation. *We all shall return to our maker,"* Clara, the old slave woman, had said. *"It's up to him how soon."* But that did not matter to Sonya; there was too much anger in her heart for sadness. She hated everything—the way people said *mornin'*, hated the way other slaves held on to their hope and optimism, but most of all she hated Jupiter. He had troubles of his own, but his portion of this burden he'd left with her to carry. When he returned—if he returned—he'd be considered a hero in spite of his abandonment. But what about her, what would she be considered? In her anger, everyone seemed happy, until the day she found someone just as angry as her—and just as angry at the same person. Colonel Smith hated Jupiter just as much as she did.

• • •

"How did you know about those herbs?"

He wanted to say that a magician never reveals his secrets, but it was obvious she was not in the mood for levity. "It reminded me of a birch flower. I saw one of the natives peddling it when we arrived. We used it on the battlefield for fever and dysentery. During the war, medicine was scarce. We often had to find relief in whatever treatment nature provided."

"You were a doctor?"

"Something like one, but not really. I was just curious and determined enough to survive."

"You never said you were in the war."

"Sebastian the Magnificent wasn't—he is far too clever to be lured into such a deadly illusion. It takes a great deal of skill to trick a man into fighting in another man's war. A man named Shadrach fought in that war, but Shadrach the Magnificent doesn't have the necessary elegance."

"Shadrach the Magnificent is not so bad. It just depends on presentation. I can't thank you enough for saving Jacob."

He thought about the money he took from her on the *Orpheus*. He told himself that it was a loan, that one day he'd find a way to pay her back, but a part of him wanted her to suffer. He had cast a spell too strong. He was more powerful than he knew. "Don't mention it," he said. "I made a promise to you on that ship and I intend to keep it."

59

Shanghai

"We're being followed," said Jupiter.

"In Shanghai it always seems as though you're being followed," said Barrett.

They hustled down the docks, forcing their way through the dense crowds. There were three men dressed in black—like the men that had rescued them from Yerby's cave. They moved in the opposite direction of the crowd, stopped by everyone they ran into. People screamed at them belligerently.

"We should separate and meet later at Wu's compound."

• • •

Archer ran, never looking to see if the men were close. He ducked into alleys, not knowing if they were passageways to freedom or capture. He passed so many sights that would have stopped the wives of businessmen and tourists in their tracks. Curious and exotic things to foreign eyes. Places that to the foreign merchants represented opportunity, but he noticed none of it. He ran until he couldn't. He looked behind himself expecting one of them to be close. No one was there.

He slipped through a red door and into a dimly lit room with men hunched over tables. He smelled the air and the place revealed its purpose.

"Back so soon?" Did he know this woman? He felt he had seen her in a dream. She touched his forehead, damp with sweat, her fingertips traced the side of his face, his neck, his chest—it heaved under her hand. His racing heart quickened.

"What is your name?"

She stared at him, then smiled. "It is Mei. Of course, I never told you. Last night, only your name mattered. Why are you in such a hurry? Did you run all this way to see me?"

• • •

A haze of smoke over her porcelain body, a flash of red nails as she handed him the pipe, a bed so soft he felt buffeted by a cloud. No ships, no guns, no fathers, and no brothers, just a dreamscape where everything and everyone was a cloud.

What are his plans? he heard a voice ask.

He did not know how to answer.

What are his plans? the voice asked again. Never mind that, thought Archer. Clouds have no plans. They go where the wind takes them. And he was now, after all, a cloud.

"What are Barrett's plans?"

Archer felt like he was falling, the details of his environment painted in with frenzied brushstrokes. He felt pain in his knees, his shoulders, and his throat. He felt the hand release his neck. "I don't know," he heard himself say.

"Why was he meeting with Tseng?"

The room was dark, cold, and wet. He could hear drops of water, echoing, echoing—revealing just how deep and cavernous the place was—whatever it was.

"Guns," said Archer, unsure if it was him speaking.

"We know."

The hand returned to Archer's neck. "Easy," he heard another voice say. "The drugs will do their work. We just have to be patient."

Archer could not turn his head to see.

"Why does Tseng need more guns? Is there a war to be fought?"

His head wasn't clear, but he could still recognize the absurdity of the question: there is always a war to be fought.

"What is your role in this? Were you brought here to inspire the rebels?"

"I know nothing about rebels," said Archer. He could see the environment better, but it was a small bit of clarity with a hazy ring. He was on the floor. He could see the shoes of the man addressing him as he paced back and forth.

"And what of the provinces? Is he planning on taking you out into the backcountry and using you as a symbol for inspiration? Turn some of the warlords into customers?"

"I don't know about any of this. As far as I know Barrett was hired to bring the guns to Shanghai." His mouth shut like a trap. Why had he said so much? It was as if someone had forced their hand through his neck and manipulated his mouth like a puppet. Where was all of this coming from—the compulsion to be forthright despite his best efforts to be evasive? "Barrett was supposed to sell the weapons to the Tseng, but his employer betrayed him."

"You see," the voice said, "the drug is taking effect. Give it time to work and it works well. So there are no plans of arming an insurrection?"

Archer's jaw clenched. He initiated a swallow, but left it unfinished and kept his throat closed. But again, some invisible hand pried everything open. "No. He doesn't have enough guns. Most of them were lost. He's running out of sources."

"Good," the voice said. "Good. Is that all?"

Archer tried to look up, but his neck would not move. He felt a surge of emotion. He began to sob. "There is so much I have to tell you. I have done so many horrible things."

"Quiet now," the voice said. Archer felt a comforting hand on his shoulder. "This isn't the time for that. You have done well here."

"I wanted to hear what he had to confess," another voice said.

"No, that's not what this is. Go ahead and take him back."

Archer felt something prick him between his neck and shoulders. The pain and the sobbing stopped. He floated away from that dark place. The echoes of dripping water became distant and muffled. The desire to confess left him. He had nothing more to say. He was a cloud again.

• • •

Jupiter ducked and dodged, losing the men tailing him, and eventually returned to the merchant's compound. Something was strange. There were no guards at the open gate. Inside, the place seemed abandoned. There was no sign of Barrett or Archer. He called out the merchant's name. No answer. He entered one of the rooms and tripped over something in the darkness. A cloud crossed the sky, allowing moonlight into the room. Wu Ping's dead eyes reflected the pale, ghostly beam.

There was a commotion outside the merchant's chambers. Jupiter peeked outside the window. An unconscious Archer sprawled on the ground.

• • •

Now that Archer had come to, Jupiter explained what had happened. Archer rubbed his head. "I thought I was dreaming."

"No, it all happened. We've got to find Barrett."

"Do we? Why not good riddance?"

"Do you know where you are? Look around you—dead strangers everywhere. Who knows what the hell is going on in this place? We've got to get out of here, and if we're ever going to get home, we've got to find Barrett. He's the only one we can trust."

Archer nodded. "Trust the devil you know . . . isn't that the saying?"

• • •

They wandered through the city as Archer wracked his brain for the location of that red door.

"Are you sure it was real?" asked Jupiter.

They stopped. At night, the streets were more crowded than ever. The people seemed to spin on a carousel. All the places began to look alike. "I'm certain." He had taken no time to construct a memory castle—the details were unprotected, connecting to something ethereal. "I feel like we're close, but I don't know why." He remembered euphoria, feeling weightless, feeling limitless, and then the sudden horror of falling, but nothing linked those sensations to reality. A ship waited in the harbor. It had an elaborate figurehead of a curly-haired boy with despair in his eyes, his wings disintegrating as he reached up. As the ship bobbed in the water, the boy seemed to ascend, and then descend, rise and fall, launch and fail. Archer followed the line of sight of the boy's outstretched arm. "There." The dark alley was a few feet away.

60

Shanghai

They opened the red door and drew their guns. The opium prevented the patrons from reacting. Archer motioned Jupiter up the stairs. As Jupiter passed one of the rooms, a fist came down on his arm, knocking his gun away. His assailant filled the width of the narrow hallway. He grabbed Jupiter, choking him as Jupiter clawed at his eyes. Archer put his gun to the man's head and cocked it. "You hear that? I don't know if you speak English, but that sound is universally understood."

Archer felt the gun barrel poke his kidney. "Indeed it is," said Mei. "It sends a message that shall not be repeated."

Archer eased the weapon from her guard's head. Jupiter fell to the floor, coughing. Mei took the gun from Archer. "Are you so anxious to see me again? These theatrics are not necessary."

"Where is he?" asked Archer.

Mei smiled. "You did not come to see me, Archer? I am disappointed. Very well, I shall give you what you want." She grabbed Archer's face. "Isn't that what I am here for?" She let go and said something to her guard in Chinese. "Follow him," she said.

They followed the guard down a dark stairwell. Archer recognized the place from his dream. Barrett was bound to a chair and was being watched by two guards who stood on a wooden platform underneath two lamps.

They passed many crates, some of which were open, revealing

sundry goods destined to be sold throughout the world: poorly made porcelain plates, idyllic scenes made poorly on inexpensive paper meant to duplicate the authentic silk tapestries. But most of the crates contained fishing poles and guns.

Archer looked at Jupiter.

"Your rescue attempts are not necessary." A voice came from the shadows. "The question is not if you can rescue Barrett." The accent was American; the man was well-dressed. Archer recognized the voice. "The question is can you rescue yourselves?"

• • •

"I am afraid your journey with Mr. Barrett has come to an end. Do you understand, Barrett?"

Barrett raised an eyebrow. "It's *Captain* Barrett. Who might you be?"

The man smiled. "You can call me Mr. *Smith*, if you like, but my name is less important than the job I was sent to do."

"And what job is that?"

Mr. Smith approached him. "My job is to find a customer for my weapons, and I have done that."

Barrett laughed. "It looks like we are all family here—same aims and the same names."

"No, Captain Barrett, I am afraid we are not family. You have caused quite a ruckus."

"Me? I merely met a man for a drink."

"Is that all? You did not try to sell weapons that did not belong to you?"

"What is this?" asked Barrett.

Jupiter thought he heard a tremor in Barrett's voice. He realized he had been holding his breath. He swallowed hard.

Smith paced behind Barrett. "There is a bounty on your head, Captain. Clinkscales, your former employer, is quite upset with you. You sold only inferior weapons to Ten Dragons." Smith pointed to the two men watching Barrett. "And you got a man who was very important to me killed. Tseng had Wu Ping killed because of the trouble caused by you and your master. Now, Barrett, your dream of supplying weapons to China is finished. Finished for you, and definitely for Clinkscales. He has lost."

"But he has already sold the weapons to Tseng."

"Tseng will have to answer for Wu Ping. That shipment will be his last. Why build a ship when you can build a factory? Why should the Chinese wait for him to gather his weapons and ship them here, when my employer shall *make* them here? And superior in quality, I might add. If Clinkscales wants to try and sell his weapons to other parts of the world at exorbitant amounts, then so be it. But not here."

Barrett seemed confused. "I didn't know."

"It wasn't for you to know. But since your little plan failed, we can't have you selling what weapons you do have to any warlord with gold. Things like that cause . . . *instability*. Your desire to raise your stature, play at the level of men with real power, sir, I can tell you, the air is thin up there. It is easy to get winded."

"So what now?" asked Barrett.

"I have no quarrel with you. I just had to clip your wings."

Barrett looked over at Ten Dragons and his men—a hungry pack ready to tear him apart.

"It is time for you to leave China. I wanted to see what your intentions were, whether peasants from the hinterlands were expecting you to arm them. Now that I know that all of that is beyond your reach I am satisfied."

"So you are just going to hand me over to them? They killed Wu Ping. If they kill me, do you really think that Clinkscales will pay them after his China dreams are dashed? What would be his incentive? How will you keep them in line then?"

Smith did not answer.

"I know when I've lost," said Barrett. "There must be an alternative."

The American looked at the man known as Ten Dragons. He nodded. Smith walked over to him.

Barrett could hear a bit of their whispered conversation. The

American spoke Chinese well. The scene troubled him. It was all too familiar: two powerful men weighing their infinite options while he watched helplessly.

Smith and Ten Dragons walked over to Barrett. Ten Dragons untied him and stood him up.

"Captain Barrett, you are in luck," said Smith. "Ten Dragons is a reasonable man. He has agreed to accept payment from me for the bounty on your head. But you still owe him for those inferior weapons you gave him. He will discuss the terms with you. Now, I must take my leave, I'm afraid. Other business awaits. It has been a pleasure." He bowed at everyone too courteously and walked into the shadows. Barrett listened as the footsteps became faint, then heard no longer.

Ten Dragons smiled. "So, Barrett, I know you are a master of the seas, but can you sail a ship that does not exist?"

61

Maggie resisted the urge to scratch her chin as Fletcher painted her portrait. Once finished, it was to be placed in the office between the portraits of Dalmore and his adopted father. Her picture deviated from the usual style. She told Fletcher that she wanted to face the viewer, for whoever saw it to look her in the eye. In the background was a fireplace and above the mantle and hearth, a portrait of a smaller portrait of the late Mr. O'Connell. On either side of her were two men whose faces were cloaked in shadow.

There was a knock. "Mrs. Dalmore," said the maid.

"Don't move," Fletcher said to Maggie.

"Come in," she said.

"Ma'am, there is someone to see you. A Chinaman. I told him to wait for you by the servants' entrance."

"Chinese? What's his name?"

"I am sorry," said the maid. "I asked for it, but it seems I have already forgotten it. But he said something about a Mr. Lin."

She dismissed Fletcher and went to meet her visitor. He wore a black suit.

"Mrs. Dalmore?"

"Yes," said Maggie. "What can I do for you?"

"I am Tom West." He bowed slightly. "I work for Gao Lin."

"I see."

"I have a matter to discuss with you," he said.

"What sort of matter?"

"A private one. May I enter?"

She looked around to see who might be watching.

"Please come in," she said.

"Thank you."

She offered him a seat. "Would you like some tea?"

"Yes. I would."

The maid served him and watched nervously.

"So what is this urgent matter, Mr. . . ."

"West. Tom West. Yes, it is strange, but I took the name of my destination."

She was unimpressed.

"Gao Lin sends his condolences regarding Mr. Dalmore."

"I thank him."

"I am here to discuss an urgent situation. One Gao Lin feels you have neglected. He did not want to summon you. Out of respect for you, he wanted to give you the opportunity to resolve it yourself. Yet you have failed to do so."

"So Mr. Lin shows his respect by sending his servant?" said Maggie.

Tom West smiled. The maid poured more tea for him. "What is your name?" He directed his question to the maid.

She looked at Maggie before answering. "Pamela—Pam. Just Pam."

"Pam, the tea is lovely, thank you," said Tom West.

"You're . . . uh . . . quite welcome."

Tom West set his tea down. "Pam, may I ask you a question?"

She looked at Maggie again. "Sure, I suppose."

"Pam, how long have you worked here?"

She straightened her posture. "Not so long for Mrs. Dalmore, but fifteen years for the household."

Tom West smiled. "Fifteen years. That is a long time."

"Indeed, and I am grateful the lady continues to allow me to serve."

"Pam, indulge me once more. If Mrs. Dalmore were to die—heaven forbid—would you then become the lady of the house?"

"Of course not. What a ridiculous notion."

"Yes," Tom West said. "That would be ridiculous. You see, Mrs. Dalmore, Pam has served this home for fifteen years, and when you die she won't replace you, she will continue to serve here or somewhere else. No such fate awaits me after Gao Lin's death. I am much more than his servant."

"What do you want, Mr. West?"

"Gao Lin wants you to honor the agreement made between him and Mr. Dalmore. A favor was done for Mr. Dalmore. In return he was to hire Chinese workers in his shipyards and protect them from any white retaliation."

"Mr. West, I can assure that not one Oriental has been harmed in my shipyard."

"That is because you do not employ any Chinese in your shipyard."

Maggie glared at Pam, who still lingered. "Pam, you can leave us now. I am certain Mr. West has had enough tea."

"Certainly, Mrs. Dalmore." Pam hurried away.

Maggie leaned in. "Mr. West, I do not know what arrangement you had with my late husband, but this is my business and I won't be told who to hire. If Mr. Dalmore promised you something, feel free to dig him up and demand recompense. I have played no part in the matter."

"On the contrary, Mrs. Dalmore, you would have no business if Gao Lin had not offered his help to Mr. Dalmore. Your late husband was drowning in debt. Gao Lin was very generous to him."

She felt like sinking in her chair, but maintained her composure.

Tom West stood. "I was not sent here to persuade you, Mrs. Dalmore. I was told to deliver a message. I shall leave you now that I have done so. I thank you for the tea." He went for the door, then stopped. "What is it about this country that makes us forget how connected we truly are?"

"I don't know," said Maggie, "but I'll be sure to summon you when I have an answer."

62

Somewhere in the Pacific

They set sail, Barrett at the helm, Jupiter as first mate. The crew was a motley mix of Chinese and other races. Most were sailors who had found work on the Shanghai docks. Jupiter thought he recognized one of them, but found it painful to admit from where. He watched him go about his business on the ship. Jupiter's mind reached back, back to the mainland, to the shores, to San Francisco and the streets of the Barbary Coast, and to a foggy night. He watched a young boy in a sordid city on a night dedicated to carousing. Jupiter emerged from the shadows and knocked him unconscious. He and Clement took him to one of the ships, where they were given twenty-five dollars for him.

He had never wondered what happened to him after that night. Jupiter had always told himself the same tale: it is better this way, at least he'll be off the streets. Working and traveling builds character—the harder it is, the better for your soul. He never questioned if it was true.

Watching the young man on the ship, he was confronted by his actions. This was a man he had shanghaied. Was he better off? He meant to approach him and ask him the question directly, but he couldn't move. He thought about Sonya and the boy. Suddenly, his hands seemed dirty. Surrounded by water and no place to wash them.

• • •

Barrett told them to be wary of the crew—it was still Ten Dragons's ship after all, and Barrett did not trust its men yet. Days passed, and except for the occasional trips on deck, under the icy glances of the crew, they spent most of their time in their quarters.

It was night. The moon seemed to be keeping pace with the ship.

"I'm going up," Archer said. "My leg's killing me."

"And you think going up will help it?" asked Jupiter.

"Been dormant too long. Need to walk out some of the ache."

"There's room for you to walk in here, you know. Just walk in circles."

"Goddamn it, I didn't escape one prison just to be held in another."

"This ain't exactly the same thing. We're going home now," said Jupiter.

"My leg hurts. I need some fresh air," said Archer.

"You just want to go up there because you were told not to go up there and you don't like being told what to do."

"If that's true for me, then it's true for my leg too. I'm saying stay down here, and it's saying, no, go up top."

"Archer, don't start any trouble."

Archer went on deck. He watched the moonlight dance on the water. A man was on watch duty, scanning the dark with his spyglass. Archer thought about Elizabeth and the boy. Did they miss him? What did they think of him when he didn't show up for the boy? Did they think he was dead? That he had abandoned him?

Archer heard crying. He thought it was a trick of the ocean, an auditory hallucination. Maybe that sailor was a more sensitive fellow than he seemed. No. He heard it again. It wasn't coming from the ocean, it wasn't coming from the sailor, but it was coming from the ship. Somewhere down below.

Archer looked over his shoulder at the sailor. The sailor returned the look and went back to his spyglass. Archer dashed belowdeck. He went down the steps to a double set of doors. They were locked. He pressed his ear against them and heard the crying. He looked up and to the left of the doors: a set of keys on a ring, like a guard might leave outside of a prison cell. He tried each key; there were five of them. None worked, except the last one.

He open the door, slowly, as it was heavy—maybe fortified with steel. It was pitch-black inside, but he heard the crying. He went back out for the lantern that hung outside the door. He shined its light inside the dark room and for the source of the crying: a little girl, maybe thirteen or fourteen, dressed in rags, sobbing. Archer moved the light. Behind her sat dozens of other women, girls, in stoic silence.

63

Archer backed away, closed the door, and put the keys and lantern back in their place. The sailor on watch met him as he came up.

"What are you doing?"

"Just stretching my legs, getting fresh air," answered Archer.

"No. You don't go down there. You stay where I can see you. If you go down there, then you'll go out there," he said, pointing to the dark sea.

"I understand," said Archer. "It won't happen again." Archer smiled and patted the sailor on his shoulder. It was all stone.

Archer headed back to the cabin.

"Jupiter, you won't believe what's down below this ship."

Jupiter looked at him. "What now?"

"They've got a hull full of women down there. Ragged and scared."

Jupiter sat up. He wanted it to be a lie. He was so close to reuniting with Sonya and the boy—closer than he had been in Yerby's cave or Wu Ping's compound. Of course he had to do something; he knew it as soon as Archer said it. How could he be delivered to his family on a slave ship?

Archer became impatient with Jupiter's silence. "Say something. We've got to do something to help them," said Archer. "We can't just sit back and watch their freedom be taken away from them."

Jupiter laughed. "Boy, this is one hell of a time to develop a conscience. While you sat around on a plantation for most of your life and watched the humanity be snatched away from every slave around you.

Now you go down below for a few minutes and come back up as some sort of abolitionist, some type of hero. You see a room full of teary-eyed maidens and all of a sudden you're some knight in shining armor. How many china dolls did you try to rescue up there in Chinatown? Maybe those girls back in 'Frisco weren't pretty enough. Those girls down below, are they real pretty? Is that it, Archer?"

Archer lunged at Jupiter and cocked his fist. Jupiter didn't react. He just smiled at Archer.

"There it is, Master Archer," said Jupiter. "Teach me a lesson about freedom."

Archer released him and dropped his fist. He lay on his mat and closed his eyes.

64

Jupiter was bothered by his conversation with Archer. His anger with Archer soon passed, so it wasn't that. The man wanted to do something to help those girls, and he was right. That's what bothered Jupiter the most. He had to see for himself. It was not that he didn't believe Archer, but there was an unidentifiable force that was pushing him, propelling him to see with his own eyes. To make matters worse, while everyone slept Jupiter thought he could hear a little girl cry over the sound of the waves.

•   •   •

"I need you men to work," Barrett told them.

"I thought he wanted us out of sight," said Archer.

"That was then, but some of the men have grown resentful that you get to rest while they work. They wanted to throw you overboard, but I talked them out of it when I told them that you have sea experience."

"Well, I'll be sure to thank them for their hospitality."

"Jupiter," said Barrett. "Hold watch tonight."

Jupiter nodded.

"You should go down there and see for yourself, tonight," Archer said to him.

Jupiter didn't answer.

•   •   •

That night, Jupiter took the keys and opened the door. He saw them. He had never been on a slave ship, but he had heard about its horrors from descriptive abolitionists and older slaves who themselves remembered or knew someone who remembered the voyage over.

The girls were corralled like cattle; some of them were downright skeletal.

One of them became very animated and spoke in Chinese.

"Calm down. Quiet," Jupiter whispered to her. "I can't understand you. They'll hear you."

"She's asking if you are a slave," the little girl said.

"You speak English?"

"Yes. I learned from English missionaries."

The woman spoke to the little girl in Chinese.

"She wants you to tell the captain to give us more food," she told Jupiter. "We are starving."

The woman spoke to the little girl again, clutching her chest. The little girl looked down. "Tell him," the woman managed to say.

The little girl looked up at Jupiter. "We need more food. Do they want us to look like skeletons when we reach shore? What men will want us then?"

"How did this happen to all of you?" Jupiter asked the little girl.

"We want to be reunited with our families. Our husbands, our brothers, and fathers. They all went to America for work. We are supposed to be making the voyage to see them, but we don't have the money to pay. So we will have to settle our debts in other ways when we reach shore."

Jupiter placed his hand on the girl's shoulder. Her eyes grew large, and he felt a hand on his own shoulder.

"You shouldn't be down here." Barrett hooked his arm forcefully under Jupiter's and led him up the steps. "Forget what you saw, Jupiter. They will be with their families again. Yes, they will have to work off the cost of their voyage in a brothel on their backs, but they will be paid more than they ever made on the mainland. And they will have access to the opportunities that the West can provide, more than they ever did back home. So it is either know their fate, which is to live the life of a peasant—or to have one that is open and limitless. They can be anything they want to be in your land. That is the choice that they have made. It is a sacrifice, but it is a worthy one."

"But how can they look their husbands or fathers in the eye," asked Jupiter, "after all this?"

"What, are you becoming sentimental? Why? Because they are women?" Barrett laughed. "How many men have you put in this same situation?"

"Never like this," answered Jupiter.

"No, worse than this," Barrett said. "These women chose to be on this ship."

"Not all; some were forced," said Jupiter. "I can tell."

Barrett was quiet. He looked back at the door and then at Jupiter. He shook his head. "It's a sorry sight, isn't it, son?"

"If you know that then why are you doing it?"

"Did you think stepping out of that dragon's den would be easy? It was a requirement of our freedom. Those women were on this ship a month before I took the helm."

"I don't understand," said Jupiter.

"It's one of the businesses Ten Dragons specializes in. Cheap labor. Prostitution."

"Slavery."

"Sadly, that describes about a third of all human interaction. The international ports are starting to frown on this sort of thing. Especially the U.S. They needed a navigator with a special knack for evasion."

"So we just arrive and turn them over to whorehouses?"

"No. I am taking what remains of the weapons to Cuba."

"So that was the plan?" asked Jupiter. "That is not how you explained it to us. You want to sell weapons to the oppressed to help them to be strong for their own sake. But if they don't want that help, the help you're willing to offer, then you have no problem offering your services to tyrants."

Barrett smiled. "Yes, Jupiter, it's true, I wanted redemption, but somehow it evaded me. It's not a straight path, it's curved and winding. When redemption eluded me, I seized opportunity. It is not wrong or right, it just . . . *is*."

"And what about those girls?"

"They will be set free," said Barrett.

"I don't like the tone of your freedom."

Barrett smiled. "I know this bothers you. I too am looking for redemption. You have convinced me, Jupiter, and I am grateful. Do not worry, this is not a step backward to profiting off the flesh of others. I am not a slaver. I can't participate in the oppression of those women."

"You confuse me."

"Some years back, before the war, the American government had a plan to relocate its Negroes. Some of them went to Haiti, others went to an island in the Caribbean called Île-à-Vache. It was pitched to them as a paradise, a pearl in the Caribbean."

"I've never heard of it."

"Most people haven't. It's a plop of shit. A group took the first Negro settlers there, and it was nothing like they promised. The weather, the lack of food, they starved and suffered. Most of them died."

"Why was this place chosen? Who brought it to their attention?"

"I was hired by a consortium that wanted to rid America of its Negroes. I am cursed. I see that now. But I can still undo it. I can't return to the Caribbean as a slaver. Those girls will be set free long before we reach land."

Barrett ushered him on deck. Jupiter had wished Archer was lying, and now he wished Barrett was telling the truth. He closed his eyes and felt the wind. For the sailor, the sea is freedom. Despite her often oppressive and mercurial moments, if you endure her moods and learn her patterns, she will offer you the world. For a man of the sea, the only alternative type of freedom was death. Jupiter looked back at that door. He knew what kind of freedom Barrett had in mind. Jupiter was about to participate in his second mutiny.

65

Somewhere in the Pacific

Raymond—that was the name of the man that Jupiter had once crimped. He'd shown him the girls, and the mutiny happened hours thereafter. Barrett gave no resistance, but he swore to withhold any assistance navigating. Whatever came of this, the men were to obtain it on their own.

Jupiter knew it was the right thing to do, but something about the crusade may have been corrupted considering Jupiter had failed to tell Raymond that it was he who shanghaied him so long ago.

•   •   •

They tried to ease the clouds from their brains, hoping their memories would coalesce as they navigated under the starry skies. They thought that between the two of them, they would have gained enough information to survive their journey. But a ship is neither a deck of cards, nor is it a toy in a bottle. It is a way of life, a philosophy. A symbol. It sails through the rivers of the blood more so than the seas of the mind. They did not watch the sea for shifts in her mood—temperamental and mercurial she can be—they were too busy watching Barrett, bound aboard a ship once again under his command.

They were hit by a squall, and then a storm that sent them off course, at least the course Jupiter and Archer thought they were following.

• • •

Barrett stayed silent through the whole ordeal. Archer and Jupiter, though their confidence waned each day, never asked him for help. Sunburned and parched, they were low on fresh water, low on food. Though he was nearby, Jupiter was no longer at the helm, he was genuflecting before it, begging for its cooperation. The sea's decisive and ancient currents set their course, and the ship went along agreeably.

Jupiter looked out on the ocean. He had made sacrifices to the wrong god—the memory goddess, Mnemosyne—not Neptune or Poseidon. No land in sight, only water on the horizon. He no longer saw it as a route to Sonya and his son. Despite how vast it was, he only saw it as one enormous place to die.

He felt the Colonel's hand over his. The weight of it stung his cracked skin. "It's over now," he said to Jupiter. "You can let go." He looked at him, his white hair ignited by a halo of sunlight. He couldn't see his face. "It's all right, you can let go. I'll take it from here."

Jupiter let go of the wheel and fell into his arms. He looked over the Colonel's shoulder—Barrett's shoulder—and saw the young Chinese girl crying with a knife in her hand, and the cut ropes that once held him.

• • •

Archer, delirious, protective, misunderstood the embrace. He lunged at Barrett with his last bit of strength. The Captain pulled out his blade and stabbed Archer in the stomach. As Archer held his stomach, Barrett kicked him over into the boat.

He turned to Jupiter. "I'm sorry, but you have to join him."

Jupiter obeyed.

The ropes were untied and the boat was dropped in the sea.

66

Her new partnership with Mr. Clinkscales—such an odd name—was paying handsomely. As a shipper and gunrunner, a woman of intrigue, she resented that Miss Ellen would have the audacity to summon her to the old woman's Octavia Street mansion—stranger still that Maggie came when called.

Maggie was greeted by the desiccated old butler and led into the opulent yet neglected and dusty interior. She sat across from the old colored woman. "You're looking well, Miss Ellen," said Maggie.

"Oh, don't lie to me, child, I look as old as I ever did. But you, child, you're looking quite regal. You're practically glowing."

"I'm doing fine, I suppose."

"Don't be so modest, child. Nothing pleases Miss Ellen more than to see one of her children living a *good* life. That's all I ever wanted for my girls. And you are definitely living the good life . . . I hear things." The old woman smiled.

"I never could have done it without you, Miss Ellen. Thank you for everything." Maggie reached across the table. "May I take your hand, Miss Ellen?"

Miss Ellen looked at Maggie and pulled away. "I'm sorry, dear, my arthritis is agitated. The slightest touch causes me pain."

Maggie withdrew her hand. "Well, I suppose I don't need to ask why you have brought me here."

"Why *I* brought you here? You brought yourself here. I'm old, but I'm certain of that. I'm so tired of you ungrateful little wenches pretending I'm some puppet master pulling your strings. All I've ever done is to recognize your potential, and to help you live up to that potential. I never forced a decision on any of you. Especially you, Maggie."

"I know, Miss Ellen, and I am forever in your debt."

"Forever in my debt? Yet you treat me as if I'm the one who owes you something. When you was a teenage girl on her back, legs spread for money, didn't I teach you how to spot the right kind of man? The big fish. When you set your sights on Mr. O'Connell, didn't I teach you how to get your hook in him and reel him in?"

"You did. But he still left me with nothing."

"He left you a *name*, child. I gave you the money for your business because of what that name could do for *us*. Now, here it is, twenty years later, and you forgot our agreement. You act as if that's all this is about. Did I ever ask you for anything? When you've needed me, I always opened that door for you. Yet you've turned your back on me so many times. Do you ever come to see Miss Ellen, just to see how she's doing? No. You come in here with a railroad scheme. You say it will earn me more than what you owe times ten. But that's not how it turned out, is it?"

"A lot of people lost money, Miss Ellen, all the investors did—including me."

The old woman laughed; phlegm rattled in her chest as she covered her mouth. "But you seem to be doing just fine now."

"Miss Ellen, that is my shipping line. I built that business up by myself."

"Is that really true, child? Think hard about the history I just laid out before you."

"Well, if you're looking for a partnership, I already have one."

"I know all about your partner. But I've been your partner from the beginning, and I am tired of being silent. Maybe I am a bad mother. Maybe I didn't teach you girls the way I should have. We are supposed to help each other. Women supposed to help women. We are stronger when we stick together. As soon as we trust a man at the expense of our sisters and mothers, we lose. There is no you without me. O'Connell, the old place in the Barbary, Dalmore and this shipping company, all of that was put into motion by your association with me. Because of my love for you. You're still young. You've got a lot of life ahead of you. I'm an old woman. I don't have much time left on this earth—but until that day comes, while I'm here I want what's mine. I'm sure the Irish would like to know what really happened to Mr. Hutchins. And I'm sure the Chinese would like to know who set them up. I hear Mr. Lin lost a grandson to Hutchins's men. I'm not saying they would pay you a visit, but it must be worth something to them."

"How much do you want, Miss Ellen?"

The old woman said nothing.

"What number should I say to get right with you?" asked Maggie.

"I'll let you decide what to say . . . but don't insult me."

Maggie rose slowly and walked over to Miss Ellen. The old woman's bodyguards rushed into the room. Miss Ellen raised her hand, and put the men at ease.

Maggie knelt and rested her head in the old woman's lap. She smelled like lavender and old linen, a perfumed corpse prepped for burial. "Thank you for everything." She inhaled the old woman's scent. "You have done so much for me. You are a part of me. Half of me belongs to you." Maggie wiped away a tear. "Including the shipping line." She felt Miss Ellen touch her head and run her fingers through her hair; the strength of her grip was undeniable.

"I forgive you. What's past is past. Miss Ellen is just grateful to see one of her children grow up to be so generous."

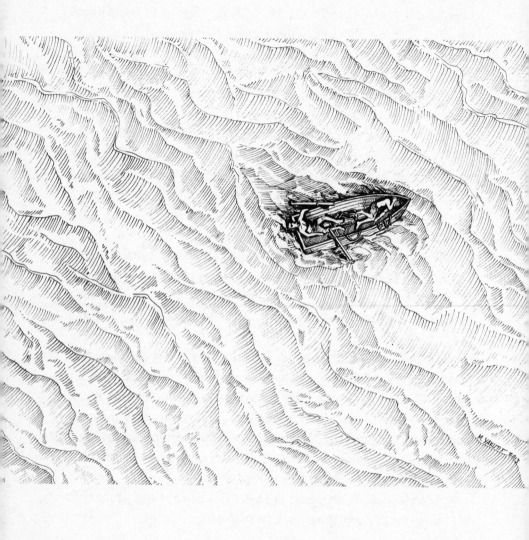

67

They drifted for weeks; they did not know for how long. Archer had lost a lot of blood, but Jupiter had stopped the bleeding with a compress of cloth and seaweed. The cut wasn't that deep. The bleeding had stopped, but since the wound wasn't properly tended to it had become infected.

"When you make it back to San Francisco, I want you to look up Elizabeth and her son, and I want you to tell them what happened to me. Tell them everything. Why I was in San Francisco. Why I did it. And you be honest with them. From your end of things you be honest too. I want them to see the whole picture. Especially the boy. You make sure the boy understands."

Jupiter smiled. It hurt to do so. They were starved and baking under the sun, and the nights were cold. "What the hell makes you think I'm gonna live? Can't you see we're in the same boat?"

Archer laughed, and it hurt his throat. "No, you'll live. You're a survivor. As someone who's tried to kill you, I know firsthand."

"If I survive, then you'll survive."

• • •

When he saw the blue ridge of mountains, he knew he was close. It wouldn't be too far now. Jupiter knew these mountains far too well. As intimate and familiar to him as the insides of his pockets. He had tucked away so many memories in these woods. He wasn't too far away now from a place he'd once called home. As he got closer, things were not as pristine as he'd left them, as unsoiled as they remained in his mind. Those unsullied hollows and creeks, the holes and hiding places, were now charred earth left in the wake of Sherman's army. Still the stray resilient tree or the obstinate house led him onward.

The Smith plantation still loomed over the charred earth like a wounded and resentful giant. An impossible fantasy came upon him all at once, and he half expected to see his family run up to him; the child, still in his mother's belly when he'd left. He envisioned a strong boy running up to meet the father he had never met, followed by a woman who longed for him and stayed true in his absence. There was no running. Just smoke coming from the carcasses of old manors, circling the air, mixing with the closed.

All had changed. He approached the large white columns stained with blood and soot and hacked saber marks for God knows what reasons. Yes, everything had changed.

He grabbed the handle and entered through the door—the front door, not the servants' entrance—of Colonel Smith's big house. Yes, a lot had changed.

But inside, it was as orderly as he had kept it in his mind. He knew this place well too: in the large white marble fireplace he had tucked away the amount of steps a private must learn to drill. On each step of the large, spiraling staircase he had placed elements of the privates' training manual for battle. On the chaise lounge were seated rules of engagement, battle hymns, psalms from the Bible. Nothing had changed.

However, he did not remember the silence—that was different. Not the silence of the absence of life, but the kind of silence that is paradoxically loud, created by someone or something trying to remain undetected and unheard.

Yes, it was all the same. Even the enormous oil portraits on the equally large walls had miraculously survived the ravenous horde of Sherman's army. The portrait of Colonel Smith's maternal grandmother was still there, as was that of his uncle, and of his father, the first Colonel Smith. He remembered everything about it—the epaulets, the white beard, the saber held just so, but he did not remember the eyes that followed him with every step.

Yes, those eyes did move—quickly—and so did Jupiter. His hand slid down the strap of his canteen and to his waist, unsheathing his blade.

"Come on out and show yourself," Jupiter said to the dancing eyes of the portrait.

"Who goes there? State your name!" came a muffled reply from behind the portrait. The eyes continued to dance, never settling on Jupiter.

"The name's Jupiter, but don't bother introducing yourself unless you intend to do it face-to-face. Now come on out here."

"Jupiter?" the portrait asked. "Yes, yes, I do know a Jupiter. One of my slaves. Fine boy, he was, but he ran off with the Yankees. Fine lad, but no, no, no you can't be him. Jupiter's a ghost, so Jupiter is dead. There's no way Jupiter survived that hell of a war. No, sir, you lie to me. You are a demon cloaked in the seemingly innocuous visage of a darkie. I will come forth, but I promise that your demon work will have no effect on me, for I am a good Christian man."

By now, Jupiter had recognized the voice. "No demon work here." There was loud banging and then a groan that echoed in the chimney. Dust and soot fell into the hearth. More groans, more soot, and then a bare foot, and the other wore a sock with holes that allowed all five toes to breathe as well as the heel. The mantel and hearth moved as one, opening as if hinged to a door, to reveal the ghostly visage of Colonel Smith.

He wore a dressing gown and smoking jacket, all covered in soot. His shock-white hair was streaked black with soot.

"So, you black devil, you've come back to kill me."

Jupiter thought about that for a moment. Had he? His skin tingled at the thought of it. There was a startling truth to it that he had not anticipated. "No, sir. I didn't come back to kill you. I came back for Clara, the young one."

The Colonel threw up a hand in disgust. "Bah! You confound me with your riddles, demon. I know not the gods you speak of from your heathen religion. I spit on your pagan rituals." The Colonel breathed in deep, unleashed a rattle from his chest, and spewed a web of sputum onto the floor beside his bare foot.

Jupiter looked at its green and yellow sickness. He looked closer at the Colonel's eyes—bloodshot. Closer still, sores about the scalp and arms. It was obvious that he was gripped by madness and suffering from something of the venereal variety. The Colonel's many dalliances with the flesh had resulted in a punishment of the flesh. "Do with me what you will, heathen. Shrink my head. Cannibalize my entrails. But know thee this: With every ravenous bite you take you are ingesting a child of God. The light of Christ will sear you from the inside out." With that, the Colonel slumped to the floor and began mumbling to himself in some dead and forgotten language or the language of madness.

"Do with me what you will," said the Colonel. Jupiter recognized the irony of that statement immediately. That the Colonel should say these words to him who was considered property just months ago—the Colonel's property at that. How many times had the motto of *Do with me what you will* been acted out on the other slaves on the plantation, as he did with them as he willed? Now here he was, asking for the same power to be expended on him as he had done to others. There was a sadness to it, yes, but definitely a twisted madness.

The Colonel's leg twitched, and then the mad mumbling stopped. The Colonel looked at Jupiter for the first time with recognition. "Jupiter," he said, eyes opening wide.

"Yes, Fath—" Jupiter stopped himself. "Yes, Colonel. It's me."

"Oh, you're a soldier now." The eyes grew weary. "I beg of you, man. Do with me what you will. Put me out of my misery. Have mercy on me."

Jupiter could see the Colonel's eyes begging for help. He went over to him, patted him on the shoulder, and leaned him against the wall, being careful not to touch his syphilitic sores.

"I sure did miss you," the Colonel said. "I took what was yours and I am sorry. I took it. Took it . . ." Jupiter removed the strap from his canteen, wrapped it around the Colonel's neck like a torch, tighter and tighter, until the Colonel stopped babbling, stopped grabbing at Jupiter's hands, and then stopped doing anything at all.

• • •

Archer was impeccably dressed in his gray uniform, broad-brimmed hat, gilded saber sheathed at his hip and nestled in the tossing but decadent carriage; he looked not like a man on the losing end of a war but a victorious soldier returning home to bask in his glory—but in reality this was not the case.

He passed the scorched earth of battle. The corpses left in the wake of destruction did not startle him for they all seemed more familiar to him than home. His carriage passed former soldiers—the wounded and amputees, both Yankee and Confederate, hobbling alongside the road together. "Never thought I'd see it," said the man next to him. Archer could not remember his name, but his rank was captain. Archer ground his teeth and his eyes welled up. "I'm now inclined to believe I could see anything." He relaxed his jaw, but sweat formed on his brow, and his eyelid began to twitch incessantly. He longed for opium.

The manor was in utter decay. He expected that. However, upon entering he could sense something was wrong—those instincts that saved his life so many times during the war told him that something was not right. He cracked the door. The smell hit him first. His stomach muscles clenched with their own assault as Archer wrestled with the urge to vomit. He looked around in a panicked search for an answer. *Someone?* No one. Nothing. Even though the horrific smell of death covered everything both living and tangible, he knew that the source of the smell was his father, Colonel Smith.

●　●　●

Heavy, heavy rain. Archer dug at the base of the gravestone until he reached his mother's exposed coffin. He worked for hours, deep into the night, with Clara holding a lantern above him. The casket, prodded open, revealed the time-ravaged bones of his mother. He pushed them aside, surprised at how light they were, and applied pressure to the coffin's bottom, revealing a deeper space—filled not with the morbid contents provided on the higher level, but with his mother's jewelry, the family heirlooms that she'd vowed to take with her, lest the Colonel lavish his slave wenches with them.

Archer stuffed his pockets with the valuables like a pirate. They would fund the search for his father's murderer—his former slave and brother. *Of course he would get himself killed when I need him most.* Archer climbed out and kicked the Colonel's body into the muddy grave.

● ● ●

Birds circled their tiny craft. Archer's wound began to smell, even above the briny ocean.

"Do me one more favor," said Archer, now almost green in color.

"What's that?" asked Jupiter, starving, barely sounding the words.

"Make sure you never give up on finding Sonya."

Strange that he said that. Jupiter had given up. He had searched for her for so many years, only to have impediments and obstacles between them become more elaborate, more challenging, and more dangerous. Obviously, the world was trying to tell him something. From the way things looked, he wouldn't have to worry about it much longer.

Hallucinations. Mermaids. The ghost of sailors Jupiter had crimped rose from the sea. The Colonel. He sat right there in the boat with Jupiter and Archer. He held Archer's head in his lap, stroking his hair. "I'm sorry. I'm sorry," he said, but Archer couldn't hear him. Most vivid of all was that large ship off in the distance.

68

Somewhere in the Pacific

The Cressida *Pacific: Captain's log. Picked up a Negro and a white man. Castaways. The white man had already died of starvation and possible complications of syphilis. The Negro was very weak. Took days to recuperate . . .*

●   ●   ●

"I finally get a job that gets me away from that city, and I run into you in the middle of the ocean. I promised myself, the next time I saw you I'd kill you."

Jupiter was too weak to move.

"You took everything from me. Least that's how I felt. When Sonya left with Jacob, it tore me apart. Soon as you came back, she pushed me away."

Jacob.

"But eventually I came to see it was the right thing for us to be apart. I was holding on to a dream that I wanted to be true. Everything that I could remember about the plantation—between me and Sonya— seemed like it was making its way to being real. We had a family, and the whole time you was tearing us apart. You were always there, even before you caught up with us. . . . There never was no *us* . . . was there?"

Jupiter turned away from Titus. His son's name echoed in his head.

"Damn, boy, by the looks of you, you been through hell. You don't have to talk. It's fine if you just listen. Did you find her?"

Jupiter managed to shake his head.

"So here's what's gonna happen now. We gonna get you better."

Jupiter swallowed. His throat felt scorched. His eyes welled.

"You seem like you was ready to give up, like you been through enough. No, you can't give up now. I can't imagine what you been through to be with them, but I can tell you that they are worth it. You all deserve to be together."

69

Sebastian brought her to Mary's home. She and Sonya stared at each other for a long time, waiting for the reunion to register as real. Maybe she had asked the universe for too much—a sister, a friend, a husband for her, a father for her son. When they finally embraced, Sonya thought for a moment that this change of fortune might be enough for her.

• • •

Mary had a large plantation-style home. She had married a wealthy merchant whose father was Dutch and mother a native African.

"Do you know that I kept that first letter you sent me?" said Sonya. "And I only lost it recently on the voyage over."

"Oh, really?" said Mary. "It's for the best, I suppose. Most of it was propaganda for the ACS."

"You didn't write it?" asked Sonya.

"Heavens no. I could barely spell my own name at the time. I didn't receive proper instruction until I met my husband, Robert."

Sonya found it difficult to hide her disappointment. "Oh, I see . . ."

Mary leaned over and grabbed Sonya's hand. "Sonya, I meant every word of it at the time, but I was just a girl excited and thrilled by the adventure. It wasn't until later that I learned of the snakes and insects, the lack of food, the belligerent natives, the malaria, the death. When I could write for myself, I put all of this in a letter, but the ACS censored it. They were worried that no Negroes would come if they knew of Liberia's hardships. And I'm glad they did, Sonya, for you wouldn't be here with me now had the letter been sent. It wasn't true then, but it's true now. Look around you, Sonya. I worked as a maid for Robert's parents in this very house."

Liberia was a strange land inhabited by familiar faces. Already, she could tell that it was not the paradise that some thought it to be. This was not a place free of conflict, free of prejudice. Tribes were tribes, no matter what part of the globe. This place was no exception. The American Negroes had already begun to see themselves as superior to the native Africans. She hadn't before, but she suddenly felt uncomfortable in this Southern plantation–style mansion, here on free soil. Maybe it did not demand the same uses, but those intentions were there, those same grandiose yearnings.

"Of course, it's all so amazing. I understand, Mary, truly I do. I know how hard and unforgiving this world can be. Maybe I was feigning innocence for my own sake."

Mary smiled. "You were always the one full of romance and optimism—no matter how horrible your life really was."

"Yes, no matter how horrible." She had not thought of optimism as an insult, but it felt like one. Sonya realized she had not told Mary about Jupiter, and she didn't feel comfortable doing so.

$$\bullet \quad \bullet \quad \bullet$$

Sonya realized that the only fantasy in Liberia is the country itself. Everything else was a raw kind of reality. She had begun to accept that she would never see Jupiter again. She'd had to chase the fantasy in order to let it go.

Mary offered Sonya one of her many rooms. Having no other options, she reluctantly accepted. Sebastian asked permission to speak to her alone.

"So what do you think of my latest trick?" Sebastian smiled. "I think it is by far my best."

"Once again I am in your debt." Sonya did not smile. "What do you expect as repayment?"

"I have already told you what I want from you. The question is what do you want from me?"

"It's not what I want for me, but what I want for Jacob. Now look," she said, "if you're going to be in my boy's life, then you'll have to be in it. If you are going to stay, then you'll have to mean it. I can't have you running in and out of his life when you see fit. I know you've come all this way, and maybe things aren't what you expected them to be, but I can't let you hurt him. I can't let you hurt me."

"I plan to be with you and the boy . . . as long as you'll let me," said Sebastian.

•   •   •

There was screaming everywhere. The chants in their language— Sonya couldn't understand. The merchant unlocked a chest and revealed his weapons cache. He grabbed a rifle for himself, another for Sebastian, and handed a pistol to Sonya. He tossed a pistol to Mary, who easily caught it.

"The Grebo," he said. "They don't respect paper treaties. They view us as the aggressors. Every so often, they raid the town and we have to beat them back."

A window was broken. Wood was smashed. A passing torch illuminated the curtain like an orange-red flag. It was as if the entire tribe was waiting for them.

"Come out, Vanderhoven. Face us."

Sebastian peeked through the curtain. "There's too many of them. We'll have to sneak out back."

"They'll just break down the door and take everything. Everything I worked for. I can't let that happen."

Sebastian looked around. "What do you have in here that's flammable?"

"Kerosene. Maybe a bit of gunpowder."

"We'll throw it out the window, create a diversion, and slip out the back." Sebastian positioned himself by the window with the barrel. "Robert, go with them out the back. I'll roll the barrel out and shoot it. The explosion should give us enough time to escape."

Robert did as Sebastian instructed and led everyone out the back into the darkness. She heard the faint screams and an explosion that gave her a jolt. She looked back and saw the blue-gray cloud, visible even at night, forming over the merchant's home. They ran farther into the darkness until the sound of their breath and footsteps were the only thing they heard.

• • •

Sebastian clawed up the hillside, struggling to lift himself. As usual, it was intolerably humid; sweat and condensation on his hands, his brow, and his rifle. Every wet breath seemed like a prelude to drowning. He reached the top of the bluff that overlooked the village. He stayed low, belly in the dirt, as he surveyed the area, watching the dense brush for any signs of movement. He readied his rifle. They would be coming soon. He tried to focus, but the predatory ritual triggered fearful memories of those anxious nights before a battle, the quiet jitters that plagued his regiment as they observed a tranquil clearing from the woods and waited for the sound of the Rebel cry.

He saw movement in the trees. A bird flew away from the treetops. They were here. There was a long silence after that bird's flight—and then there were screams. The attack had begun. Sebastian steadied his rifle and picked them off one by one. He thought he had gotten them all, then gunfire came from the woods. *Where the hell did they get guns like that?*

He fired blindly in the direction of the gunfire. Two screaming men emerged firing at him. He tried to take them down but they were too fast. He rolled and slid down the muddy hill. One of them drew a knife and followed him down. The blade almost cut his shoulder—but it caught the wrist. Immediately he was aware of how small the wound was. Sebastian knocked the knife out of the assailant's hand, grabbed it, and then plunged it into his belly. It was not until the frenzied anger left the native's face, and death took it over, that Sebastian realized that he was just a boy of twelve or thirteen. He still held the knife in the boy as his knees buckled. Sebastian withdrew the knife and eased him down. He held the boy until the life left his eyes.

Sebastian heard someone behind him. He turned. All he saw was a flash of light, then complete darkness.

• • •

Sonya came back to town looking for Sebastian. They were already clearing out the bodies of the natives. It was as if he had performed one last disappearing act, rendering his audience speechless.

70

Cuba

Jupiter arrived in Cuba, where most of the fighting was. Wherever there was chaos to be exploited, Barrett would be close by. He tried to ingratiate himself with the locals, but he soon found he was in danger. There was a revolution going on. The angry slaves, now turned infuriated rebels, fighting for their freedom from Spain and the sugar plantations, had caused the white population to panic. There was a lot of fear and distrust to go around, and now the American Negro was on a strange island, an island in upheaval, looking for a white man who sold weapons.

"Look around," he was told on more than one occasion. *"Choose one."*

He did look around, and he saw plenty of the kinds of crimes that Barrett was guilty of. He thought Barrett was a special case, but now he wasn't so sure. He spent some time in Havana getting his next plan together. How would he get to Liberia? He was closer now than ever before, but that would take money. He didn't have any. He had been a fool to come, thinking he could change the world again. But he felt he needed to do it if he was to ever look his son in the face and not be ashamed. He had tried to rid the world of a bad man. Was he removing a bad man from the world, or just one from his life? When would it end? He could go on this self-righteous path until the end of time, and the world would still not be free of bad men, men like Barrett or worse than him. In the end it would amount to nothing more than a killing spree. Somewhere he had gotten it wrong. It wasn't about ridding the world of bad men. The path that he needed was one that he had never tried before: becoming the best man that he could be, not just for his sake, but for his son's sake as well.

He gathered his things. He had to get the hell off this island. Two men appeared. A third one stepped behind him and put a knife to his throat. They had other plans: they intended for him to stay a while longer.

• • •

He awoke on a raft. The sound of the river. The sounds of the jungle. The night sky. Two of his captors hovered over him. Negro—*mulato*—like him. The other one steered. He was going to ask questions: where, who, why? But he knew these were not the types of men who liked interrogations. Besides, his Spanish was not that good.

The longer the trip took, the more certain he became that he was going to die. What did these men want, and if they were willing to tell him, was it something that he wanted to hear?

Then he looked closer at one of his captors: his collar; the buttons; it was the kind of coat worn by a sea captain.

• • •

They docked the raft and blindfolded Jupiter. They led him through the shallow water at the shore, then a muddy bank and into the dense jungle.

"What does he want with this one?" one of them asked in Spanish.

"Doesn't matter," said the other one. "He asks, we get."

They slowed to a standstill. Jupiter heard a voice from in front of him, not one of the men he was with. One of his captors responded. The sound of a door opening. They let Jupiter take a step closer, then he felt a strong shove to the back and he fell, rolling, tumbling down.

When he stopped rolling, he took the blindfold off. Complete darkness. A match was struck. A torch was lit.

"You've come a long way to see me, Jupiter," said Barrett. "I knew you'd find me, son." He sat in a simple, modest chair, but it still invoked the throne of a mad king. "I'm so glad you're here. We need each other now more than ever."

"I haven't come here for that," said Jupiter.

"I know. You think you've come here to kill me, but really it's to join forces. There are things—limitations—since I've been here, that I have encountered as a white man. Limitations that you still encounter as a Negro, but the two of us together," he interlaced his fingers, "the two of us together can be a force to be reckoned with."

"I don't see how I can be any help to you," said Jupiter.

"Some of the Negroes buy my guns, some of them don't. But some of the plantation owners and the government have discovered who has been arming the rebels—not all, but some, including me. They're hunting us down."

"Something tells me that you'll survive. You're still doing well for yourself. Not your usual operation, but still ruling with an iron fist."

Jupiter tried to stand. Barrett came over to assist him.

"It only appears that I am in charge," Barrett whispered to Jupiter. "I am really a prisoner. Get me out of here."

Jupiter stepped back in shock, but also to look into Barrett's eyes.

"Barrett, if what you say is true, then there is nothing that I can do for you. You may be safer here than you are out there with the Cuban government looking for you. And I know for a fact that there is someone who would love to know your whereabouts."

Barrett's eyes grew large. "My, how you have come up in the world, Jupiter Smith."

"No," Jupiter said. "I'm down at the same level. So if you're a prisoner, what does that make me?"

"When they heard that you were asking around looking for me, they assumed it was to free me, and they could hold the two of us for ransom. So it seems that, once again, the two of us are in the same boat." Barrett smiled.

"Not exactly." Jupiter called to the guards. A door opened above him. "Listen," he said in Spanish. "I am not a friend of his. I haven't come here to rescue him. I came here to talk to him. I've done so—now I am leaving."

"I have a ship waiting for me at the eastern port. The *Liverpool.* I will take you to your family. I've sold a lot of guns since I came here, Jupiter. I have more than money, I have gold. Help me, and I'll show you where I've hidden it," Barrett said.

"I don't want your gold," said Jupiter. Just then he saw a glimmer in Barrett's eyes. Most of the signs of his previous fear and terror had vanished.

"Of course you want my gold," said Barrett. "You want the gold of my charity, the remuneration of my allegiance, the lucre of my validation and approval. Set me free, and I will spread a tale so grand and heroic from these Caribbean isles to the Isle of Nantucket. Every inn, every saloon, will be filled with the retellings of all you have accomplished on our extraordinary voyage. Let me go, and I promise that in the company of white men, both high and low, that when the subject of the Negro and his limitations surfaces, as it inevitably will, I will knight you as the exception, and name you so. And talk of your intrepidness, your courage, your resolve, and above all your humbling, awe-inspiring intellect. When people are confronted with fine specimens from your race, they may be impressed but ultimately they will say, 'He may be something, but nay, he is no Jupiter.' I promise you this: I'll scream from the mountains, and whisper it in the brothels, and in your lifetime you will see its effects. One day you may be crossing a street, and the dark shadow that follows you—the one that causes white folks to eye you suspiciously, or bold ones to spit at your feet—will be no more. You will pass a white man, and I promise you he will tip his hat to you, and then you shall be confronted with your own legend—"

"I'll take it from here, Jupiter," said a voice in the shadows.

"Good-bye, Barrett. The two of you have some catching up to do."

"Who is that?" said Barrett. "Show yourself."

Jupiter turned to leave.

"Are you sure you don't want a part of this?" asked the man in the shadows.

"I'm certain. You don't have to do this. You can let him rot here," said Jupiter.

"I can't. I have already paid our friends their money. I guess you did more growing on those waters than I did."

Jupiter did not respond. He looked at them—the man in the shadows, and Barrett—then walked into the jungle. "Who are you?" he heard behind him.

"You shall learn soon enough."

71

Cuba. A few weeks earlier . . .

Jupiter stared at the disfigured face. "May I help you?" Jupiter asked a bit too politely. The burns made him uncomfortable.

"You don't recognize me, Jupiter?"

He knew the voice. "Singleton."

"Yes."

"How did you survive?"

"Drifted on wood for days—God knows how long—until I was picked up by a whaler. I think you went through a similar experience."

"If you have all the answers, what do you want with me?"

"I need to find Barrett."

"I wish I knew where he was. I haven't seen him since the last time you did."

Singleton made an expression that could have been interpreted as a smirk. He revealed a dossier, revealed some papers, and then read aloud. "*Captain's log. Picked up a Negro and a white man. Castaways. The white man had already died of starvation and possible complications of syphilis. The Negro was very weak. Took days to recuperate. Upon recuperation spoke of being set adrift by a Captain Barrett. Claimed to be on his way to Liberia, to find his wife Sonya and son. Informed him that we were not headed to Africa. He insisted on being let off at the nearest port. I insisted that he was not well enough. However, upon docking in the harbor, he slipped off into the night."*

Jupiter was speechless.

"Impressive, no? My employer, the same man who hired Barrett, also owns the insurer of the ship that picked you up. It's a small world, controlled by a small group of people."

Jupiter thought of the longitude and latitude lines on a map; they quickly metamorphosed into puppet strings. "What do you want?"

"I want to trade information for information. You tell me where Barrett is, and I will bring you to your wife and child. My employer has a ship headed there very soon. It seems that the people of Sierra Leone and Liberia are in desperate need of weapons to hold back the natives. Just tell me where Barrett is, and you can be on your way."

"Can we be honest with each other? You seem to have all the answers, or at least you work for a man that has all the answers, and yet you come to me. What is this really about? You already know where Barrett is. Can we stop playing this game?"

"By all means."

"You want me to help you kill Barrett?"

"Yes. Is that so wrong?"

"I am not a mercenary. When I meet my son, I want to do it with clean hands."

"It's a little too late for that, isn't it, Jupiter? I am trying to help you."

"I don't need your help. I already knew that my family was alive. The same way you sensed that Barrett was living—because of your hatred for him—I knew they were alive because my love told me so. I will find them without your help."

Singleton ran his hand across his stiff, scarred brow. "I am trying to be civil with you, Jupiter, but you don't seem to understand. I told you I know where your family is, exactly. You see the difference? If you upset me, I can make things happen to them. I can make things happen to you right now. Before you can even get to them. Do you see now what I am offering? Help me and they live, don't and they die."

"One thing that I learned from your employer is that the confident do not have to threaten; their reach is felt with every breath, as every hair rises on the back of your neck. They have no need to threaten. Threats are for desperate men. Clinkscales is not a desperate man. He has already sold his guns. The world is as he sees it, whether Barrett lives or dies. Besides, as far as he is concerned, it was you who failed—not Barrett."

"So you have learned about my employer?" said Singleton.

"Somewhat."

"We've had a number of men get close to Barrett, but with all the turmoil going on there, people are easily corrupted. Money is in short supply."

"They must have really wanted Barrett to hunt him down so."

"Certainly," said Singleton.

"What kind of man would ask another man to do these things?"

Singleton leaned forward. "The kind of man that could make a fortune selling guns to both sides of the war, then play the bond markets, seizing advantage after said war causes much upheaval. That's the kind of man we are dealing with. Scruples are in short supply with him. But I've said too much."

"It wasn't the first time that Barrett had let down my employer. He can be surprisingly merciful at times. He's being quite kind by merely eliminating Barrett."

"Aren't you asking me to 'eliminate' Barrett?"

"Yes. But you would do it at his service."

"But, why? If this Clinkscales is as powerful as you say, then he can get in and out of Cuba as he pleases. Find Barrett himself."

"He's tried that," said Singleton.

"And he failed?"

"Clinkscales does not fail—he just defers success to a later date. He sent a man there to find Barrett, promising a bounty to any man who could give him information on Barrett's location. That man has since disappeared, along with the money."

"Ran off with it?" asked Jupiter.

"Died for it. Everything is flipped in Cuba. If Barrett is making a play there, then it is probably on the side of the Negro peasants, the rebels. Clinkscales hasn't been able to retrieve much information from the Cuban aristocracy. He plays in many circles, but unfortunately a circle of slaves is not one of them. His influence lies mainly within the Cuban aristocracy and no one has seen hide or tail of Barrett, which leads him to believe that Barrett is making a play to arm the rebels."

"And that's where I come in . . ."

Singleton nodded. "You have the right relationship with him, the right amount of knowledge of the language—"

"The right color," Jupiter added.

"Well, it's finally come in handy, has it not?"

"Why me? I'm sure there are plenty of desperate Negroes on the island who can speak Spanish a helluva lot better than I can, and get hold of Barrett a helluva lot faster than I can."

Singleton said nothing.

"Oh, I see," said Jupiter. "I'm not the only one."

"Advances have been made to others. Clinkscales knows how to hedge his bets."

"What happens when I cross paths with one of these other fellows looking for Barrett, and they are not so keen in giving up the bounty?"

Singleton shrugged. "I don't know, Mr. Smith. You have proven to be a resourceful fellow. I'm sure you will think of something. Clinkscales hedges his bets, but I'd place my mark on you. You're the one with the family at stake."

"What do you mean by that?"

"Clinkscales knows the location of your wife and boy. They are living in a small village in Liberia. Find Barrett, and Clinkscales will provide you with passage and you will be reunited with your family."

Jupiter sighed. "Since we are being honest with each other, I know your story isn't worth an ounce of pig shit. Clinkscales has no use for Barrett, but he also has no use for you. I know the signs of a man all alone. Clinkscales has taken away his influence. With that face and without his name, you're finding it difficult to get what you want. You think if you serve Barrett on a plate, Clinkscales will be satisfied, but men like him are never satisfied. I know Barrett is out there and I intend to find him—but not for the reasons you think. I need to know that I can live my life without killing him. I don't know what I'll do when I see him, but my actions will be my own."

• • •

Spanish soldiers patrolled the harbor, inspecting the cargo of the ships at port. There were five ships docked, as far as Jupiter could tell. Which held the weapons? Which had secreted Barrett there right under the nose of Spain? Crews unloaded shipments of cotton, foodstuffs, and rum, sugar, and tobacco. Items that had their trade suffer due to the revolution. Jupiter noticed a ship with a very high waterline. There was something heavy in its hold.

Jupiter walked up the gangplank and tried to board the ship.

A tall man—presumably the first mate—with two of the crew behind him stopped Jupiter just as his foot hit the deck. "What the hell do you think you're doing?"

"Is this the *Liverpool*?"

"Aye, it is."

"Then I am coming aboard."

The man laughed. "The hell you are. Now get your black ass off this ship before I rig your hide to the sail."

"Barrett isn't coming." It was a guess, a gamble. They looked the rough sort with which Barrett would have associated.

The man drew his pistol.

Jupiter raised his hands.

The man grabbed him and placed the barrel under his chin. "The hell you mean Barrett's not coming?" he whispered in Jupiter's ear.

"He's not coming. He's in the jungle out there. The insurgents didn't like the idea of Barrett selling weapons to the other insurgents."

The man spat. "Fucking mambi."

"They wanted all the guns. Barrett wouldn't sell them."

The man pressed the barrel harder into Jupiter's chin. "How do I know you weren't a part of it? Who the hell are you?"

"My name is Jupiter."

He lowered the gun. "Bloody hell. Barrett's black bastard son. I think I see the resemblance. He spent many a night talking about you. He said he lost you during a squall when you took the boat out to retrieve a man fallen overboard."

Jupiter almost laughed, almost grabbed the man's gun and shot him, almost screamed *He is not my father*. "That's right," he said.

"Old Barrett knew you'd turn up in Cuba. Didn't he, lads?" The man turned to his crew. They gave *aye*s in agreement. "He said, 'My boy's not the sailor I am, but he's a survivor. He understands the nature of things. I'll see him soon enough.' And here you are. I guess the old man taught you more than he realized, eh?"

"Yes. He's taught me a great deal."

"Well, we will have to cross the Atlantic with more weapons than intended. Not much rum and tobacco to trade. The trip can still be profitable. Hopefully, there are enough Africans in dire need of guns."

72

San Francisco

Maggie's eyes drifted around the room. The late Preston Dalmore had had impeccable taste. Her exotic pieces seemed out of place and like gaudy trinkets within his old world refinement. *She* was out of place. Although she was not far from her former place of business, Nob Hill was a world away from the Barbary Coast.

She stepped out onto the balcony, into the night air, and it was . . . *quiet.* It was quiet even though at that moment the docks and saloons of the Embarcadero were raucous and quaking. A part of her could still feel it—the part of her that was still whole, the part of her that had survived a journey across an ocean and a continent, the part that didn't allow her to dawdle in the slums too long, and that quickly discovered with whom to align herself. Once, she had compared San Francisco to Sodom and Gomorrah, but that city would never suffer the same fate as the biblical one.

The late Mr. O'Connell, like her, had started with nothing. He parlayed a dockworkers' strike in '49 into an import and export concern that thrived—and then went bust. The only way O'Connell could save it was to marry the daughter of a wealthy financier. He did so, but Maggie by that time was already in his heart, his mind, his bed. While alive, he did his best to take care of her, but upon his death, there was nothing to give her except his name—he adopted Maggie posthumously. All the money belonged to his wife. The other Mrs. O'Connell was astonishingly wealthy, she hobnobbed with royalty—or so went the story that Maggie used to torture herself.

She wasn't really Mrs. O'Connell, was she? With O'Connell, she had been a glorified concubine. If she was honest with herself, Preston Dalmore was truly her first husband. In a sense, the Dalmore Shipping Company was something that they had built together, and there were people that wanted to take it away. She chose Clinkscales over Miss Ellen and the Chinese Tom West. Clinkscales could reach around the world—and he was alluring in a strange way. She explained the problem of Ellen and Tom, that they were of the type that failed to see reason, that they did not understand the true meaning of a partnership, and that they should be eliminated. Ellen and Tom were rats scurrying through the city's dark alleys, swift work for Clinkscales's men. She expected word that she was rid of them—

The hand came over her mouth. *Whose could it be?* She had so many enemies. His hand was rough. He could have easily worked on a ship. She could feel his calluses as she struggled. *Don't look back and everything will be all right.* Why would she tell herself such a thing? She couldn't breathe, a flash of metal, and then her throat opened—blood and air. As her lips parted, she tasted salt on the hand and thought of Lot's wife.

73

Somewhere in the Atlantic

He was taught to give the experience details, adorn it with the most lurid and vivid ornamentation; build a place in his mind to house the images, where they could live forever. The truth housed in a dream: this is memory. By itself, memory isn't strong enough to live on its own. Desire, fear, imagination, they comprise the fertile soil—without them memory dies. Memory is when the dream meets truth. He thinks of the plantation, and he sees not the faces and details, but stark silhouettes against a sky that's blue and golden-red, and he watches a female figure hold that of a young boy, and the cotton fields are clouds and stars, and he hears that woman tell the boy the truth about his father, how that doesn't have to be his destiny, and the boy nods his head. Jupiter watches all of this from the window of the house floating in his mind; does that make it any less true?

Jupiter entered his memory palace. It had been a long time since he had to search for something within it. He passed a room filled with facts—arcane and trivial—dusty from neglect and disuse. Another room housed all of his sexual conquests and victories in physical conflicts. A teenage version of Jupiter watched the contents with lust and desire.

He passed a room that appeared empty, yet when he entered he saw himself as a little boy sitting alone. Jupiter sat next to the little boy and saw the room from the child's perspective. Large, menacing, beastlike things loomed over him. The room housed all of the moments when he felt humiliated and powerless.

He left that room and went upstairs to the attic. He worried about how he would feel when he saw her again. He searched the attic of his memory to remember how to feel the same. He found what he was looking for: Sonya on the day he first saw her, the day he fell in love with her.

Something doglike and feral watched her from a dark corner. As Jupiter approached, it moved aside and revealed a box. He opened it, releasing a conversation between the Colonel and Archer that Jupiter had once overheard.

The time is coming when you'll want to be with a woman. Don't be afraid to visit one of the slave girls at night. You're master of this house. She won't embarrass you . . .

Under that memory and in the same box, Jupiter saw all the other house slaves. They had different mothers but they all looked like Jupiter.

Another memory was under that as well . . .

• • •

Jupiter entered the Colonel's study. He was hunched over his desk and held a reading glass over a book.

"Colonel?"

The Colonel lingered over the text, then looked at him. "Jupiter, have you read all of the exciting advances in the steam engine? Fascinating."

"No, Colonel, I have not."

"Oh, you should familiarize yourself with it. It's all quite revolutionary."

"Yes, sir. I will keep that in mind."

The Colonel put down the reading glass and leaned back in his chair. "Don't ever miss any opportunity to expand your mind. Haven't I always taught you that?"

"Yes, sir. You have."

"Good. So what is it that you want, Jupiter?"

He straightened his posture. "Sir, it is about Sonya."

"What about her?"

"I intend to marry her."

"I see. And I suppose that this love affair came about after I allowed you to teach her to read?"

"Yes, sir, it did."

"Did you come here seeking my blessing? Why are you wasting my time with this?"

"Out of respect, sir."

"Don't insult me, Jupiter. If you want to get married, you will do so in your own way. Don't think that I am unaware of those secret heathen unions that go on in the woods. I know it's not my permission, so what is it that you really want?"

The Colonel stared at Jupiter. Jupiter felt it was a look that dared him to ignore decorum, dared him to scream, *You can't touch her, Colonel. If you ever lay a hand on her I will know, and I will kill you for it.*

There were screams outside the window of the Colonel's study. Jupiter looked out and saw people running toward the source.

"Leave it," said the Colonel. "Stay where you are."

Jupiter heard the crack of the whip and more screams. "Who is that?"

"I do not know," said the Colonel, "and I am grateful for it."

"You don't want to know why a whipping is being given?"

"I know nothing of whippings, Jupiter. That's the overseer's business."

Jupiter looked out of the window again. A young girl named Molly was at the painful end of the whip. "It's Molly, Colonel."

The Colonel raised his eyebrows. "Oh, I see. I understand she is with child again. This causes a problem for me. This plantation is profitable only by a hair's-breadth. To add another belly to the ledger might be catastrophic for us. Yet she did not hesitate to become with child— or to seek out other . . . alternatives. Despite the family atmosphere I have built, this place is a business."

There were more cracks of the whip. Jupiter headed for the door.

"Jupiter, don't," said the Colonel. "War, my father's plantation:

they made me sensitive to atrocities, Jupiter. I do not care to see them again. That doesn't make me a monster—that makes me a victim. Maybe the girl would not be in this situation if she had practiced some restraint, or at the very least wasn't so tempting."

Jupiter thought of Sonya.

"But enough of that. I believe we were discussing marriage."

"Never mind, sir."

"Everything on this plantation costs money. You want something of mine to claim as your own. I believe I paid eight hundred dollars for Sonya. If you want my permission to play make-believe like a child, then you have it," said the Colonel.

"Thank you, sir." He turned to leave.

"One more thing, Jupiter. Please do get acquainted with these steam engines. I need someone to discuss them with . . ."

•   •   •

The box seemed endless, and Jupiter found a memory that he thought he had placed somewhere else. He was back at the moment of the Colonel's death, convincing himself it was the right thing to do.

74

Liberia

"Sonya Smith?"

"Yes."

"I am an employee of the ACS. I have a letter for you."

"For me?"

The envelope was stiff and warped. She unfolded the letter.

Dear Sonya . . .

Her heart surged. Some anonymous child outside let out a gleeful scream.

> *They told me that you are alive and well in Liberia. I pray to God that it is true. I have so many things to tell you. I am sorry for all that you may have endured in my absence. I feel foolish and selfish for asking you to do this once again, but wait for me, Sonya. Wait for me. I will be with you soon.*
> *With Undying Love, Jupiter*

With a strange formality, she closed the letter. She pressed it against her neck; stiff and rough, her skin told her it was real. She opened the letter again and repeated the ritual. She should have been happy—and she knew that she would be at some point—but at that moment, she was back on the plantation. She thought about the way Colonel Smith put his arms around her that night. The way she looked at him and saw so much of Jupiter in his face, saw what Jupiter had inherited—all that brashness, arrogance, and strength.

A voice brought her back to the present.

"Mamma, why are you crying?"

Jacob

He had strange dreams during the fever. He was haunted by his mother's ghost stories. A child's dreams are not always harmless and innocent: adult fears seep in and haunt the outskirts of the dreamscape without becoming full-fledged nightmares.

That is what concerned Jacob while he fought for his life. His memory palaces, the ones that he had spent so much time constructing, breathing life into them through the details, all those things were beginning to erode. All he could think of was what would happen to his mother if he were to die. Although he knew the story of their harrowing journey from the South to the West, and he had seen evidence of her determination, how formidable she could be once she set her mind to something, how she would do anything to protect him, despite all of that, he still sensed her fragility. He couldn't die, for her sake. What would she become?

He awoke when the fever passed. The relief gave way to guilt. He had put her through so much, and now his illness had put her through so much more. He looked around at the half-corpses shrouded in netting to keep the insects at bay—all of this because of him. She had lost so much already, and yet now he threatened her with more loss. He did not like the idea of being a burden, and though his mind was still foggy, he set out to restore his skills of memory. He saw that as the best way to display his value.

Before all of this, in order to hone his memory skills, he would read his mother's letters. It was good practice, and it allowed him insight into a woman who was so closed off emotionally. The secrets in those letters, things she would have never told him and he would not have learned otherwise. They were gifts to him. He liked knowing her, even though he did not fully comprehend what it all meant. He liked having a secret—he knew her better than she thought he did. Despite her best efforts to hide the ugly parts of herself, the parts that shamed her, the parts that caused her fear, he knew those things and loved her even more for it.

Yet on the way to Liberia, those letters were lost. She did not have the ability to build a fortress around the things that were dear to her like he did; she had to write them down. The only thing that was left for her was the feeling associated with the letters, the ache felt in their absence.

At one point, he had remembered all of them, but the illness had chipped away at some of them. He found a piece of paper and began to write.

We had a child. A daughter. She passed three months after you went away. She is buried under the tree just outside the Smith family cemetery. I named her Tess, after your mother.

Soon after she passed, I became with child again. I shall not relive the details. They do not matter.

Jupiter, you have a son. Yes, in my heart and mind he is yours. I see you in him. And if after reading this letter, you wish to set eyes on him, you will see the same.

It was a cryptic letter. It began and ended abruptly. However, he always could sense the letter's importance.

•   •   •

She could not remember much of what had happened. The Colonel stood over her—bloody scratches on his neck and chest—and fastened his britches. She lay on the floor, the wetness under her buttocks getting colder. She could feel the strange stirring inside her. She knew she would soon be with child.

75

Liberia

A clerk at the ACS office told him where to find her. When he learned that she was staying with someone named Mary, he wondered if it was the same Mary that left for Liberia so many years ago.

As he approached the house, he thought of Jacob. He thought of his son and decided that he would no longer call himself Jupiter. That name belonged to a different person—a person with no family, a person with no history. Like his son, he would go by Jacob; a father and son should share a name.

He had seen himself as someone who was perpetually wronged, a man in constant pursuit of retribution. Could he stop building altars to perceived injustices? He needed to know that if he ever saw Barrett again he could resist the temptation to kill him. He had his answer.

Sonya and Jacob stood on the porch of the plantation-style home. When he saw them, something akin to an earthquake happened in his mind. His memory palace, his shrine for things that were meant to be forgotten, collapsed.

ACKNOWLEDGMENTS

Many books aided in the research for this blend of myth and history, and those—to name a few—that proved to be especially helpful were: *Shanghaiing Days* by Richard H. Dillon; *The Price of Liberty: African Americans and the Making of Liberia* by Claude A. Clegg III; and *Rulers, Guns, and Money: The Global Arms Trade in the Age of Imperialism* by Jonathan A. Grant.

My thanks and gratitude go out to the following:

Scott Mendel, for his advocacy and gentle nudging. Malaika Adero, for her patience and support. Todd Hunter, for his diligence and dedication to seeing this through. The hardworking folks at Atria Books. Michael Yakutis, for turning my strange visions into compelling illustrations.

Debra and Jennifer, my very own Dynamic Duo.

My family and friends who offered their invaluable support to this book as well as my previous book: Doris, Roy, Dena, Mildred, Earl, Moses, Paula, Tom, and Steve.

To the newest member of the family: Son, you have inspired me in more ways than I can fully express. Much of what I've written contains messages for you, yet their contents remain a mystery to me. When you are older, we will decipher the code together.